JANE B. MASON

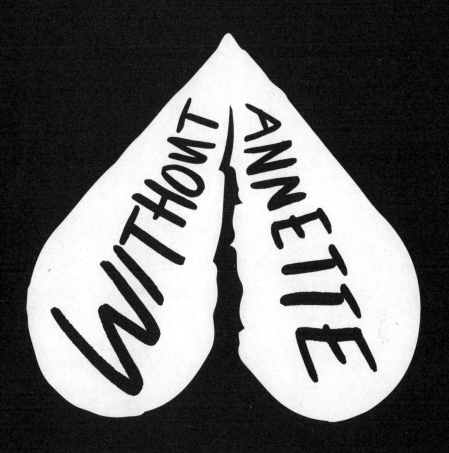

WITHOUT ANNETTE

Scholastic Press / New York

All rights reserved. Published by Scholastic Press, an imprint of Scholastic Inc., *Publishers since 1920*. SCHOLASTIC, SCHOLASTIC PRESS, and associated logos are trademarks and/or registered trademarks of Scholastic Inc.

The publisher does not have any control over and does not assume any responsibility for author or third-party websites or their content.

This book is a work of fiction. Names, characters, places, and incidents are either the product of the author's imagination or are used fictitiously, and any resemblance to actual persons, living or dead, business establishments, events, or locales is entirely coincidental.

Library of Congress Cataloging-in-Publication Data available

ISBN 978-0-545-81995-4

10 9 8 7 6 5 4 3 2 1   16 17 18 19 20

Printed in the U.S.A.   23
First edition, June 2016

Book design by Nina Goffi

FOR CRAIG WALKER,

WHO BECAME A FRIEND THE FIRST TIME WE MET,

AND UNDERSTOOD.

CHAPTER 1

♥

I stared at the piece of paper posted on the dormitory door as if it were committing perjury, feeling the blood drain from my face. "We're not roommates?" I blurted.

"Apparently not," Annette said. She found my hand and gave it a quick squeeze, then dropped it again. My head spun crazily. *We weren't roommates.* "We're in the same dorm at least," she added quietly.

I scanned the list again, double-checking the room numbers. Annette's name was right where it always was, at the top: Annette Anderson, room 108. I was lost among dozens of other names in the middle: Josie Little, room 316.

Behind us, sunlight glinted off the luxury SUVs and station wagons that lined the curb. Dads in sherbet-colored button-downs and loafers hefted luggage, while moms in printed blouses, skirts, and low heels gathered in conversation nearby.

Our parents were thirteen hundred miles away, in Virginia Falls, Minnesota. Which was probably just as well, since most of the shirts my dad owned were lumberjack plaid, and my family drove a ten-year-old, rusty Dodge Caravan.

Annette and I had both spent our entire lives in Virginia Falls, right up until three o'clock this morning, when we'd piled our luggage and ourselves into said minivan and departed for the

Minneapolis airport. A three-hour drive and a two-and-a-half-hour plane ride later, we'd arrived in Hartford, Connecticut. And just now, at Brookwood Academy, elite coeducational boarding school in picturesque rural Connecticut.

Turning, I looked out at the main circle, at the ivy-covered brick buildings and giant elms—the biggest I'd ever seen. At the people who somehow reminded me of Easter-themed tablecloth and napkin sets.

"It looks just like the catalog, doesn't it?" Annette asked as a silver-whiskered golden retriever lumbered past, sniffing the grass in search of the perfect place to relieve himself.

"Sure does," I agreed. A pair of girls in sleeveless sweaters embraced not far away, laughing. Their tanned, slender arms linked easily as they crossed the lawn—they could have been starring in the catalog shoot. I tucked a wayward curl into my headband and adjusted my backpack. I'd pored over that catalog a hundred times and imagined our arrival just as many, but somehow I hadn't pictured anything like this.

It wasn't as though I expected balloons. Or a bunch of people standing on the curb, holding hot dishes with crocheted hot pads. I knew Brookwood wouldn't be like Virginia Falls. I didn't *want* it to be.

I'd wanted it to be different. I'd wanted to be someplace else. I'd wanted to go to a school that challenged me. But most of all, I'd wanted to get Annette away from her mother, to keep her safe.

I'd wanted Annette to be my roommate.

"I see you've found the list of room assignments," Dean Austin said, setting our luggage on the curb and mopping his brow with a handkerchief. "I'll send someone over to bring your luggage up so you can settle in."

I watched as the golden retriever finished his business and trotted over to the car, hopping onto the seat I had occupied moments ago, panting and looking pleased with himself.

I swiveled my head to look at my butt. Sure enough, the entire tail end of my dark denim capris was covered in blond, silky dog hair. I swiped at my ass, glancing over at Annette's, which somehow remained hairless-terrier bald.

"Hey," a pair of girls dressed in sporty above-the-knee skirts, who had just come out of the dorm, said as they passed. One of them turned back, giving me a skeptical once-over. And why wouldn't she? I was the only female in sight who didn't have long, straight, shiny hair, and had dog hair all over her butt.

"Should we go in?" Annette's voice was crazy quiet, the way it got when her mom had been drinking and she was trying to avoid a blowup.

Half of me wanted to go home, and none of me wanted to go in. But we couldn't just stand there on the stoop, staring—especially since Dean Austin and the shed machine had already driven away.

"May as well," I said as lightly as I could. "I am in serious need of a bathroom."

Annette chuckled and stepped into the foyer. "Peeing all over yourself would not be good," she agreed.

It took about ten seconds to find Annette's room. It was right there, a few steps down the hall, as accessible as her name on an alphabetical list. The door was open a crack and I could see a girl unpacking inside. She was tall and slender, with a blond ponytail running halfway down her back. *Of course.*

"I'll come find you as soon as I settle in," Annette told me, giving my hand another quick squeeze.

I gazed at the pale yellow shadow of a bruise under her left eye—a parting gift from her mother—and tried to disguise the fact that I longed to barge through the door and explain to the girl with the ponytail that there'd been a mistake, that there would be two girls moving into this room, that *her* roommate was actually upstairs in room 316. But even in my state of disbelief, I knew that doing such a thing would be ridiculous, as would giving Annette a passionate good-bye kiss in the dormitory hallway. Or any kiss right then, since Annette and I had decided to wait a little while— get our boarding school bearings—before going public as a couple. So I mustered up the best smile I was capable of and turned toward the stairs, unable to avoid overhearing Annette introduce herself to her roommate, picturing her expression based on the cadence of her voice, and then my mind's eye going blank as I heard her roommate reply, "I'm Rebecca."

The stairwell was concrete and metal, and my footsteps echoed as I shuffled my way up. Floor three was at the top, 316 at the end of the hall. The door was closed.

"Hello?" I called quietly, opening it a crack and peeking inside. *Speak up, Josephine!* my deceased grandmother said in my head. She was practically deaf by the time she turned seventy, so shouting was required if you wanted her to hear whatever it was you had to say. And in this case she was right.

"Anyone home?" I said a little louder as I pushed the door open wide and saw for the first time the space that would be my home for the next nine months. It was smaller than I expected, and already full of stuff—presumably my roommate's. She was lying on the bottom bunk, which was covered in a funky duvet, with her eyes closed and buds in her ears. A matched set of partially empty suitcases covered most of the floor, along with a stack of oversize art books, and one of the dressers was piled with everything from toiletries to magazines to jewelry to a mountain of lacy underwear. I was wondering how many pairs of underwear were in that heap when my roommate did a little shimmy and belted out part of the song she was listening to.

I laughed out loud, and she opened an eye.

"Hi, I'm Josie." I stepped forward so she wouldn't have to get up.

My roommate stared at me for a long, hard moment, her eyes a mixture of resentment and ambivalence. Then she momentarily looked past me, rolled over, and turned her entire body to the wall.

Face flushing, my hand dropped limply to my side. "Nice to meet you, too," I mumbled.

CHAPTER 2

♥

I stared blankly at my roommate's back, grimly thinking that I probably should have been grateful. After all, she did not have long, shining hair and was not wearing pastel. Her dark hair was short and spiky and she was wearing black. All black.

The door behind me swung open, and a tall boy with shaggy brown hair stepped into the room, carrying my suitcases—all three of them—like they were rag dolls.

"Hey," he greeted. "Where do you want 'em?"

Room 108, I thought, thinking maybe I could just move in with them. Annette and I could sleep in a twin, no problem—we did it all the time. "Uh, anywhere is good," I replied.

He put the suitcases down and held out a hand. "I'm Penn," he said. "Penn McCarthy."

"Josie Little." I extended my own hand and hoped it wasn't clammy. Clammy hands, along with bitten fingernails, were gross.

"Rocks," he said loudly.

I blinked in surprise. Rocks? He'd just carried my suitcases in as if they were filled with feathers.

Penn swiped at my roommate's foot. "Roxanne!" he said, a little louder.

My roommate rolled over and pulled her earbuds out.

"What?" she asked, a little annoyed but clearly not at all fazed by this boy's presence in our dorm room.

"Just sayin' hey," he said with a shrug. A lock of hair hung over his eyes, making it hard to see what color they were. Brown, maybe. Or hazel. "How was your summer?"

"Not terrible," Roxanne admitted, propping herself on an elbow. She had dark eyes, a long face, and blue-black nail polish. "My dad was gone the whole time, of course, but my mom let me help out at the gallery."

"Sweet," Penn said. "New self-portrait?"

I followed his gaze to a small painting that leaned against the wall above one of the desks. It was a girl with piercing dark eyes standing alone on a crowded city sidewalk, the people around her a blur of motion. It did in fact look a lot like the girl lying on the bed, though the face in the painting was more gaunt and pale, more ghostlike.

"Yeah." She shrugged.

Penn stood there for a second, as if waiting for more detail, or for Roxanne to ask him about his summer. She didn't. Nobody said anything, and you could almost hear the silence between them. I wondered what it meant.

"Well, I'd better get back to delivery," Penn said. "Duffels await. Nice to meet you, Josie. Welcome to Brookwood. Catcha later, Rox."

"Later," Roxanne agreed, sticking a bud back into an ear.

"I'm Josie Little," I said quickly, before she could get the second bud in and tune me out entirely. "Your roommate."

There was that look again—ambivalent resentment. I was expecting her to roll away from me a second time, but she opened her mouth instead.

"Hello, Roommate Josie Little," she said in a voice that was practically impossible to read. It wasn't mocking, but almost. "I'd tell you my name, but Mr. McCarthy has already taken care of that. And it's obvious that I'm your roommate, unless of course I'm some sort of vagrant who's stumbled into Cortland Girls Dormitory, which seems extremely unlikely. So if you don't mind, I'll get back to my music. Feel free to make yourself at home. The top bunk is yours, as is the empty dresser and half the closet. The bathroom is through that door. I haven't finished unpacking in there, so go ahead and spread out a little. But not too much, or I'll have to reclaim what's rightfully mine, which won't be pretty." She smiled wanly and stuffed the second earbud in, flopping back on her bed.

Bathroom. I was through the door before Roxanne pressed PLAY, unzipping my capris and sighing in relief. I felt myself relax a little and perused the room, which was covered in tiny, off-white octagonal tile. The sink and tub were both huge, and the slightly open window had leaded glass and ran practically up to the ceiling. Roxanne already had a bunch of stuff next to the sink and a huge toiletry bag on the wall shelf.

I was done peeing, I realized, but had no desire to get up. The view from the toilet seat was surprisingly pleasant, looking out over rooftops and between sky-reaching elms to the seemingly endless fields that surrounded the campus. *How long can I sit here?* I wondered. Ten minutes? An hour? Roxanne clearly wouldn't give a damn. But what about Annette?

I grabbed my phone, typed *Miss u already*, and hit SEND before I could change my mind. I felt like a barnacle as I watched the screen for a moment, waiting for a response before leaning my head back against the wall and trying to wrap my brain around the fact that we were here. In Connecticut. At a boarding school. Thirteen hundred miles from home.

And that, so far, nothing was going the way I'd thought it would.

A typo—it was all because of a typo. Well, okay, it wasn't *exactly* the typo. It was actually Annette's mother, Shannon, a mean drunk who had a tendency to flip out and rail on her only daughter. Shannon had been mean for as long as I could remember, and was getting meaner. So when I tried to look up *bookworm*, but typed in *brookwoom*, and my search engine kindly translated it to *Brookwood*, what I saw on my computer screen wasn't just Brookwood Academy, elite boarding school in pastoral Connecticut. What I saw was an exit strategy—a path to something better.

I'd thought that coming to Brookwood would solve everything. It would put six whole states between Annette and her mother, between *us* and her mother. Annette could live without the constant fear of her mother going on a rampage. We could be together without our parents hovering over us. And we would also get out of Virginia Falls, our tiny Minnesota hometown, where the priorities were hockey, homecoming, football, and more hockey. Plus, it certainly didn't hurt that Brookwood offered twice as many classes as VF High, or had fewer than a quarter as many students.

I'd been one hundred and one percent certain that coming to Brookwood was the right thing to do. Even when Shannon became so enraged she hit Annette and declared that she wouldn't let her go. Even when Annette herself got so nervous she balked. I never panicked—I just kept believing that we were coming, right down to the moment we got on the plane. Right down to the moment we pulled in and I saw the place. Because even though it *looked* exactly like the catalog and the pictures on the website, it *felt* totally different.

Now here we were, at Brookwood, with 418 other students and (according to the catalog) an extremely qualified faculty. Half of me still couldn't believe we'd both gotten in, with scholarships. I turned my gaze back toward the fields, remembering the day the letters came. I could still feel the envelope in my hand, my thudding heart as I dialed Annette's number.

The phone rang—once, twice, three times. I'd stripped down to my T-shirt even though there was still snow on the ground—spring was late. Finally, she picked up.

"Did you get it?" I asked without saying hello. I'd set the envelope on my desk, where the full-color return address and its embossed, crested logo stared up at me.

"Yes," Annette said a little breathlessly. "Do you want me to come over?"

Uff-da. That was a tough one. I did want her to come over—I always wanted her to come over. But I didn't want to wait for her to get here, and what if our letters weren't the same? What were the odds that we'd both been accepted?

"How thick is it?" I'd read somewhere that rejection letters were single pieces of paper, while acceptances were three pages or more. My envelope looked suspiciously thin.

"How thick?" Annette echoed. "I don't know. Kinda thick, kinda thin."

That was so Annette—always coasting down the middle. She just glided easily along, no matter what. It was her gift.

"Should I come over so we can open them together?" she repeated.

A wave of nausea engulfed me as I eyed the Brookwood logo on the envelope. "Let's just open them," I blurted. I still felt like throwing up, but suddenly had to know.

"Are you sure?" Annette asked. I could picture the expression on her face, the concern in her flecked green eyes. She knew me better than anyone, knew how compulsive I could be. "It might be better if . . ."

Too late. I was already ripping it open, completely mangling the envelope and tearing a corner of the letter itself. My hands shook as I unfolded the paper.

Dear Miss Little,

    After careful consideration by our Admissions Committee, we are pleased to offer you a contract with financial aid for enrollment at Brookwood Academy.

"I got in!" I shrieked into the phone. "Annette, I got in!"
Silence, and then a very quiet "That's great."
I pulled my lips together, feeling like an idiot. Duh. My getting

in was only *half* the plan. But of course Annette got in. There was never any question in my mind about her being accepted. She was a much better student than I was, if a little less driven. "You did, too, right?"

"Not exactly." Her voice was steady but soft.

I took a breath. Not exactly?

"I got wait-listed."

Wait-listed? I had heard about wait-listed, of course, but hadn't really considered it a possibility. Through the seemingly endless process of applying to boarding school, I'd always assumed that the letter in the mail would be a kind of deliverance—a yes or a no. After everything, a maybe seemed unfair. Cruel, even.

A shuddering exhale made its way across the phone line and into my ear, and it wasn't the good kind.

"I'll be right there." I hung up the phone and dropped the letter onto my desk, slipping my feet into Converse and arms into down. "Going to Annette's!" I shouted as I headed out the door.

I raced down the sidewalk and hurdled a pile of sooty snow, the word *wait-listed* repeating itself in my mind. I had no idea what it really meant. How many people were on the wait-list? How many got in? And what would we do if she *didn't* get in?

Breathless and a little sweaty, I pulled open the Andersons' front door, only to stop short. Shannon was coming toward me from the kitchen, her green eyes narrowed and her mouth set in a straight line. I could smell the gin on her breath.

"You again," she said, weaving just enough to make the ice cubes in her lowball clink. Out of the corner of my eye I could see Annette sitting on the living room sofa, holding her letter and staring at the floor. "Annette isn't going anywhere—that boarding school of yours doesn't want her."

Shannon didn't mince words—especially the cruel ones. I forced myself to swallow my anger and walked over to Annette, gently tugging the letter out of her hand. If we'd been alone, I would have reached out an arm or given her a kiss, but under the circumstances, it was best to keep a careful distance.

Dear Miss Anderson,

The Admissions Committee has carefully reviewed your application . . .

Blah, blah, blah.

. . . because we have more qualified applicants than spaces . . .

Yadda, yadda, yadda.

. . . we have placed your name on our waiting list. Your position is fifth.

Blah, blah, blah.

If you are still interested in attending Brookwood this fall, please let our Admissions Office know as soon as possible.

Blah, yadda, blah.

"They don't want her," Shannon repeated, sinking heavily into the faded armchair by the fireplace. "Not that I blame them." She paused to take a sip. "Am I the only one around here who saw this one coming?"

Annette's eyelids fluttered closed and I heard her exhale with

13

almost inaudible raggedness. I leaned a tiny bit closer and pressed my knee against hers, wishing I could put a protective bubble around her—around us. Something her mother couldn't penetrate. Or burst.

"That's not what the letter says," I said, keeping my voice calm. I'd had years of practice. "It says they don't have space for every qualified applicant."

Shannon swirled her cubes and eyed her daughter on the couch. "She's not qualified."

Annette's dad came in from the kitchen, wiping his hands on the apron Annette had given him for Father's Day several years before. The words *King of the Kitchen* had mostly worn off, but you could still see the gold crown in the middle. His skin seemed stretched over the bones of his face, his thinning hair unusually messy. "Of course she's qualified—it's just a matter of numbers."

"And she's fifth," I added. That was probably pretty good— there were maybe thirty names on that list. She'd get in, in the end. She *had* to get in.

Annette's eyes were focused on the nail polish stain we'd made on the carpet years before, during our makeover phase. Her body oozed defeat.

"I'm not going without her," I said.

"Oh yes, you are," Shannon pronounced with utter clarity (it was still pretty early—she was probably only on drink number two).

Annette turned to me. Her green eyes—the color of birch leaves just unfurled—glistened with sadness. "You have to go," she said, half pleading and half resigned. "If it weren't for you, we wouldn't even know about Brookwood." She bit her lower lip to keep it from trembling, and I squelched my urge to lean in and kiss it. "I really wanted to go," she added in a whisper.

"You're not going anywhere but that god-awful Virginia Falls High."

I watched Annette's shoulders sag forward, watched the last ray of hope disappear from her eyes, and steeled myself. I didn't usually go up against Shannon—especially when she was drinking. But she had Annette in a cage, and I held the key in my hand. I hadn't gotten it into the lock yet, but I was close. Oh so close. If I said nothing and Annette stayed in Virginia Falls, it would be like dropping the key on the ground, like walking away from Annette when she was still behind bars.

Which would rip my heart out.

"This isn't a rejection," I said, fixing my eyes on Shannon, and then Michael. "She's fifth. The other people on that list probably applied to a bunch of schools. If Annette tells them she really wants to go, she'll get in. That's how it works."

Was that how it worked? I had absolutely no idea, but it *sounded* reasonable.

"You think?" I could see a sliver of light in Annette's eyes— sunlight on spring leaves.

"I know." I reached for her hand. "You are going to Brookwood Academy this fall. *We* are going."

Shannon opened her mouth to say something, but Michael beat her to it. "Well, then. I believe you girls had better let Brookwood know that Annette is still highly interested," he said, avoiding his wife's death stare.

It was all I could do not to leap off the couch and throw my arms around him. Annette's father wasn't exactly a pillar of familial strength—this was a rare showing of some major backbone.

Shannon stared at him in a kind of stupor (maybe it *was* drink number three), and I thanked him profusely with my eyes as Annette and I got to our feet and hurried toward the stairs and Annette's laptop. We did, indeed, have a letter to write.

The sound of voices drifting in through the open bathroom window filtered into my daydream, and I realized I'd been sitting on the toilet so long my butt was starting to ache. And also that I had a reply from Annette. When did that come in?

Going on campus tour w roomie—will come get u 4 Vespers. Xo.

Was she already unpacked? Knowing Annette, this was entirely possible. The girl took organization to a whole new level.

I stood up and washed my hands, wiping my wet palms on my sweater since my capris were still covered in dog hair and there wasn't a towel in sight. In front of the mirror, I noticed that my hair was even more riotous than usual due to the eight-hour trek, making my head look like a sheep in need of a shearing. And thanks to my ridiculously pale skin I had bags under my eyes. I looked like a zombie, and didn't feel much better.

I had a sudden urge to turn the water on full blast, strip down, and take a scalding-hot shower. But I didn't have a towel or a bar of soap—they were, along with everything else I'd brought with me, in the next room along with a black-clad stranger. A stranger who barely had two words for a classmate she obviously knew, much less some freaky-looking girl from out of state whom she had never laid eyes on.

I let out a sigh. I'd wanted to come to Brookwood and here I was—here *we* were. Annette was safe from her mother, probably already unpacked and definitely touring the campus. Me? I was sitting in a bathroom having a pity party.

That's not going to do you a lick of good, Josephine, said my grandmother's voice, and, again, she was right. I gave myself a stern look in the mirror on her behalf. Then I finger-combed my tangled curls, squared my shoulders, and opened the door. "Ready or not," I murmured. "Here I come."

CHAPTER 3

♥

"You are truly fortunate to be here," Headmaster Thornfeld said from the carved podium at center stage. The entire student body was gathered in the auditorium, seated in red velvet-upholstered chairs that curved gracefully to match the unusual shape of the hall. "For every one of you sitting in this room, a dozen were turned away. Some of you have just arrived, while others have been here for a year or two. We expect the exceptional from all of you, equally."

Is he serious? I tried to imagine Principal Hansen giving a speech like this at Virginia Falls High and almost laughed out loud. VF High was a big public school, the only high school in town. Even the mascot—the lumberjack—was big. But exceptional? Definitely not.

"We take our motto," the headmaster went on, " 'Achievement, Honor, Respect,' seriously at Brookwood."

"What a load of bull," a boy behind me said with a snicker. Newcomb, his name was. Or Newhall. An *N* name. I was in a row of *L*s, next to someone named Oscar Lord and smack-dab in the middle of my class, the mids. I'd learned from the website that lower mids were freshmen, mids were sophomores, and upper mids were juniors. Seniors, it turned out, were just seniors.

The mids essentially occupied the rear third of the auditorium, because there weren't that many lower mids (freshmen) and they only needed three rows in the back. The seniors and upper mids were up front, and in that order. Annette and I had found our seats before Vespers started, so I knew she was three rows in front of me, off to the left. Penn and Roxanne, the only other students I actually knew (if you can call a two-minute conversation knowing), were somewhere in the sea of students behind me.

I tried to focus on what Headmaster Thornfeld was saying but was suddenly finding it hard to keep my eyes open.

"The Honor Code is the backbone of our educational and social community." Thornfeld's balding head looked a little fuzzy. My eyelids drooped. "Your signature on the contract is your personal pledge to abide by its . . ."

I just need to close them for a minute. I slipped down in my chair.

". . . rigorous class schedule . . . academic expectations . . . students who do not . . . put on probation . . ."

Something jabbed me in the ribs.

"Quit it!" I heard myself say in the screechy voice I generally reserved for my three brothers when they were being extra annoying.

"You were snoring," Oscar whispered in my ear.

My eyes shot open and I bolted upright. Half the row behind me snickered, and several people in H through J turned around just in time to see me wipe the drool from my chin. Annette's eyes scolded, then softened into a look of bemusement.

I pushed my back against the velvet seat, focusing intently on the stage and pretending that nothing unusual had happened.

"Just a little narcoleptic," I mumbled. Oscar chuckled and tugged at his collar.

The headmaster had been replaced by a boy in a blue blazer and red necktie who was explaining the importance of student government at Brookwood.

"Head Monitor William Spencer," Oscar whispered. "Total geek."

I had no idea if this was an insult or a compliment, so I didn't respond. The boy on the stage was tall and lean and looked a lot like everyone else in the room. Or at least like every other *male* person in the room . . .

Did they look the same because they were dressed alike? This was Vespers—a coat-and-tie assembly that took place four evenings a week, on the nights that students had sit-down dinner. Both were semiformal, which was why I was surrounded by boys in khakis, blue blazers, button-down shirts, and ties (mostly red and either striped or dotted with miniature animals—I'd noticed a lot of bears, in particular). The girls' outfits were more varied—dresses and skirts and sweaters and blouses, with a unifying theme: the pearl necklace. Some were graduated, some multistrand, and still others were partially gold chains (aka, I would learn, add-a-pearl necklaces). I fingered my gold chain with its opal pendant—a gift from Annette on my thirteenth birthday—and listened to the boy onstage.

William Spencer spoke with an impressive combination of enthusiasm and confidence, as if he'd been addressing huge groups of people since he was in kindergarten. He explained that the formal dinner seating was assigned, and students who had not already done so should consult the list in the foyer outside the main dining hall. "So without further ado . . ."

Without further ado? I thought as conversations broke out all around me. I considered thanking my alarm clock, but he was yakking it up with some boys from row J.

Exiting the auditorium was like exiting a completely full airplane with multiple exits, so I knew almost immediately that my plan to wait for Annette was doomed. Out in the hall, things were no better—I was quickly swept up in the mob of students moving down the long, stone-arched corridor.

At least I don't have to worry about finding the dining room, I thought.

"Feeling rested?"

I turned and saw Penn, the boy who'd brought up my suitcases, grinning at me. He was wearing one of those ties with the bears on it.

"Don't worry," he consoled me, seeing my expression. "You're not the first Brookwood student to fall asleep on Thornfeld's auditory watch. The guy is notoriously long-winded."

"Was I loud?" I ventured.

"Like a sumo wrestler."

"Uff-da."

Penn stared at me. "What was that?"

I flushed. *Uff-da* was one of those weird Minnesotan expressions I swore I'd never use but somehow did, anyway. It basically meant you were overloaded and so close to speechless that something as dumb as *uff-da* was all you could get out. "Um, nothing."

He eyed me warily. "Well, it wasn't that bad. I'm pretty sure the seniors didn't even hear you."

"That's a relief." I was still mortified, but also reassured that Penn thought my inadvertent performance was more funny than offensive.

"Do you know where your hot seat is for your inaugural Brookwood banquet?"

"My what?" I replied, feeling a vague sense of panic.

"Relax, Josie Little," he said. "Where are you sitting at dinner?"

I let out my breath. "Table 37, but I'm not exactly sure where the dining hall is. We never made it here to see the school—it's all new."

"We?" Penn inquired.

"My . . . friend and me," I replied. "Annette. We're from the Midwest and applied toge—"

"Penn-y," a broad-shouldered boy called, approaching from behind and thumping Penn, hard, on the back. I watched the boys engage in a complicated wrestling embrace without halting their forward progress. Weirdly impressive.

"Hank-est," Penn replied. "How was it?"

"Excellent," Hank (was it Hank?) replied. He had blond hair and a round face with a square, cleft chin. "France was a highlight—I fully recommend Parisian women."

"You dog."

I was ambling along behind them when Penn turned back to

me. "Hank Jeffrey, meet Josie Little," he said, waving a hand in my direction. "She's from . . ."

He looked at me with one eye closed, and I saw that his other eye was green-brown.

"Minnesota," I finished.

"I was gonna go with Wisconsin," Penn admitted.

"I'm no cheesehead."

"Ahhh, but you are, quite apparently, a football fan."

I held my hands in the air. "Guilty, but not necessarily by choice. I have three brothers and a dad, and since it's often below zero for weeks on end, we're forced to entertain ourselves indoors on the weekends . . ."

"I can think of some indoor entertainment," Hank mused, the edges of his mouth curving upward in a smirk.

I'd stepped right into that one, and I blushed as I considered indoor entertainment with Annette. *Way* better than football, no question.

"Below zero? Dang, that's cold," Penn said with a sympathetic shiver. "How do you deal with that?"

"A lotta layers."

Up ahead, the hall herd was breaking up as some students made their way into the dining room while others checked the list. Hank peeled off, and I followed Penn toward a sea of white tablecloths and china.

"The Brookwood dining hall, like a long-lost friend . . . or enemy," he said, spreading his arms. "See you later, Subzero," he added, cracking a smile as he moved away.

"See you," I replied distractedly as I scanned the tables for numbers. A small bronze-colored plaque sat in the center of each table, several of which were already filling up. I searched the room, looking for table 37, and instead found Annette standing next to her roommate at table 19.

I felt a pang of envy as I watched the two girls bend their heads together. Annette looked happy, and had clearly landed a room-mate, a friend, and a tour guide in the space of a few hours.

That's what she does—she fits in, I reminded myself as the noise in the dining room rose to a din. All around me, students were laughing and talking, and I felt as though I'd walked into a party several hours late, when everyone else was already having a good time. And then, cutting through the sound came the ring of a little bell—a signal that everyone was supposed to take a seat.

Thirty-seven, a tiny voice said in my brain. My feet moved, taking me to the other side of the room, where I found my table and slipped into the last empty chair. No sooner had I sat down than a faculty member, a sharp-eyed woman with short, salt-and-pepper hair, told me I had to get up.

"You're in one of the waiters' seats," she explained, looking over the top of her glasses. "You and Mr. Jeffrey are tasked with bringing food to our table." She gestured palm up to the boy who'd just been wrestling with Penn in the hall, then to a long buffet table covered with platters of food, on the other side of the room.

The meal, surprisingly, looked delicious. Roast chicken with potatoes and carrots, rolls, and a green salad. "I got the fowl and tubers, you grab the carbs and roughage." Hank pointed with his chin to the other end of the table.

"Got it." I grabbed a basket of rolls and a wooden salad bowl off the buffet and followed him back to our table, where we set everything down near the salt-and-pepper professor. She served herself, then passed everything to her right. By the time the chicken platter got to me, only thighs remained, just like at home, where I was perpetually eating my brothers' leftovers. Out of the blue I felt an ache so sharp it was as if I was being squeezed and pierced at the same time, as if a giant had reached in from through the ceiling and grabbed me around the chest. It was all I could do to choose one of the remaining chicken thighs and pass the platter along, and I was still reeling when the vegetables arrived. I served myself and tried to breathe, tried to hide the fact that I was losing it.

I was just getting a grasp on a normal inhale/exhale pattern, when Salt-and-Pepper cleared her throat. "I am Carol Blackburn, classics professor," she said. "I have been at Brookwood for seventeen years. We have three new students seated here, and I think it would be nice to go around the table and introduce ourselves. Tell us who you are, where you are from, and something surprising about yourself. Erica, you may start us off."

Erica was an olive-skinned girl with dark eyes and a round face. Her pearls were double stranded. "I'm Erica Goodspeed, and I'm an upper mid from Manhattan. This is my second year at Brookwood. I'm a triplet."

As luck would have it, I was sitting right next to Erica. "My name is Josie Little, and I'm from Virginia Falls, Minnesota. This is my first day at Brookwood, and . . ." The first thought that came to me was *I feel like a mutant*, which was clearly not a good choice. Next up in my brain was *I came here with my girlfriend*, which was also unacceptable, since blurting out your sexual orientation on your first day at a new school in a new state was never a good idea. (And would get me in hot water with Annette, since we'd agreed not to be out at first.) So I blurted out the third thing that came to mind, "I was born in a Red Lobster."

Somebody's fork clattered, and Hank Jeffrey laughed out loud. The girl sitting across from me choked on her roll. Clearly, my third idea was as bad as my first two. I felt my face grow warm as the boy next to me started to talk.

"I'm Jake Flemming, from Darien, Connecticut. I'm a senior, and this is my fourth year here. I skipped second and fifth grades." He said it as if it was his shoe size or something—like it wasn't really something to talk about.

I took a bite of chicken and tried to chew through the introductions, thinking I might get lucky and chew my tongue off.

Amanda Collins was a senior from Cambridge, Massachusetts, and the granddaughter of some famous writer. Hank Jeffrey was an upper mid from Philadelphia and had been a Gerber baby. Cynthia Wu, a mid, was from Westchester and spoke five languages. Fluently. And Patrick Mahoney, whom I recognized from my row at Vespers, was a mid from Manhattan who was training for his pilot's license. Maybe when he got one, he could fly me the heck out of here.

I looked down at the food on my plate, trying to ignore the lingering ache in my chest and wondering if anyone would notice if the girl born in a mediocre seafood chain restaurant slid under the table and stayed there, indefinitely.

CHAPTER 4

♥

"Thornfeld hates it when you scrape at the table, but everyone does it anyway." Hank skillfully heaped everyone's uneaten food onto a single plate. He'd tucked his tie, dark blue with narrow stripes, between the buttons of his shirt to prevent splatterage. "If we didn't, we'd never make it to before-study-hall Scene in the T."

I nodded as though I knew exactly what he was talking about and picked up a couple of serving platters. Spotting Annette waiting by the door, I made a little detour on the way to the dish drop.

"I have to clear," I explained quickly. "I'll come find you as soon as I'm done."

She nodded and I scurried over to Hank, who was dumping the food into a giant bin of slop and sliding the plates onto the stainless counter. On the other side of the window, a college-age boy was hosing down the dishes and loading them onto a giant plastic rack. He looked a lot like my brother Ben (except for the hairnet)—tall, dark hair, straight nose. I pushed the platters toward him, painfully aware that Ben, like the rest of my family, was seriously far away. "Hey," I said, then added, "Thanks."

He didn't reply, and I wondered if he'd heard me. Then I wondered if I'd offended him. Then I wondered how saying hello or thank you could be offensive. Ugh. Why did everything seem so hard to figure out?

Turning, I saw that Hank was already on round two of table clearing. Ugh again.

"Steve lives in town," he said as I approached.

I looked at him blankly.

He pointed to the boy doing dishes. "He's a townie."

Meaning . . .

"I think he graduated from the public high school a couple of years ago, but I'm not sure. We don't really talk."

"Oh," I said lamely. Why did that matter, exactly?

He picked up the scraper again and grinned conspiratorially. "Whatever you do, don't let Lola No see you scraping at the table. Or breaking any other rules. That woman has a serious pole up her butt and lives to bust anyone for anything."

"Lola No?" I repeated.

"Penelope Lassen. Associate professor of chemistry. Total hard-ass. I have the unfortunate privilege of spending the year in her lab." He leaned in closer, his blue eyes narrowing slightly. "Rumor has it she uses a spreadsheet to keep track of the busts she makes, with dates and levels of offense and every other detail she can come up with. I think her goal is to get us all kicked out so she can retire early." He shook his blond head and handed me a tray of glasses before picking up the last few items on the table and carrying them to the drop. I followed after him like a golden retriever puppy.

"Well, Josie Born-in-a-Red-Lobster," he told me. "I believe our table is fully cleared, and therefore we may adjourn to the T in the main hall for a little Scene before they whisk you away for your ritual first-year orientation. Said orientation is somewhat painful—especially for an unlucky few—but not as painful as Professor Roth's final exam." He headed for the door and I paused, wanting to get to the main hall as soon as possible but unclear on whether we'd walk there together.

"Are you coming or what?" Hank called over his shoulder.

He led the way back through a pair of stone archways into the main hall, which was crowded with students. But unlike the en masse parade to the dining hall after Vespers, this gathering felt sort of . . . electric. Students grouped together in clusters, obviously aware of who surrounded them. Eyes darted—searching, scoping, doing a kind of evaluation dance to see how everyone was measuring up. One minute Hank was next to me, and the next he had ambled into the crowd. I stood on the edge of the Scene as if I was not only late to the party but crashing, too.

Wishing I wasn't thoroughly opposed to heels, I rose up on tiptoe and tried to spot Annette. I saw myriad heads, but none stood out as hers, which befuddled me. I'd thought that I was infinitely familiar with every angle, every posture. How could I not identify her in a crowd of strangers?

Standing on the edge of the swirling mass of students, I longed for something safe and familiar. Two days ago, being in Virginia Falls seemed drab and uninteresting, but it was starting to dawn on me that it was *my* drab and uninteresting, that everything about it was part of me. At the moment, being squished on the faded living room couch, fighting a losing battle for the remote, sounded like heaven.

"Josie!" I turned to see Annette a little farther down the hall in a cluster of girls. She stepped away and came toward me.

I rushed forward, as if she'd just tossed me a rescue buoy and was towing me in.

"Finally! Come on—I want you to meet some people." She turned and I reached out, barely touching the back of her sweater as she led the way to the other girls. I'd done this a thousand times, but instead of relaxing into my touch, Annette hurried forward, leaving my hand hanging awkwardly in midair for the second time since I'd arrived.

"This is my friend Josie," Annette said to Rebecca and another girl I didn't know. "She's from Virginia Falls, too. Josie, this is my roommate, Rebecca Ryder."

"Becca," Rebecca corrected, holding out a hand. Rebecca was tall and extremely fit—her biceps were more sculpted than Ben's—and her eyes were the color of a lifeless lake, an incredible turquoise blue. Her eyes swept over me in approximately three seconds, making me feel inside out. "Welcome to Brookwood," she said.

Oh my God, I thought. *She's gorgeous. My girlfriend's roommate is freaking gorgeous.* I did my best to muster a friendly, nice-to-meet-you expression.

"Isn't this place amazing?" Annette said excitedly.

Amazing? I thought dazedly. More like Overwhelming. Confusing. Foreign.

"I'm Marina Carlisle," the other girl said. "I'm in the room next door."

I looked at her blankly.

"To these two," she finished. Marina was tiny—barely five feet—and chesty. *Impressive rack*, I heard my brother Ben say in my head, immediately followed by the sound of my mother whacking him on the arm with a rolled-up magazine.

I laughed aloud and the conversation halted, eyebrows clashing together. Annette's lips curved into a small frown.

While I tried to let the awkward silence roll off my back, I spotted Penn and Hank down the hall, yakking it up with a bunch of boys. I watched them guffaw and wrestle and act like buffoons, and momentarily wondered how long it would take to undergo sex-change therapy, a thought so ridiculous that I laughed again.

It happened while I was still chuckling. A shift. I didn't see it, but when I refocused on the girls, it was obvious that something had changed. Becca and Marina had turned ever so slightly, just enough to move me out of their conversational circle, leaving Annette in an in-between position.

Annette's eyes dimmed as if the sun had slipped behind the clouds, her expression clearly saying "what is going on with you?"

"Can we go for a walk?" I asked under my breath. I wanted to take her hand—that's what I would have done at home. I didn't, but Annette pulled away as if I had, and regained her position in the group of girls. The one I'd so rudely interrupted. And was, clearly, no longer a part of.

I felt my jaw slacken in bewilderment. Annette had just chosen these girls, whom she'd met a few hours ago, over me. I stared at the tiny moth hole in the back of her grandma Ruby's sweater and wondered what to do while my eyes started to well.

Don't just stand here, I told myself. I needed an exit, or better yet, a portal. Turning, I saw stairs at the end of the hall and somehow moved myself forward. Half tripping over my own feet, I rushed down them and pushed blindly through a pair of massive double doors.

CHAPTER 5

♥

Gulping in air, I wiped my cheek with the back of my hand. *You're such an idiot!* my brain shouted. I was angry. Angry with Annette for choosing those girls over me, and even angrier with myself. How could I not have known how different Brookwood would be? How overwhelmed and awkward I would feel? How much I would miss my family?

I was walking fast, trying to pull it together. I couldn't stop crying, though. And I had no idea where I was or where I should go. I walked up a paved path and out across the athletic fields, which seemed to stretch on and on. Every so often, I'd go up a little rise, only to find another field at the top. And from what I could gather, every field was perfectly rectangular, perfectly level, and perfectly mowed. Freakin' everything at Brookwood was perfect.

I want to go home! I thought. I kicked my shoes off my feet, hard, sending them flying into the air. Two seconds later, I heard them plunk onto the soft grass somewhere in the darkness.

The grass was cool and squishy under my feet, and I wriggled my toes into it. I took a breath, felt a tiny bit better. I was getting a momentary grip. But now I had to find my shoes in the dark.

Padding forward, I aimed for the spot where I thought maybe the left shoe had landed. But thanks to a mostly overcast sky, there was no moonlight, and I couldn't see a thing. I zigzagged in an attempt to be logical. *Could it have come this far?* I wondered as I scanned a section of grass near the goal. Probably not . . .

Turning around, I headed in the other direction and came almost immediately upon my right shoe. Well, that was something. I slipped it onto my foot.

In the distance, I heard voices and laughter. The new students were on their way to Orientation in the auditorium. I knew I should be going, too, but also knew I couldn't show up wearing one shoe.

I retraced my steps and kept searching, but it was as if my shoe had disappeared, as if the field had swallowed it up. I could feel my heartbeat accelerating, my palms getting sweaty. I was going to miss Orientation and had no idea whether or not it mattered. At VF High, they never bothered to take attendance at assemblies—it took too long. But I was far, far away from my Midwestern high school.

My search became urgent. I raced up and down the field, not really paying attention to where I was looking. How hard could it be to find a shoe? As my feet moved quickly over the grass near the painted center line, I heard a familiar gurgling sound that I couldn't place. My phone beeped, a text. *Where are you?* Annette wanted to know. *It's starting!* And then, just as I realized what the gurgling sound was, the sprinklers came on.

The water was surprisingly icy, and I was drenched in seconds. I didn't even bother to run. I was smack-dab in the middle of the field; there was no easy way out. So I just stood there in the freezing sprinkler shower getting soaked, holding a cell phone and wearing one shoe. I shuddered as water dripped into my ears and down my back. And then, all of a sudden, I couldn't take it anymore.

"I hate it here!" I screamed.

I heard my voice echo off the buildings in the distance, the garbled words rushing back at me in the darkness. And then my mother was there, in my head, telling me not to be so rash. Not to judge. To give it a chance. Just like she'd been telling me since pre-school, when I spent the first two weeks screaming my head off.

"I hate it here!" I shouted, louder this time.

The sprinklers turned off as quickly as they'd turned on, and the fields were silent except for the settling water that gurgled in the irrigation tubes. I took a step forward and heard the water squish between my toes, felt my foot sink into the wet earth. Two steps later, I found my shoe.

I bent over to retrieve it as a breeze came up, and shivered. Like the rest of me, the leather flat was soaking wet. I tipped it and a thin stream of water ran to the ground, flooding my memory with the first time I met Annette.

It had been raining for almost two days, and everyone in the house was cranky as anything when the doorbell rang. I opened the door and there she was, on our porch, smiling.

"Can you play?" she asked without telling me her name. Her family had just moved into the neighborhood.

I nodded while my gaze dropped to her boots, which were brand-new, polka dot, and shiny as all get out. They had every color of the rainbow.

Her eyes followed. "You want to wear them?" She didn't wait for an answer—just slipped her feet out and handed them over.

I put them on and tromped to the closet to find my brother's army green hand-me-downs, watching her face when I brought them out of the closet. She didn't balk, even when she had to squeeze her feet into them because they were two sizes too small.

"Let's go!" she said, tugging on my hand. We splashed in mud puddles all afternoon, tromping across the greener-than-green-from-rain grass dotted with yellow dandelions that we stomped on with all our might. Back and forth we marched, the water sucking and slurping against our boots while the rain poured down and my brothers threatened us with dripping earthworms. We ignored them in unison, totally absorbed in our own water-logged world. Annette's long, wet eyelashes clumped together, making a single dark fringe above her green eyes.

I fell in love with those boots right away. Falling in love with Annette took a little more time. I can't tell you exactly when I realized that the way I felt about Annette was different from the way I felt about, say, Maureen. Or Henry. I think my first clue might have been that she was my favorite thing to photograph during my middle school photography phase. I took pictures of other stuff, too, but somehow Annette always found her way into the frame.

Our parents didn't notice at first, probably because we had been best friends for years. Weekly sleepovers were part of the regularly scheduled programming. Years later, we were still having sleepovers, though what we did after lights-out was not so regularly scheduled, at least not in our small Minnesota town. Where we came from, girls like boys and boys like girls, or at least that's what they wanted us to believe. Not that we were constantly going at it or anything. Mostly we spooned each other—her back against my front—fitting together perfectly and talking in the dark.

"You might want to keep that opinion to yourself," someone said bluntly.

My head snapped up and I squinted across the wet field toward the sound of the voice. It was female and, I was pretty sure, not an adult's. But I couldn't see anyone.

I could, however, hear someone walking toward me.

"Not that I disagree with you. Sometimes it freaking sucks here. But being miserable is not the kind of thing you want to advertise at Brookwood."

Roxanne. It was my roommate Roxanne walking toward me. I felt a moment of relief, and then wondered why I would be relieved to see her.

I didn't say anything as she closed in on my dripping, shivering self. "You look like you could use a drink," she said. "Come on."

I dumped the rest of the water out of my shoe, slipped my phone into my pocket, and followed her across the grass into a patch of woods that was bizarrely situated in the middle of the fields. The thickly clustered trees made everything even darker, but I could make out the shape of a bench near a small open area.

Roxanne sat down on it and pulled a two-liter bottle out of her giant book bag. Unscrewing the top, she tilted it and took a drink. "Brookwood Balm," she told me, handing the bottle over.

I hesitated. I wasn't a prude or anything, but I didn't drink a whole lot, and when I did, my usual beverage of choice was beer. I definitely wasn't accustomed to swigging hard liquor out of a bottle the size of a milk jug.

She shook the bottle. "This thing weighs close to eight pounds," she said. "Are you going to take it or not?"

I took the bottle, lifted it to my lips, and let the vodka, I now knew, fill my mouth. I held it there for longer than I should have, wondering if I'd be able to get it down, and when I finally swallowed, a wash of dinner and vodka belched into my mouth, making me gag.

Roxanne chuckled. "You have to get it down fast—otherwise it burns too much." She took another drink and handed it back.

Shivering, I took the bottle again. This time I swallowed almost immediately, and down it went, leaving a trail of heat in my throat that spread into my belly.

Roxanne screwed the cap back on the bottle and buried it in her bag. "Drinking rule number one," she said. "Two shots is generally the limit, especially on school nights. You can do two shots and still function well enough to walk past Lola No, do your schoolwork, and not make a total ass of yourself at post-study-hall Scene." She pulled a box of Altoids out of her pocket, flipped open the lid, and extended it to me. "Rule number two. No drinking if you do not have a method for disguising the alcohol on your breath. After extensive research that lasted my entire lower-mid year, I recommend Altoids, three of them, eating them one at a time, and dissolving, not chewing, though sometimes you will be in a hurry and chewing will be necessary."

I complied, even though Altoids were too strong for me—I was a Pep O Mint Life Savers kind of girl. As the first mint dissolved in my mouth, I felt the booze slipping into my bloodstream, making everything a little hazy. For the first time all day, I felt myself relax. Plus, I was no longer shivering.

Roxanne slid the box of Altoids back into her pocket. "Do you talk?"

I laughed, because at home everyone wondered if I was capable of shutting up. And, to be honest, sometimes I wasn't. Which was one of the reasons I didn't really want to start talking.

"Listen, I wasn't kidding before," she went on. "Brookwood can really suck sometimes. But if there's one thing I've learned, it's that weakness is universally frowned upon—even more than weirdness—so whatever you do, don't look vulnerable. Especially not to the Soleets."

"The what?"

"Soleets. The Social Elites. They're sporty and rich and beautiful and, for the most part, so busy thinking about themselves they don't give a rat's ass about anyone else. There are a lot of them around here, so watch out."

My mind flashed to the Scene after dinner, and I knew instantly that Becca was a Soleet.

"They make me feel inside out," I blurted.

I heard Roxanne exhale slowly. "Exactly," she agreed. "Inside out and upside down."

CHAPTER 6

♥

I had just stepped out of the shower and was wrapping my hair in a towel when Annette burst into the bathroom.

"Where were you?" she demanded. "I texted you like ten times and practically got busted for having my phone in public—totally against the rules. Josie, you missed it!"

A brief flash of happiness—she'd missed me!—was followed by a free fall into annoyance. Didn't she realize how hurt I'd been when she brushed me off in the main hall?

"My phone died," I said, yanking the towel off my head and wrapping it around my torso, as if a rectangular piece of cotton terry cloth would protect me, would make me less vulnerable. She raised an eyebrow, silently reminding me that we'd been naked together countless times.

"I went on a walk."

"But you got picked!" she said. "They told your life story!"

"My what?"

"Your life story. Becca says they pick three new students every year and do a little slide show about them. You know, so people can get a snapshot of some of the kids who're new at Brookwood. And they picked you!"

What the . . . ? I suddenly remembered what Hank told me after dinner—that Orientation was especially painful for an unlucky few. Only I'd had no idea what that meant, or that I was one of those few. Uff-da.

I steadied myself on the old-fashioned radiator. I already felt like I had a sign around my neck saying "I'm not like any of you people." Did I really need a slide show, too? "What did they say?" I asked, slumping onto the toilet.

Annette could see my worry and crouched down to my level. "It's all right, Jo. It was nothing too embarrassing, and your baby pictures were adorable. Your mom did a great job picking them out."

"My mom?"

"Of course. Where else would they get baby pictures of you?" Her fingers rested on my forearm. "She did an awesome job, too. The only one Becca said she'd have edited out was the one from two years ago of you with your face covered in birthday cake. She said it seemed kind of . . ."

I bolted to my feet, knocking the plastic cup of toothbrushes off the sink and sending them to the floor with a hollow clatter. My thirteenth birthday party had a carnival theme, complete with a cake-eating contest in which I beat all three of my brothers and emerged victorious. I did *not* need Rebecca Ryder to tell me how ridiculous I'd looked!

Annette calmly gathered the toothbrushes and set the cup down on the edge of the sink. "Josie, what's wrong?"

"Nothing. I'm fine," I murmured, pulling back slightly. For some reason, I didn't want to tell her how hard the last several hours had been, how uncertain I was feeling.

"Well, that's clearly not true." Annette was gazing at me, not letting me off the hook.

I shivered and shrugged simultaneously. "I just got a little cold on my walk."

The corners of her mouth tugged into a smile. "Oh, is that all?" She stepped closer. "I can fix that." She let go of my hand and found the small of my back, nudging me closer until our breasts were touching. Then she leaned in and kissed me.

I felt her soft lips settle onto mine and tilted my head, opening my mouth slightly and breathing her in. She smelled like Pert shampoo and strawberry and everything that was good, that was familiar. As I reached my arms around her shoulders, the whole day began to disappear. Why had I been so upset again?

Annette leaned the length of her body into mine, pressing me against the wall and kissing me a little harder. I gave in to everything then—to her lips, her tongue, her body, until I forgot where I was. Then Annette's hand was on my breast and my towel was slipping and I suddenly remembered exactly where we were, and everything that had happened that day, and was starting to cry. Only this time, Annette was here, kissing me—my cheeks, my chin, my eyelids. And then she reached for my hand and kissed that.

"It's going to be okay," she told me as she retrieved my towel from the floor and wrapped it around me, tucking the flap next to my armpit. We'd reversed our usual roles—I'd gone from pep talker to pep listener—and I felt like a little kid as she pulled me into a hug. "You said it yourself. They're going to love us."

I tried to shake off my uncertainty and just be here and be happy, to think of nothing but Pert shampoo and Annette and kissing.

And then Roxanne opened the door.

"Oh!" Annette said in surprise, stepping away so quickly you'd have thought I was made of molten lava.

I straightened and made sure my towel was covering but couldn't quite manage to offer an excuse. And anyway, what was the point? I already knew Roxanne well enough to know that she wouldn't believe some half-baked lie, and at the moment, I wasn't particularly interested in hiding my relationship with Annette anyway. Which, admittedly, wasn't entirely fair since I'd actually been the one to suggest we keep our relationship under wraps for the first few days.

It was our last Saturday night in Virginia Falls. Annette rolled over, throwing an arm across my chest and tucking her head against my shoulder. During the day, she was the calm one, moving through life as if it had been scripted and she'd been rehearsing for years. At night, though, she thrashed around like a wild pony, tangling the sheets and our limbs.

"Josie? Are you asleep?" she whispered, wriggling closer.

"No."

I heard her exhale, and knew what she was thinking before she spoke again. "I'm kind of freaking out." Her voice had that nervous edge—the one that emerged when Shannon got nasty after drinking too much. She rolled over to face me and I glanced at my clock—it was one thirty a.m.

Neither of us said anything for a long time, and I could feel Annette's heartbeat through her pajama top, hear her breathing in the dark. I slid down, wrapping my arms around her waist.

"It'll be fine," I said. "It's not like Brookwood is a foreign country. I think they even speak English . . ."

She let out a whoop and I smiled into her collarbone, loving how her laughter could suddenly erupt from her belly. I lifted my head to find her lips, her warm, minty breath on my face.

I loved kissing Annette. Her lips were fuller than mine and so, so soft. She opened her mouth and I pulled her closer, my palm against the curve of her waist. I was starting to drift when, just like that, we weren't kissing anymore.

"What if they don't like us?" I couldn't see her face in the darkness, but heard the worry in her voice loud and clear. "What if they're weird about girls who like girls?"

"You think they're lesbophobic?" I asked, trying to make her smile. That word had always seemed funny to me.

"Josie, I'm serious. We have no idea what it's like there."

I'd thought about this, of course, and wasn't surprised that she had, too. "We don't have to broadcast that we're a couple," I said reasonably. "We can keep it quiet at first."

"You'd be okay with that?"

"Sure. We'll be roommates, and still a couple—just not public about it for the first week or two. We'll break in those Brookwood lesbophobics easy."

"They still might not like us."

"Annette, they're going to love us. Well, you at least. Everyone adores you. Plus, you're smart and funny and not a total dog . . ."

She pinched me, hard, on the butt.

"Hey!"

"You deserved that."

"I think you broke the skin."

"You still deserved it."

I could taste the remnants of her hint-o-mint lip balm on my own lips and kissed her again, quickly this time. "I forgive you."

"Really?" she asked.

"Of course. You're impossible to stay mad at."

"I mean about them liking us." She was whispering again, the anxious edge resurfacing. Having Shannon for a mother had seriously eroded Annette's self-esteem.

I sat up on my elbow. "Annette Anderson, where is your confidence? You are a fabulous human being, and everyone at Brookwood Academy will see that the minute we step foot onto that campus."

I watched her face shift into a smile, felt her shoulders relax. I snuggled back down and she curled into me, draping an arm over the edge of the bed. "You always know exactly how to make me feel better, Josie," she said, turning to kiss my cheek. "I swear I'd be lost without you."

———

"Um, we were just talking," Annette babbled to Roxanne. Then she seemed to remember her manners, because she stepped forward and held out a hand. "I'm Annette, Annette Anderson."

Roxanne raised an eyebrow and shook, but didn't point out the obvious fact that talking was clearly not all we were doing. Then she grabbed a tube of moisturizer off the shelf above the sink. "No problem, girls," she said lightly. "A little female pow-wow is always a good thing. And I totally should have knocked.

But for future reference, this door has a lock." She slipped out the door and closed it behind her.

Annette steadied herself against the pedestal sink. "I'm totally not ready for this."

I knew exactly how she felt. "It's ridiculously overwhelming, isn't it?" But as the question came out of my mouth, I couldn't help but wonder if she was talking about what I was talking about—making a life halfway across the country from our friends and families and everything we knew—or about being ourselves, a couple, in front of people who didn't know us.

"Overwhelming, yes," Annette agreed, leaning fully against the sink and looking tired for the first time since we'd arrived. "It's like being on a roller coaster." Her eyes softened. "I'm sorry about what happened in the main hall, Josie. I didn't mean to hurt you. But I didn't want to offend them, either. We're not in Virginia Falls anymore—we can't just go off by ourselves whenever we feel like it."

"We can't?" I half joked. I knew she was right—or at least partly right—but didn't want to admit it.

Annette shook her head. "No. And anyway, why would we want to? We moved halfway across the country to go to school here, and this place is incredible."

I didn't say anything.

"Did you know they have sixty-seven clubs and organizations? I was thinking of doing filmmaking, or maybe baking. What are you going to try?" Annette was filling my silence with her excitement, which only seemed to drain whatever fumes of energy I had left. I hadn't even considered extracurricular activities. We'd only been here for ten hours!

"I'm not sure yet," I admitted. "Can we decide later?" I pulled my pajama bottoms off a hook and slipped them on. "I'm about to fall over."

Annette gazed at me with a "you can't avoid deciding forever" look, which I almost *did* avoid by pulling my tank top over my head—but didn't protest. She half smiled and tilted herself forward, giving me a quick kiss on the lips. "Okay, later, then. I'll see you tomorrow."

I watched her disappear out the door with a wave to Roxanne, remembering with a pang that I thought we'd be roommates, that we'd be falling asleep whispering in the dark. Instead, we were both bunking with virtual strangers.

Tomorrow couldn't come soon enough.

CHAPTER 7

♥

Oh jeez, I thought, gazing at the handout on the table in front of me. Until that moment, I'd had no idea that a single sheet of plain white 8-1/2 x 11 paper could be capable of striking terror into my heart. And yet there it was, the syllabus for mid English, staring up at me and making me feel like it was my first day of classes in a new school, I didn't know anyone, and my family and friends were extremely far away.

Oh, wait, that was actually true.

To begin with, the type on the syllabus was so small I could hardly read it. But that was clearly necessary if Mr., um, *Professor* Drake was going to fit it all on one piece of paper—even if he used both sides. Second, it was filled with a painstakingly detailed, well-thought-out plan for the entire year, during which I would apparently be writing *innumerate* (his word) essays and engaging in both debates and *recitations* (also his word).

Frankly, it was all a little much for seven forty-five on a Monday morning . . . especially since I'd overslept and hadn't had a single sip of coffee, much less my usual cup. And since every other English class syllabus I'd seen was barely thought out and fit easily on an index card.

The class was small—eleven students—less than a third the size of my freshman English class at VF High. Brookwood prided itself on its small class size, which sounded great in theory but at the moment felt more like a choke hold.

Penn was at one end of the oval table, Becca right across from me. She fingered her add-a-pearl necklace, looking very sure of herself. I was starting to suspect that she always looked like that. Next to her sat Patrick Mahoney, from table 37. His eyes kept darting to the syllabus and he was beaming as though he'd just been handed the keys to his dad's Mercedes.

Professor Drake, dressed in a tweed blazer and a red patterned bow tie, stood at the front of the room, gazing out at us over the top of his tortoiseshell glasses. "The goal of this class is to turn you into thoughtful human beings who are capable of reading, writing, and discussing literature both analytically and critically," he stated. "Not an easy task, I assure you, but there we have it."

He wrote four words on the board and proceeded to define each one out loud and in detail, as if he were some sort of oral human dictionary.

"*Emotion*, noun, an excitement of feeling that is separate from reason or knowledge.

"*Logic*, noun, the science or art of exact reason or formal thought.

"Are you with me?" He paused in his definition spouting and looked over his shoulder, catching my eye and making me wonder if I looked as slow as I felt.

"*Rhetoric*, noun, the art of persuasion in composition or speaking, often without conviction or sincerity."

I eyed Becca, who I already sensed was some kind of rhetorical genius.

"And finally, *authenticity*, noun, the quality of being authentic," and then, "*authentic*, adjective, of approved authority; true, trustworthy, credible.

"These are the primary tools we will use to discuss our readings," Professor Drake said. "I suggest you get to know them intimately so that you are able to form opinions about the effectiveness or ineffectiveness of everything you read and write."

No pressure, I thought, remembering with a sinking feeling that Brookwood held classes six days a week. I looked to the clock for comfort, but found none. It was only 8:19.

Professor Drake plowed through the next thirty-one minutes at warp whiteboard-writing speed, then gave us our first assignment. Read two poems: "The Wood-Pile" and "Stopping by Woods on a Snowy Evening," by Robert Frost. But that was not all.

"I'd like you to come to class with detailed notes on whether or not you found these selections to be effective or ineffective, and why or why not based on two of the four components we've just discussed. And please try to sound like the intelligent creatures the admissions committee believes you to be. I don't want to be bored to tears for the next nine months, and neither do you."

He caught my eye then, and nodded slightly, as if he knew I could do it. And in the space of a single forty-five-minute class, I had reconsidered everything I knew about English class. I'd never had a teacher who (1) operated under the assumption that his students would do what he asked, (2) assumed I was really smart, or (3) expected me to use my brain pretty much all the time.

Not sure how to respond, I nodded back before shoving my

books into my backpack and getting to my weary feet. The academic part of Brookwood appeared to be *authentic*, at least.

"He's not as tough as he seems," Penn said as we filed into the hall. "He just likes big words and tiny bow ties."

"And essays," I added, remembering the syllabus.

"That too," Penn admitted. "What's next for you?"

"Algebra Two. Professor Roth."

"Male or female?"

I hesitated.

"There are two Roths."

"Oh. Female, I think."

Penn winced. "Ouch."

Great. "That good, huh?"

"They call her the Dragon Lady."

"Ouch," I repeated. "Does she breathe fire?"

"Quite possibly. She's definitely tough, but most of them are. Academics are of the utmost importance here at Brookwood Academy," he intoned.

"Yeah, I'm getting that."

We dropped down a couple of stairs into the arched junction, where students veered off in all directions. Penn raised a hand in a partial salute. "I'm off to Latin with Blackburn," he said. "See you later."

I nodded and started toward the exit—math and science were in a completely different building. By the time I slid into my seat in algebra, my midsection was making so much noise I thought I might have a couple of semis rumbling through my stomach. I needed food.

Professor Roth brought preppy to a whole new level with her tortoiseshell barrettes, baby-blue Fair Isle sweater, and pink wide-wale corduroys, but I could tell right away she was tough as nails underneath her ridiculous appearance. Her nostrils did, in fact, flare out a little. Her syllabus was considerably shorter than Professor Drake's, but just as detailed, and the longer she talked, the more stressed I became. I hadn't exactly flown through Algebra I but had tested well enough to make it into this class. Which had seemed like a good thing . . . until now.

I was sensing that a lot of things about Brookwood sounded good from halfway across the country. But now that I was here and actually had to face them? Um, not so much.

By the time I stumbled into anthropology, which was thankfully in an adjacent wing of the same building, I was feeling downright faint. I took a seat at the end of the table and looked around. The classroom was cluttered with all kinds of weird stuff—masks, headdresses, feathers, and skulls, most of which appeared to be human. Professor Mannering looked sort of like an artifact himself—the guy was seriously old, with jaw-length gray hair that was impossibly frizzy. He wore a wrinkled button-down shirt that was rolled up to the elbows but also tucked in. His pants were neatly pressed, and belted at the waist. He was so thin he looked like he might break at any second, and yet he buzzed around the classroom, jotting things on the board, arranging papers, and generally looking like an excited little kid in the wrong body.

"The guy's a legend," Penn said, appearing beside me and pulling out a chair. "To the students, anyway. The board has other ideas," he added in a low voice. "We're lucky we got in here before they kicked him out."

"Why would they do that? Because he's old?"

He tossed his backpack onto the desk and sat down. "Not exactly. Mannering isn't a company man, so to speak—he likes doing things his way. He was supposed to retire three years ago— the board and the administration threw him a big party and everything. But the next fall, he was right here in his classroom like nothing had happened."

"Seriously?"

Penn nodded. "Seriously. He's been teaching here forever. Taught my father *and* two great-uncles." A look of resignation moved across Penn's face. "I come from a long line, I'm afraid."

"A long line of what?"

"The jury's still out on that one." He sighed. "And unfortunately, I'm the only boy in my family—the only one to carry on the esteemed McCarthy name." He leaned in close. "It's as if my parents have forgotten about McCarthyism," he confided, rolling his eyes.

A loud rapping sound echoed through the room, and we turned our attention to Professor Mannering. Some kind of antler, I realized. He'd been rapping an antler on the table.

"Welcome to Anthropology Four Hundred, known affectionately as Ant Four," he said, beaming at us from behind his glasses, which looked as though they hadn't been cleaned in, well, ever.

He handed a stack of syllabi to the boy at the other end of the table, who took one and passed it down. It was handwritten—a scratchy scrawl—and photocopied crookedly on the 8-1/2 x 11 sheet.

I stared down at the paper. The syllabus contained only two sentences, which, together, created a single line of text: *Humans are both biological and cultural creatures. What does this mean?*

Next to me, Penn chuckled. "Get ready, Subzero," he murmured. "Assuming old Mannering doesn't keel over or get booted in the next couple of months, this is going to be good."

I had no idea *what* it was going to be but was pretty sure that Professor Mannering wasn't going to keel over anytime soon. I was also sure that he was nothing like the other Brookwood professors I'd met so far, who were nothing like the teachers at Virginia Falls High.

At VFH, teachers had too many students and too many discipline problems. The entire staff was overworked, right down to the office aids. Classes were big, and getting extra help wasn't easy. Not that a lot of students even *wanted* extra help. Sure, there were a few kids who worked their butts off, but the vast majority did the bare minimum, which basically meant that they usually showed up for school. And some didn't even do that.

Brookwood was, clearly, the polar opposite. From what I could tell, students and teachers alike took academics *extremely* seriously. This fact fell into the category of "sounded good from halfway across the country" but was, up close, feeling a little scary. Especially because I was on a good-size scholarship, and if I didn't keep up my grades, the school had the right to renege and give the money and the spot to someone else. Which, according to Headmaster Thornfeld's Vespers statistics, could be accomplished at the drop of a hat.

Professor Mannering spent our first class barraging us with questions: What did it mean to be human? How much did culture shape our actions? Our ideas? Do cultures dictate our ethics? What about human rights?

If I was tired and hungry after English and tired, hungry, and overwhelmed after algebra, I was tired, hungry, overwhelmed, and confused after anthropology. Penn wanted to talk to Professor Mannering, so I stumbled out of the science building, around the pond, and into the dining hall alone.

"Hey," a voice said. It was Steve, who was standing behind the grill in the servery (yes, they actually used the word *servery*), where I had ventured on autopilot.

"Hey," I said back, eyeing the food like a hungry dog. "Got anything that'll cure ridiculously low blood sugar?"

"Definitely." He leaned forward conspiratorially. "And for the record, my grilled veggie feta wrap kicks the pineapple pizza's ass."

"Really," I said. "Maybe I should be the judge of that?"

"Be my guest," he replied, setting a delicious-looking grilled sandwich on my plate, followed by a dollop of green sauce. "Cilantro pesto," he explained. "I created the recipe myself. You want the chipotle sour cream, too?"

"You betcha," I replied, forgetting for a moment that I was no longer in Minnesota.

He gave me a sideways glance as he plopped a healthy spoonful next to the wrap. "You're not from around here, are you?"

"Um, no," I admitted. "And I'm not in Kansas anymore, either."

He laughed. "Are you really from Kansas?"

"Actually, no, but I am feeling a little bit like I've landed in Oz." I squinted at him, wondering why I seemed utterly unable to act like a normal person. And what possessed me to tell him this? Was it because he was a . . . what was the word again? Towner?

"Well, watch out for the winged monkeys," he said, deadpan.

This time *I* laughed. "Excellent advice," I said. "Thanks."

The dining hall was crowded, with a long table in front clearly designated for faculty, and I paused at the edge of the tables to look for Annette. We didn't have any classes together but had lunch at the same time most days, which would have to suffice. The academic schedule at Brookwood was nothing like the academic schedule at VF High. Classes did not meet at the same time every day—or practically at all, from what I could tell.

The smell of the grilled wrap drifted up to my nose, and my mouth started to water. Being careful not to drop my tray, I picked up the sandwich, dipped, and took a bite.

"People usually sit down to eat here at Brookwood," a voice said behind me. Penn. How did he get his food so fast?

I chewed and swallowed. "Where's the challenge in that?"

"Ahh." Penn was smiling. "The challenge lies in finding a seat with people you actually want to eat with . . ." He trailed off and scanned the crowd. "Not a lotta room, I see."

"Nope." I was still searching for Annette. Unfortunately, her blondish ponytailed head continued to be essentially indistinguishable from the one hundred *other* blondish ponytailed heads. It was beginning to make me uneasy.

"Penn!" Hank was on his feet and shouting from halfway across the room. "Dude, are you blind?"

Penn responded by raising his chin. "Twenty-twenty," he shouted back. Then to me, "Care to join us?"

I chewed, wondering if this was a genuine offer. The table was all boys, and they appeared to be in their usual state of shenanigans. It looked appealing. Funny how boy goofiness drove me crazy at home, but here it sort of pulled me in.

"We don't bite," he added.

"No, thanks," I said. "I'm good."

"No one was doubting that, Subzero," he said. "Just try not to fall asleep—that would be messy."

I laughed as he ambled over to the table of guys, then acted like I knew where I was going and started walking. And then, thankfully, I spotted Annette.

And Becca.

And the rest of the girls from the main hall that first night.

"Hey," I said, setting my tray down next to Annette's just as I'd done every school day for years.

"Hey," Annette replied, "I was wondering when you'd get here. Becca is filling us in on the Dress to Impress Dance this Saturday."

"It's a rite of passage at the beginning of each school year," Marina explained. "We all dress up, but not fancy—crazy. The wackier, the better."

"Remember last year?" said fluent-in-five-languages Cynthia Wu from table 37 (in English, thankfully). "Penn McCarthy's outfit was hilarious."

"He's such a ham," Becca pronounced.

"A gorgeous, meaty ham," Marina added with a giggle.

Taking the cue, the girls cast their eyes toward the table of boys not far away. Penn was on his feet, adding to the chocolate chip cookie and toothpick bridge they'd been building, his face tight with concentration despite the silliness of the task.

Gorgeous? Penn? Funny, yes. Quick-witted, definitely. But gorgeous? That had been lost on me.

When I turned back to our table, Annette was watching me knowingly. *Lost on both of us*, I thought with a small smile.

"Watch out for your lateral bracing, McCarthy," Becca called out. "You wouldn't want it to get stuck in one of your stringers."

At that moment the bridge collapsed, leaving a heap of cookies on the table. "Your fault!" Penn called accusingly, though it was clear he didn't really care as he picked up a cookie and bit into it. His smile was wide.

"Faulty design!" Becca retorted before turning back to us with a wide grin of her own. "Powwow in my room on Saturday to figure out what we're gonna wear," she said. "I have cross-country until five, so come at five thirty."

"You're running again?" Cynthia asked. "Girl, you have got to get with real team sports. Field hockey is where it's at."

"Are you kidding?" Becca countered. "There's no way I'm going to run around chasing a tiny plastic ball so I can whack it with a stick."

I felt a flash of respect for her, since I was in total agreement. Despite my little brothers Josh and Toby's obsessive interest in hockey, chasing something with a stick had always seemed a little ridiculous. And team sports in general kind of . . . teamy.

"Especially when I can be kicking butt in cross-country," she finished, turning to Annette. "Last year we had a 7-2 record, and almost went to regionals. We rocked it. You should run with us."

Like that's *gonna happen*, I thought as I took a bite of wrap. I almost felt sorry for Becca, since Annette despised running. She'd never run a day in her life . . . unless you counted the early days when the neighborhood kids played freeze tag in our backyard, and sometimes even that took coaxing.

"I do not see why anyone in their right mind would want to spend extra time with Lola No," Marina said, blowing her bangs out of her eyes.

Becca stared her down with her turquoise blues. "Just saying," Marina added lamely.

"She might be a nightmare in the dorm, but she's an amazing coach. Plus, she looks out for her girls, so to speak. Being on Lola No's good side is *definitely* a good thing."

"Annette's not exactly a runner," I said, taking a swig of iced tea.

I felt Annette stiffen next to me, even as Becca babbled on, providing details about the practice schedule and their fiercest competitor, the Sutton School.

"I'd love to try out," Annette announced as I took another bite.

I choked on a piece of feta cheese. "No, you wouldn't." I knew I should just keep quiet and talk to her about it later, when we were alone, but I seemed unable to control myself.

"How do you know?" I could see the challenge in her eyes, in the tilt of her head.

"Because I've been listening to you complain about having to run more than fifty feet since you were eight," I said. "Remember those laps Coach Thompson made us do in fifth grade? You pretended to have the stomach flu almost every Thursday."

"Most of the class did that," Annette said woodenly.

That was true, actually. But so was the fact that Annette did not like to run.

"Why don't you try out, too?" Becca said, raising her chin. This was obviously meant to be a challenge.

"No, thanks," I said. "Running isn't my bag, either."

Becca narrowed her eyes at me as if to say "no, of course it isn't," and then actually opened her mouth. "I think you forgot your dessert," she said. "That cake looks delicious, and you don't have to worry about getting it on your face." She pushed a fork across the table in my direction.

Did she really just say that? I wondered. Nobody at the table acknowledged the snub, and Becca immediately refocused her energy on Annette. "Just think about it," she was saying. "Tryouts for new students are Wednesday."

"Sounds great," Annette said.

My girlfriend skillfully avoided my gaze—a talent she'd perfected on her mother—and I wondered if she had lost her mind, her backbone, or both. Not knowing the answer, I slathered my last bite of veggie wrap with chipotle sour cream and shoved it into my mouth.

CHAPTER 8

♥

"Orientation? It was great," I lied into the room phone I shared with Roxanne. My cell was permanently dead, thanks to a combination of my own foolishness and the Brookwood sprinkler system. I stretched out on the top bunk and gazed out the window at the pond, where a group of people lounged in the Saturday afternoon sun. I watched Becca and Cynthia and Hank, and several others I'd seen a dozen times in the past week but couldn't identify by name if my life depended on it.

"It took forever to pick out those pictures!" My mother's excitement reverberated through the phone line.

"She made us all crazy!" my dad put in. "I'm officially certifiable."

"You've been certifiable since Josh was born." I heard the breathy sound of a spoon swat—probably on the arm—and wondered which spoon it was, the short one with the hole in the middle or the longer one with the scorched handle. My mom had an entire collection of wooden spoons, thanks to years of Christmas gifts, but used these two over and over while the rest collected dust in a drawer.

"What's for dinner?" I asked, turning away from the window. I could picture them as clearly as if I were right there at our kitchen table, and found that I wanted to be. Which was surprising, because a couple of weeks ago, that seemed like the most boring place in the world.

"Chicken cacciatore," my mom said. "Your grandfather is coming."

Crap. I loved my mom's chicken cacciatore. I could smell the oregano, taste the falling-off-the-bone-tender chicken and mushrooms.

I heard Ben come into the kitchen and imagined him slouching against the Formica counter with his hands shoved in the pockets of his tattered Levis, but he opened the fridge instead.

"How's it going out there in preppy land?" he asked as he popped the tab on his Mountain Dew. "Are you working your butt off?"

"Uh-huh. That's pretty much what everyone does around here."

"Well, then, you should fit right in."

I considered trying to explain that working hard at VF High and working hard at Brookwood weren't even in the same orbit, but decided it might just depress me. Being on a grade-based scholarship was stressful enough.

Luckily, Ben changed the subject. "Did you freak when you saw the pictures?"

"Pretty much," I said. "And hey, thanks for the warning."

"Mom swore me to secrecy," he intoned before taking a gulp of Dew. "Said she'd take away the car if I spilled."

"Maybe she should take the car away anyway."

"That's cold, Jo," Ben said. "But we both know she won't, because then she'd have to drive Josh and Toby everywhere herself."

"I *do* drive those maniacs practically everywhere," my mom insisted.

That crack is almost the exact shape of Turtle Lake, I thought, looking up at the ceiling above my bed and wondering if Mom was glad to have one of her kids out of her hair. Maybe my leaving had simplified things.

I closed my eyes and rubbed my temple, even though it was my chest that was aching. I missed them so much it actually hurt.

"Hey, I have to go—Roxanne needs the phone." Total lie.

"All right, sweetie," my mom said. "Say hello to her for us. Tell her we can't wait to meet her."

"Right. Especially if she's hot."

"Benjamin!" More spoon swatting.

"She is smoking hot," I confirmed.

"Really?" my dad wanted to know.

"I give up," my mother said, sounding completely exasperated. Maybe all the testosterone in the house was getting to her. Maybe she missed me after all.

"Well, don't go cheating on Annette," Ben advised. "Or I'll have to pound you at Christmas."

My family knew I was gay, and they knew about Annette— none of us were good at keeping secrets. I didn't tell my parents right away, though—I needed some time to sort things out in my head. For a long time I didn't tell *anyone*. And then, all of a sudden, I told my parents I wanted to have a powwow. Half an hour later, my mom, my dad, and I were all in the kitchen.

63

"What'd you do this time, Josie?" my father asked, pulling out a chair at the table. "Crash the car?"

"I don't think that's it, Peter," my mother said quietly.

My dad heard the tone in her voice, and the creases on his forehead instantly revealed themselves. He leaned forward, linking his fingers together on top of the table. "What is it, then?"

The words felt heavy to me, and I wished I hadn't called this little meeting. Why had I felt compelled to tell them? It wasn't like I was in trouble or anything.

"Just tell us." My mother's voice was quiet, but steely. "I'm sure we can figure out what to do."

My father looked confused for a moment, and then his face crumpled. He shook his head slowly. "Oh, Josie, no."

All at once I understood what they were thinking, and wanted to laugh. Of course that's what they would think. How could they help it? Virginia Falls High had a couple of teen pregnancies every year—it was the obvious guess. But nothing could have been further from the truth . . .

"I'm not pregnant," I said.

"You're not?" my mother asked.

"Of course she isn't, Caroline. She doesn't even have a boyfriend," my father explained rationally.

Well, that was true.

"Oh, thank God," my mother said. "You're so young, Josie! But when you find the right boy, just let me know and we can make an appointment at Planned Parenthood. The nurses there are excellent, and there are *several* preventive choices these days."

My mother could be oh so helpful. "Um, that's the thing," I

said slowly. I could feel my face flushing, and my palms were all sweaty. It wasn't that I thought my parents were going to freak out. I knew they loved me, and telling them I was gay wouldn't change that. But I suddenly had the feeling I was somehow letting them down.

I cleared my throat. "I don't think I'll be getting a boyfriend anytime soon."

"There's no rush!" my mom babbled, the relief visible on her face. She looked like I had just gotten an A in geometry. Problem was, me getting a boyfriend was even more unlikely.

I opened my mouth to do some calm explaining. "I'm gay" is what came out.

My dad's eyebrows shot up. "What?" he exclaimed. "That's impossible."

"Peter!" my mother scolded.

He clamped his mouth shut and sat back, rubbing his hands over his thighs. He didn't say anything for a long time. "Could this be a phase?" he finally asked.

"Um, no." I tried to ignore the fact that he was making me feel like a moldy piece of cheese. I sighed. "You like girls," I pointed out.

He stopped thigh rubbing. "That's true," he agreed. "I do. And one girl in particular. Two, actually," he added, reaching out to squeeze my hand. He looked into my face and smiled, a real smile, and I knew that we would be okay. There would definitely be more to talk about, but my dad and I were still us. I felt relief wash over me, then looked in the other direction. "Mom?" I ventured.

She fiddled with the paper square at the end of her Lipton string and stared down at the table, saying nothing.

"Mom?" Her silence was making me nervous, and I shifted in my hard kitchen chair while panic started to rise.

Finally she looked up. Her bright blue eyes were glistening, but, thank God, she was not actually crying. Her eyes, though, were full of sadness.

"Look on the bright side, Caroline," my dad said. "She's not a druggie, she *didn't* crash the car, and she's not pregnant. Heck, she's not even having sex."

That was only mostly true, but since he probably meant heterosexual sex, I decided it was close enough. And I was grateful to him for trying to lighten things up, even if he was kind of missing the point. Being gay had little to do with not doing or being those other things.

"I'm still the same girl, Mom," I said softly. "I'm still your Josie."

My mom did something funny then. She lifted my hand off the table and kissed the back of it. "Of course you are, Jo," she said. "It's just a lot to take in."

"You had no idea?" I asked. I'd often wondered if they'd been suspicious. I mean, I was almost fifteen and had never shown any interest in boys.

"Of course not," my dad said. "How would we . . ." He trailed off, and I could almost see the lightbulb—a hundred-watt—glowing above his head. "Annette?" he asked.

What an idiot! I'd practically led him right into that one. I hadn't planned on telling them everything—not yet. But maybe this was my subconscious at work. Maybe since I was at it . . .

"Yes, Annette."

My parents were silent for several minutes, no doubt trying to count the number of times Annette had slept over in the past two years, which was about a zillion.

My father exhaled really, really slowly. "How long?" He wanted answers now. No more kidding around.

"How long what?"

"How long have you been . . . intimate?"

He bit down on that last word, and I could tell he was trying not to blow his top. Part of me wanted to tell him it was none of his business, but that wasn't the way we were in my family. Everything was pretty much everybody's business, like it or not. I sighed. "Over a year." Actually closer to two, depending on your definition of the word *intimate*.

My mother gasped.

"Mom, I'm practically fifteen."

Dead silence. I had to start talking, fast.

"I know this is probably pretty freaky for you. But Annette and I have known each other a long time. I honestly don't remember when we realized how we felt, but I know I'm lucky to be with her. Lots of girls date boys who treat them like crap. Annette and I are a team. We decide things together. We talk about stuff. She's my best friend."

More silence. Finally, my dad cleared his throat. "You should be a lawyer," he said grimly. He looked across the table at my mom. "She has some valid points, Caroline."

"Of course she does," my mom said. "And we all love Annette—she's practically family. It's just hard to find out you had no idea what was really going on."

"Or that the girl you think of as a second daughter is dating your actual one," my dad said bluntly.

A wave of guilt washed over me. "I know," I agreed. "I totally get that. I wasn't trying to be deceitful—it's just not an easy thing to say."

"Or hear, apparently," my dad admitted. We were all quiet, but it was a comfortable quiet this time, and I was so relieved I wanted to cry.

"Josie?" my mom's voice came through the phone line. "You still there?"

I rolled back to the window. "Yeah, still here," I replied. "But I've got stuff to do, so I'll let you people get back to your little freak show."

"Call anytime!" my mom said.

"We love you, Josie," my dad added.

"Love you guys, too. I'll call you next week. Bye!" I hung up the phone and brought my knees up to my chest. I felt the tears and willed them away, but they didn't listen. Through the blurriness, I could see Annette had joined the group by the pond. She was wearing a flowered skirt I didn't recognize. Sunlight reflected off her ponytailed head.

Why didn't I know how hard this would be? I wondered as I watched Annette stretch her legs out on the lawn. My girlfriend was sliding into our new life as easily as a cracked egg slid into a mixing bowl. Walking down the hall exhausted me, and she was going out for cross-country. It was as if she'd taken a course called

How to Fit In at Boarding School and had passed with flying colors. Not that that fact was surprising. Annette loved new places, new people, new experiences. She saw them as opportunities for something different, something good. Life at Annette's house wasn't pretty, so something different was almost certainly something good, or at least something better. So really, her sliding in was to be expected. What *hadn't* been expected was just how hard totally different would be for me, and I felt like a fool for allowing myself to be blindsided by my own plan.

Get over it, I told myself. The pond party was still happening, and for a moment I considered rallying. But it was almost dinnertime and I was wiped. So I lay there watching the pond posse until my eyes drooped and my breathing slowed. The next thing I knew, someone was kissing me awake all over my face.

"Hey there, sleepyhead." Annette was standing on the bunk bed ladder, leaning over my pillow.

"Hey," I replied, opening my eyes and smiling into her face.

"I've been looking for you," she said, smiling back. "I've got some good news."

"Awesome," I said, stretching a little. "What is it?"

"I made the cross-country team."

I felt my smile fade despite the excitement on her face. Recognizing my less-than-thrilled reaction, Annette hopped down to the floor, her back to me.

I searched for the right thing to say but was utterly unable to figure out exactly what that right thing *was*.

"Aren't you going to congratulate me?" she asked, pacing a little.

I sat up. "Congratulations."

She planted her hands on her hips. "Don't sound so sincere, Josie."

"I'm just being honest," I said in my defense. "Annette, you hate running, and I don't see how moving halfway across the country could change that."

"Maybe *I've* changed."

"In a week?"

She shrugged.

"Any other changes I should know about?"

"That's not fair, Josie."

It *wasn't* fair, I knew, but I was at a loss. Annette was supposed to be the one thing at Brookwood I truly understood, but her decision to go out for cross-country was something I didn't understand at all.

I was also struggling with our in-the-closet status. Even though Annette and I had agreed not to be an obvious couple right away, now that we were actually here, it felt icky and wrong. It had only been a week and I was tired of it.

"I need you to be happy for me about cross-country."

I wiped the sleep from the corner of my eye and hopped to the floor. "I'll try."

"That's the best you can do?" her voice sounded stretched, like Toby's slingshot just before he let something fly.

"I want to be happy for you," I said slowly, "but I still don't understand why you chose something you dislike so much."

Annette raised her chin, eyes flashing. She looked like her mother. "It was my decision."

"Of course it was," I agreed. I didn't want to fight with Annette—it just seemed silly, and I needed her. "Maybe I'm just jealous," I admitted. "So far Brookwood isn't exactly smooth sailing for me."

Annette's face shifted. "I know, Jo," she said, "but you're actually doing fine." She bit her lower lip. "Maybe you should try to stop overthinking."

This wasn't the first time Annette had given me this advice. "I don't feel fine," I said. "I feel weird."

"Well, you *are* kind of a weirdo . . ." she teased. Except right then it wasn't the slightest bit funny.

"I really don't like lying about who we are," I told her.

"We're not lying." Annette stepped closer and tucked aside one of my overabundant wayward curls. "We're just not telling."

"Isn't that the same thing?"

"No, not exactly." Her fingers wrapped around mine. "I still need a little more time. I'm not like you, Josie—I don't stand out. I need people to see me for myself before they see me with you."

Ooof. That was a lot more reasonable than I wanted to admit, especially since I *was* the one who stuck out. I was louder, more sarcastic, more opinionated. I had a hard time keeping my thoughts to myself.

"Can you just wait a little longer?" She was asking with her eyes as much as her voice.

I wanted to say no, to tell her that I couldn't. I was that tired of pretending. But I also wanted Annette to be happy, and knew that her feelings counted just as much as mine did.

"Oh, all right. But hurry up and show everyone how fabulous you are, will you? Patience isn't exactly one of my strengths."

Annette chuckled as she let go of my hand and linked her own fingers behind my back, drawing me toward her. "You're the absolute best. Thank you." She ducked her head and her lips fell onto mine, warm and open and soft.

CHAPTER 9

♥

"Oh, Annette, that's perfect," Becca said, pushing the desk chair aside and giving my girlfriend a nod of approval in the full-length mirror. We were piled into Annette and Becca's room, putting the finishing touches on our Dress to Impress getups. Or at least the others were. I was scoping out the space, noting how Annette had transformed her half into a miniature version of her room at home and wishing we were living together for the hundredth time.

Annette's bed was covered in the ancient patchwork quilt her grandma Ruby had made eons ago, and I stretched out, leaning against her pile of flannel pillows. The shelf above her desk was decorated with photos of family and friends from back home. There was the snapshot of us diving off the cliff at Turtle Lake, one from our ninth-grade school carnival, and a giant collage of the people we'd spent the last eight years going to school with. The smash of our smiling faces beckoned, making me realize that this was the first Saturday night in practically forever that Annette and I wouldn't be heading out to Giovanni's for pizza, overdressed salad, and a giant pitcher of Coke.

"Josie, what do you think?" someone asked, jolting me.

I looked up, blinking at Annette's reflection, and gawked. My girlfriend looked fabulous. Outfitted in a denim miniskirt, giant hoop earrings, and a sequined halter top that I'd never seen before, she was definitely dressed to impress.

"Delicious," I said.

Annette's eyes glinted at me in the mirror, but the other girls didn't seem to pick up on my slip.

"That's what the guys are going to think," Becca confirmed.

I tried to ignore that comment and shoved one of Annette's pillows under my head, breathing in her smell.

Annette looked uncertainly at her reflection. "It's not too much?"

"No way," Cynthia Wu assured her. Cynthia, I'd learned, was Marina's roommate. Right now she was also animal print, covered from head to toe in leopard. She even had leopard-print clogs. "Everyone is going a little over the top. Plus, Becca's right. The boys are gonna love it."

My eyes stretched out to Annette's in the mirror. I knew I'd just agreed to give her a little more time, but I *so* wanted her to tell them that boys were irrelevant, that the person who mattered was sitting right here. If anyone at Brookwood knew her already, it was this group of girls. Annette shook her head the tiniest bit, invisible to everyone but me.

"The final touch," Becca said, putting a feathery plum-colored boa around Annette's neck and standing a little closer to her than I liked. *Back yourself up, girl.*

"How're we doing, ladies?" called a voice as the bathroom door swung open and Marina appeared. She was dressed in an old-fashioned barmaid's getup, her breasts cinched together and spilling out over the top. Everyone stopped for a second. "What?" she asked.

"Nothing we can do anything about," Cynthia said, glancing down at her own flat chest. Marina's boobs were everywhere, which, from what I could tell, was exactly how she liked it.

"I believe my work here is finished," Becca announced. She spun my girlfriend around to face the rest of us, and everyone woo-hooed and whistled. "Beautiful work," Cynthia declared.

"Beautiful canvas," I murmured under my breath. "Annette has always cleaned up good," I said a little louder.

"How long have you two known each other?" Marina slid into a chair and blew her bangs out of her light brown eyes.

"Since we were five," Annette and I answered in unison.

"We were in the same kindergarten class," Annette explained.

"Alison Krupp tried to steal her away in first grade," I added, "but I fought her off."

Everyone laughed, and Annette's face relaxed into a smile. I *did* fight off Alison—and her bag of bribery M&M's—with a vengeance. And that was long before Annette and I were even a couple.

"Josie, is that what you're wearing?" Becca's gaze made me feel slightly compressed, as if I were vacuum-packed. Suddenly, all eyes were on me.

I looked down at my jeans and tie-dyed tee. "Um, I thought so."

"It's not that terrible," Marina said. "I mean, her hair is already off the wall. Maybe we could do something with a tiara, or . . ."

"I don't do tiaras," I said, bristling about the off-the-wall part. What was I supposed to do, shave my head? My hair was my hair!

"How about a bandanna and some earrings?" Annette suggested, getting to her feet. Her eyes were pleading—she knew dress-up wasn't my thing. But here I was in a room full of girls who were dressing up. Girls Annette was getting to know, girls she was excited about knowing. Girls she wanted me to know, too. *Oh, why not*, I thought.

Hoisting myself to my feet, I walked over and plopped myself into the hot seat in front of the mirror. "Transform me."

Thank you, Annette mouthed.

In a flash, Marina and Cynthia were in the closet, searching for something to swap out for my jeans. "No short skirts," I told them. "Or high heels."

"She's not kidding," Annette confirmed, stepping behind the chair and gently running her fingers through the back of my hair. I wanted to tilt my head back, beckon her down for a kiss, but her face was turned toward the closet (from whence my probable doom would come at any moment). "If we put her in heels, she'll take us all down on the dance floor."

"Let's leave her hair wild," Becca suggested, studying my locks in the reflection. "God, I've always wanted curls like that."

"They're amazing," Annette agreed.

"They're a pain in the ass," I assured them, surprised that Becca was envious of my crazy hair. Despite the fact that they often made me look like an unshorn sheep, I secretly loved my unusual auburn curls.

"Hand me the blue bottle from the bathroom shelf," Annette said.

I watched Marina flip through Becca's side of the closet with remarkable speed—clearly a professional.

"How's this?" she asked, holding up a denim mini.

Annette shook her head. Her fingers were still entwined in my hair, and I was grasping at a moment of intimacy in the crowded room. We'd moved thirteen hundred miles away from our families and lived under the same roof (if tragically not in the same room), but it felt like we'd hardly touched each other since we'd arrived. I closed my eyes and reveled in the sensation of Annette's hands in my hair.

"Hey, no falling asleep!" Cynthia called with a laugh. I opened my eyes in time to see Marina rehang the skirt and continue flipping through, making her way toward Annette's side of the closet. "Ooooh, Annette! This is fabulous." She held up one of my favorite dresses—an above-the-knee orange knit with an asymmetrical chenille trim. It was sixties vintage, and Grandmother Ruby's.

"That's perfect." Annette leaned down until I could feel her breath on my ear. "I've always wanted to see you in that," she whispered.

How funny. I had always wanted to wear it.

She gave my hair, which was especially big tonight, a final scrunch and disappeared into the bathroom to rinse her hands. By the time she emerged, Marina had the dress unbuttoned and off the hanger.

I dropped my jeans to the floor. Pulling my tee over my head, I slipped my hands into the sleeves while Annette tugged it down around my knees, which felt strange. She had undressed me a hundred times, but I wasn't sure she'd ever dressed me. While she and Marina did the buttons up the side, I studied myself in the mirror.

The dress looked completely different on me than it did on Annette, and yet I felt good in it immediately. The fabric hung just right and had a wonderful stretchiness to it. Annette was taller, so the dress fell all the way to my knees, but I was chestier, so my breasts filled out the V-neck more fully. And the color, surprisingly, worked great with my hair.

"Scrunch her curls a little more."

"And we still need shoes."

Annette looked down at my Converse, which were the same off-white color as the trim. "I think the ones she's wearing are fine."

Becca held a pair of dangly earrings up to the sides of my face. "These are great. Should we swap out the necklace?"

Annette shook her head as my fingers touched my opal pendant protectively. "No, let's leave it."

Relieved, I watched the final flutter of activity. Becca handed the earrings to Marina and in they went. Cynthia told me to pucker up and efficiently applied some coral-colored lipstick, which felt surprisingly smooth, and Annette gave my hair a final scrunch.

I watched it all in the mirror and smiled, because at that moment, every piece of it felt good.

CHAPTER 10

♥

When everyone was dressed, Becca locked the door and turned off the overhead, plunging the room into a sudden semidarkness. Annette's bedside table lamp dimly lit the space, casting off a pale disk of yellow light.

Marina giggled.

"Shhhhh," Becca warned. "Lola No is on tonight." She vanished into the closet.

Cynthia sat down on the bed, pulling Marina next to her. "Pipe down, girl. We don't want to get busted the first weekend of school."

"We don't want to get busted at all," Becca corrected in a whisper, reappearing with a blue bottle of Skyy and a pair of tiny glasses with Brookwood's main building etched on one side. No bottle swigging here.

"Is that vodka?" Annette asked.

"It isn't water," Becca replied. "Who's first?"

"The Minnesotans," Marina said. "It's their virginal Brookwood drink."

Not exactly, I thought, remembering the giant bottle I'd tilted back in the woods my first day here. I hadn't pegged Becca for a party girl but couldn't say it was totally unexpected, either.

Becca handed Annette and me two shot glasses and we held them while she filled.

"You don't have to," I said quietly to Annette. She didn't really drink.

She shot me a "don't say anything" look and her hand wavered, sloshing a bit of vodka on her wrist.

"To your first year at Brookwood," the girls whispered in unison. And then, "Go!"

We lifted, tilted, poured, and swallowed. The alcohol burned, but went down easily enough. It wasn't the cheap stuff. Annette's green eyes widened and she put her hand on her chest, sputtering. By the time she got it down, she was coughing wildly.

"She's not much of a drinker," I explained.

"She will be," Marina quipped, snatching the glass from Annette's hand and wagging it in the air for her own ration.

Without waiting for a partner, she raised her glass. "Embrace the horror," she said, downing its contents like water. Well, that was one way to approach it.

Cynthia and Becca finished the round and then we went full circle a second time. "That's enough for me," I said, remembering Roxanne's two-shot rule. I could feel the alcohol seeping in, shifting everything a little, and half wanted another shot. But I didn't want to make a fool of myself, and *did* want to let my girl-friend off the drinking hook. I could tell she was already a little misty.

"Speak for yourself," Marina said, holding her glass out for a refill. "I was just getting going." It was becoming clear that bar-maid was an appropriate costume for her.

Becca filled the shot glass just above the roofline of the main building and Marina downed it in less than two seconds. "One for the road?" she asked, holding out the glass again.

"Last one, piggy." Becca filled the glass not quite as full.

"Who're you calling piggy?" Marina protested, downing the shot and setting the tiny glass on the bedside table with conviction. "Thanks to the No Carb Diet, I wear a size four petite, and my nose is not even the slightest bit pugged." She turned her head, giving us a nice long look at her profile. Then she got to her feet, tottering for a second on her heels, and made her way to the bathroom mirror. She turned from side to side to side, trying to see her profile for herself.

"You need two mirrors to see your profile, dopey," Cynthia said.

Marina glared at her roommate in the mirror and fiddled with her straight, mousy brown hair.

"But everyone tries with just the one," Annette added with a giggly laugh I'd never heard before. Where did that come from?

"Thank you, Annette," Marina said, pulling a lipstick from the medicine cabinet. She smoothed a layer of waxy red onto her lips and smacked them with satisfaction. "Now let's get out of this hellhole."

While Becca stashed the bottle in the depths of their closet, Cynthia took the shot glasses into the bathroom to rinse them out, returning with a bottle of Listerine. "Time for another quick shot," she said, "but you definitely want to spit this one out." She took a swig and passed the bottle. Annette took a sip and, sputtering nearly as badly as she did with the vodka, sped into the bathroom to spit it out. I took my required breath-cleansing mouthful and followed suit before trailing everyone else out the door.

The dorm was unusually quiet and we sounded like a herd of elephants as we traipsed down the hall and pushed open the door. Outside, the air was chilly, the sky clear and dotted with stars.

As we crossed the circle drive, I couldn't help but notice Annette's relaxed shoulders, the easy way she glided over the pavement. I'd never seen her this tipsy before, and she seemed simultaneously relaxed and exhilarated.

About halfway across, she fell back a bit and we walked shoulder to shoulder, letting the other girls go ahead, and she extended a hand just enough for the backs of our fingers to touch.

"I think I'm a little drunk," she whispered giddily.

I slowed and stepped in front of her. Her eyes glistened from the alcohol, and I could smell the vodka-tinged mouthwash on her breath, minty and distilled and sweet. "Is it okay?" I asked.

"It's great. I feel sort of tingly and warm all over."

I felt tingly and warm just standing next to her, and could see the outline of her lips in the lamppost light. God, I wanted to kiss her.

"I wish I could kiss you," she said.

So kiss me, I thought. But I could hear the girls chatting just a few yards away, and knew she wouldn't, so instead of encouraging her, I said, "Who says I want to kiss you?" stepping away fast and almost tripping on the edge of a cobble. It was either move away or move in, and everything felt off-balance, as if we hadn't been a couple for three years, as if we were back in seventh grade.

It was the night of our middle school Fall Foliage Dance. The dance itself was a total bust, right down to the lame decorations—orange and yellow construction paper leaves hanging from the ceiling. The music was no better. Someone had brought in an iPod and some speakers, and Harold Atmore had made a terrible playlist.

"I can't dance to this!" I half shouted to Annette, whose long legs were doing an impressive job making sense of the halting rhythm. Everyone knew that Harold Atmore was no dancer, so how could he possibly pick out dance music? Bottom line: He couldn't.

I held still for a second and scoped out the dance floor, which wasn't exactly crowded. Most of the kids were huddled together in small groups—by the punch bowl, up by the stage, next to the double doors in case they needed to make a break for it. A break for it was a pretty good idea, actually.

"Let's get some air," I said to Annette, tugging on her flowered sleeve.

She stopped dancing and blew a wayward strand of blond hair out of her eyes before taking my hand and leading us past the stragglers on the dance floor, past the punch bowl, past the cheesy popcorn and pretzels, and toward the double doors. Pushing hard on the metal, we swung onto the blacktopped yard, welcoming the air.

The school yard was nearly empty. "Where is everybody?" I asked, secretly happy to be alone with my best friend.

"Not on the dance floor," Annette replied with a snort. "That was lame."

"Totally lame," I agreed. Something was tugging inside me—something I didn't totally understand.

"Do you want to leave?" Annette was asking. "We could go to your house and watch a movie."

I looked up at her, at her spring-green eyes and the ponytail wisps that framed her face. At her lips, which were so much prettier than mine.

I want to kiss them, I thought. *I want to kiss those lips.*

I stepped back, worried that I'd spoken the words out loud, that I'd already ruined everything.

"Josie? Are you okay?"

I dropped my hands to my sides. Was I okay? I had no idea. I certainly didn't feel okay.

Annette moved forward and laced our fingers together. Did she know? Did she feel the same way?

I turned to face her, tugging on her arm so we were standing very close. I could feel her Juicy Fruit breath on my face. "I . . ."

"What?" She crouched a tiny bit so she could look me in the eye.

I felt tingly all over. *Just do it!* a voice said. *No way, Josie. Don't be crazy*, said another. *She'll never speak to you again.*

"Josie?" Annette was whispering now.

My heart was pounding so hard I was sure my chest was going to burst open and the bloody blob would fall to the ground, throbbing.

Just do it, said the voice again. *Unless you're too chicken . . .*

I was a lot of things, but I was *not* a chicken.

I leaned in, and our lips touched, lightly at first and then with more firmness. Annette's were warm and soft and she tasted like tropical fruit. Happiness spread through me as I realized she wasn't pulling away.

When I drew back breathlessly, Annette's eyes were wide. "Oh," she said.

Oh what? I thought nervously. *Oh great or oh no or oh what?*
"Oh . . ." I repeated.

Annette beamed at me. "Wow," she said. She leaned and kissed me again, more quickly this time. Then she let out a horsey whoop and pulled me toward the gate. "Forget the dance," she said. "Let's go to your house and watch a movie!"

"Josie?" Annette was peering at me with hazy intentness. I blinked at her fifteen-year-old self, at her gray-flecked green eyes and her slightly open mouth. Damn, she was beautiful.

"Are you girls coming or what?" Marina called. She yanked the door open and music rushed toward us as a group of kids in difficult-to-describe outfits came out of the building, shimmying and laughing into the night.

Annette turned toward the other girls. "Yes, coming," she said.

The air inside was ripe and warm, the music so loud the floor, even out in the hall, vibrated. "Let's get in there, girls," Becca called as she disappeared around a corner. We followed, plunging ourselves into a pulsating darkness. A few chairs and tables were abandoned at one end, next to which stretched a remarkably wide chasm of empty space, and finally a mob of gyrating bodies crammed together on an invisible dance floor.

"I love this song!" Marina shouted, hurtling herself onto the floor. Becca and Annette and I followed, slipping into spaces that weren't spaces and becoming part of the grooving mass.

I wriggled past a pair of dancers behind Annette, whose arms were already above her head, waving like wide strands of seaweed in the current. She turned, her eyes closed, her body loose and uninhibited. I felt the music seep up through the soles of my shoes and started to sway.

The song faded to a single beat and Annette opened her eyes, seeing me and smiling. She leaned in close to my ear. "This is way better than Harold Atmore's dorky playlist."

I laughed as a mash-up started, feeling the music, feeling tipsy, feeling happy. We danced, letting ourselves go and riding the wave of it all.

"Nice moves," a voice said behind me. Right behind me, actually, or I wouldn't have been able to hear him.

I turned and saw Penn, who was wearing jeans, a yellow T-shirt, and a jester hat—pretty tame overall. I wondered whether the other girls would be disappointed.

He bowed in a very jesterlike way, then swiped a curl that had escaped the hat and threw his arms in all directions, nodding his head like the bobble figure my dad kept on his dashboard and looking utterly ridiculous.

Becca sidled a little closer to Penn while Marina squealed with laughter, her barmaid boobs bobbing like buoys in a lake and threatening to spring free from their cinching. I found myself between two dancers wearing bowler hats and bow ties.

Annette was now several bodies away from the group, her head swaying from side to side. I was starting to make my way over when Hank appeared out of nowhere.

"Game time, my man," he half shouted in Penn's ear. "The cards await."

"Cards?" I echoed, curious.

Penn waved an arm and leaned in. "Just a little gambling among friends. Hank here loves to give me his money."

"He is either a seriously demented individual," Hank confided, "or fails to understand the difference between addition and subtraction."

"Delusions, delusions." Penn shook his head, ducking out of the dance-floor crowd to the obvious disappointment of Becca and Marina. I watched his dark head and Hank's blond one disappear into the hall, thinking that they reminded me of Ben and Josh. Being away from my family was starting to get a little bit easier, but I suddenly wanted to know what my brothers were doing. Playing Ping-Pong in our basement? Arguing over a video game? Watching a movie? It all sounded good.

Trying to re-find my groove, I made my way over to Annette, who was still a body of lost-in-the-music movement. I sidled closer, swaying and trying to connect amidst the throng of dancers. But the music was rushing from my feet up and out the top of my head without pausing anywhere inside, without letting me feel it. Our moment of connectedness—to each other and to the music—was gone. I stopped moving entirely, right there in the middle of the dance floor, and blinked at the scene that surrounded me.

On the surface, it was just like the dances at home—writhing teenage bodies, a thumping bass line, and some guy working a board in the corner. But underneath, it felt foreign and strange, not at all mine.

When the song ended, I reached for Annette's arm and pulled her off the dance floor.

"What gives?" she asked, blinking, when we were in the hall. Her skin gleamed with a layer of perspiration and her hair was the perfect amount of messy. She looked happy and alive, like when we'd first started to touch each other.

My ears were ringing. "I just needed . . ." What did I need, exactly? "I just wanted a break," I said, overwhelmed by the impulse I'd felt to pull her out of there.

"From dancing?" she asked, turning her head toward the music. She hadn't stopped moving.

"From everything, I guess." I moved down the hall a little, slipping into a semidark alcove under the stairs. Annette followed, still half dancing. "Are you all right?" I asked.

She gazed at me confusedly. "Of course," she said, as if the question were ridiculous.

I felt myself deflate. Wasn't it okay to ask how she was?

"The music is awesome. Can we get back in there?"

I attempted to exhale my disappointment. I wished I could let go of whatever it was that made me pull her out here, that I could get back in there and enjoy the dance. Problem was, I didn't want to.

"Could we do something else?" I asked. "I really just want to be with you."

Annette's hips wriggled to the beat. "Why? I was having a great time."

I reached out a hand. "So we can have a little time together."

"We *are* together."

"I mean together by ourselves."

"Oh." Annette stopped moving and looked at me for a long moment, as if finally seeing me there in the hall. "Oh, Josie," she said. "Why do you want to be alone now? It's our first Saturday night here, and there's a *dance*. Can we talk about this later? I just want to be on the dance floor."

I didn't say anything—I didn't have to. Annette sighed. "Why is everything so hard for you, Josie? Why does everything have to be so complicated? It's just a dance."

But it wasn't just a dance. It was feeling uprooted, untethered. It was trying to figure things out when you were surrounded by people you didn't know. It was feeling lost.

"I don't want to dance with them," I said. "I want to dance with you."

Annette shook her head ever so slightly. "Josie . . ."

Something about the way she said my name sent my heart into my throat. "What?"

Her eyes were bright, and I could see the flecks of gray in them. "I just don't think we can—"

"It's them, isn't it?" I blurted, stepping back so fast I almost careened into the wall. "The Soleets."

"The what?"

"Your new *friends*," I said, spitting out the last word as if it were snake venom. "They don't like me, don't think I'm good enough."

Annette's eyes held mine. Did I really just say that? It was unbelievably cliché.

"Are we talking about how they see you, or how you see yourself?" She spoke so softly I could barely hear her.

"What did you say?" I asked, feeling my face get hot.

"Nothing." She bit her lower lip. "Josie . . ." Annette stepped closer. Her face was full of sadness, of softness, of empathy.

No, I thought. *No, no, no.*

She leaned in and kissed me, right there in the main building. We were sort of in a corner, but still.

I wanted to kiss her back, to put my arms around her, to melt into it. But if this was a good-bye kiss, I didn't want it.

I pulled away. "I can't," I told her. "I just . . ."

"Josie," Annette said.

Behind her, Marina stood watching us, her mouth open in a ruby-red O.

CHAPTER 11

I don't know why I didn't head back to my dorm. Maybe because Marina was standing between me and the door. Maybe because that's where we'd come from an hour before. Or maybe because I wanted to get as far away as possible and the dorm was right there, a mere stone's throw. Whatever the reason, I soon found myself at the other end of the main building, propping myself against the auditorium door and sobbing like a deranged lunatic.

Shit! I said, pounding my fists against the carved oak. *Shit shit shit.* My hands throbbed with every pound, but that felt right since the rest of me was already aching.

How did this happen? I asked myself, opening my fist and laying my palm against the smooth wood. I'd moved halfway across the country from everything I knew to be here with Annette, and now she was dumping me.

Or was she?

I wiped my face and leaned my forehead against the door, willing myself to think logically, to get a grip. Instead, I got footsteps, coming down the hall behind me. Just what I needed—another audience. I yanked open the auditorium door and slid into the quiet darkness. Autopilot led me to row K, to my seat, seventh from the end. I slumped heavily into the chair, staring at nothing.

Without Annette, I thought, my mind shifting the words into *without a net*. That was precisely how I felt—like a tightrope walker a hundred feet above the ground, teetering dangerously with no net below.

My gaze settled on the podium and the empty stage behind it. I felt empty myself, as if someone had sliced me open and everything that was me just oozed out, leaving nothing but a skin-and-bones shell.

I replayed the scene in the alcove with Annette. What was she trying to say, exactly? That it was over, or that we needed to find a different way to be together? And what was the difference?

I was still sitting there trying to figure out whether I had a girlfriend when the door opened and a shaft of light passed over me, then momentarily cast itself across the aisle to my left. A soft giggle broke the silence, followed by the shuffle of movement and series of intent muffled sounds.

"There's never anybody in here," a boy said as the couple stumbled over their making-out selves on their way down the aisle. Thoroughly entwined, they slithered right past my row and sprawled themselves across several seats three feet in front of me.

That can't be comfortable, I thought as their soft, eager moans filled the auditorium. A faint waft of alcohol drifted past my nose, but I couldn't tell if it was mine or theirs.

Unbelievable, I thought. And yet somehow the fact that I couldn't find a place to be by myself wasn't entirely surprising. Still, I had no intention of staying around to listen to their steamy tryst. Not even bothering to be discreet, I got to my feet and made a beeline for the door.

Back in the hall, I wasn't sure what to do. Go to my room? Take a walk? Find Annette and attempt to have a reasonable conversation? This last idea was seriously tempting, but something warned me against it. It was too soon. So I descended a few steps down a wide concrete staircase and pushed out the heavy doors marked EXIT.

I found myself at the open end of a large, grassy courtyard that bordered a baseball field. Beyond the outfield was a low rock wall and Route 6, and beyond that, I'd heard, town. A row of giant elm trees lined one side of the field, their branches casting twisted shadows on the grass. I found myself staring up at their wide, barely visible yellow-leafed limbs, suddenly wanting to climb one. *Don't be silly*, I told myself. And then, *Why not?*

I strode forward with purpose, keeping to the edge of the field while I scoped out the trees. I needed a pretty low bottom branch, the right distance between the higher ones, and more than one obvious route to the top. My brothers and I had logged many an hour in massive oaks and elms back home and I was a decent climber, but there was no reason to be stupid. I was, after all, wearing a dress.

A breeze came up, making me shiver. The sweat from the dance mob had dried on my skin and I was now officially chilled. I squinted at the tree in front of me. It wasn't the tallest in the row, but its branches fanned out like nicely spaced fingers, and both sides of the tree seemed climbable. Plus, it was pretty close to the building and happened to be out of the light, making my ascent potentially incognito. I was already the weird girl who fell asleep during Vespers and ate dessert without utensils—I didn't need anyone to notice that I spent Saturday nights climbing trees, too.

Glancing behind me to make sure I wasn't going to trip on anything, I sprinted forward, took a flying leap, and grabbed ahold of the lowest branch. My fingers slipped on the rough bark, but I dug in and walked my feet up the trunk until I could swing a leg over the branch. Grateful that the dress I wore was stretch knit, I hoisted myself upright, heart pounding. I hadn't climbed a tree in a long time.

I didn't hesitate. I got to my feet and up I went, reaching for each eye-level branch, finding places for my feet, pulling myself higher and higher. I could hear the blood rushing in my ears, pushing me forward, urging me on. I was breathless but didn't stop. Soon I was above the first floor of the brick building, then the second and the third, and closing in on some kind of tower at the top. I was almost as high as the chapel steeple, and the houses and fields stretched out below me. A gust of wind rustled the yellow leaves and sent a smattering into the air. I shook my head, inhaling and feeling air move into my belly. A flat crook in a large branch near the top of the tree beckoned. I climbed up to it, settling myself next to the trunk.

The moonlight cast the top of the tree's shadow onto the infield and I could see the shape that was me down there on the ground, small and bloblike. *How appropriate*, I thought with a sigh. But except for the looming shadow of the main building behind me, the entire campus seemed small and sort of bloblike. I spotted a group of kids hanging out by the athletic center, next to the patch of woods where Roxanne had introduced me to Brookwood's beverage of choice. Others were clustered by the pond. They were equally tiny and indistinguishable. *Maybe that's what this place does*, I thought. *Shrinks people.*

The door outside the auditorium slammed shut and the make-out couple emerged, holding hands as they walked across the field and lay down beyond second base, the girl resting her head in the crook of the boy's armpit. I could hear the faint, occasional murmurings of their voices and outbursts of laughter, and I wondered who they were, what they were talking about. Were they a new couple just getting to know each other, or had they been together for a long time?

I felt a pang for Annette and found myself wishing we were still at home, wishing I could press REWIND and go back to life before I stumbled upon the Brookwood website. Before I decided we should apply. Before Annette agreed. Before everything else . . .

You wanted to leave, I reminded myself. I'd always been clear about the fact that we had to get away from Shannon—especially Annette. Watching Shannon be cruel to Annette was like watching the evil queen in a Disney movie, and it got worse as Annette got older, as if Shannon couldn't bear to watch her daughter grow up to be a beautiful person. Because Annette *was* beautiful—the kind of beautiful that made people stop to look. But she *also* made the people around her feel good.

I looked down at the group of kids by the pond, memories of the night Annette and I had gone to the Full Moon Party at Turtle Beach the September before surfacing in my mind. Our going was a big deal because we went together—as a couple.

Annette and I had been best friends since we were five and a couple since we were twelve, but for two years, nobody knew we'd gone from best friends to girlfriends. And then came the fall of ninth grade.

We came out by accident. Annette and I had gone to poetry camp for a week of mornings that summer, and she'd written me a poem—a haiku. With our names in it.

Imagine and dream
Annette and Josie so sweet
The perfect heartbeat

Unfortunately, the poem ended up in the hands of Eric Stewart, the giant goalie on the hockey team and your basic asshole. In the space of a day, Annette and I went from a couple of freshmen to freshmen freaks. We got heckled, harassed, and bullied. Annette cried herself to sleep for a week.

And then came the Full Moon Party. That summer had been cold and buggy, but the fall was glorious. Bright blue skies and the rich green of a wet spring and summer all around us. And it was hot—in the 80s until well after sunset. The whole town shimmered like a mirage. Perfect weather for the party.

Annette and I had agreed to go to the party together in spite of Eric and his big, mean mouth, but as the date approached, I could tell she was losing her nerve. By the morning of, she was a total wreck.

"Let's bake something," I suggested, knowing that sugar and chocolate always made Annette feel better.

We spent the afternoon making fudge, Annette's specialty, using extra marshmallow creme. Marshmallow creme is the key ingredient to perfect fudge, along with not scraping the bottom of the pot when you stir (so you don't get grains of burned sugar, Annette told me, just smooth, chocolate-and-marshmallow deliciousness). Shannon was visiting her sister for the day, which meant we didn't have to worry about getting yelled at for messing up the kitchen, and we made batch after batch, each one smoother and more chocolaty than the last. We stacked the empty jars of marshmallow creme into a giant tower on the counter.

When we arrived at Turtle Lake with our Tupperware of yum, everyone watched us approach without actually looking. When we got within speaking distance, nobody acknowledged us, as if we weren't there, or didn't even exist. I was wondering if we should just forget the party when Annette's eyes narrowed and her mouth twisted into a scowl. "I'm sort of sorry I didn't spit in it," she whispered, walking right over to Eric Stewart.

"Fudge?" she asked, smiling her sweetest smile and pulling off the lid to let the chocolate smell drift up to his nose.

Eric blinked into the plastic box, at the dozens of squares of fudge lined up in rows (Annette didn't let me cut—I was too sloppy with the knife). His nostrils flared and his eyes widened. I think he was practically drooling, which was nothing short of a miracle since he definitely had cotton mouth. Eric was a stoner in the off-season, and right now the smell of weed wafted all around him.

He looked up at Annette, grinned, and reached in.

"You're welcome," Annette said as she held out the box to the rest of the group. Within ten minutes, the box was empty and everyone was licking their fingers and laughing. That fudge turned out to be our ticket out of being "those girls"—out of ridicule and harassment. In public, anyway. In private, we knew, it was another matter. Because even though nobody said anything, there were definitely people who just couldn't deal, who thought we were freaks. Like the religious kids who were sure we needed to be fixed, or the kids who were grossed out by what we did together.

Then there were the people who just seemed curious. We knew who they were by the way they looked at us. Their faces were more open, or something, and they seemed like they wanted to ask us questions. Once in a while I found myself wanting to blurt things out, things I thought they wanted to know. But I never did.

We stayed late at the party, dancing on the beach and gazing at the stars. It was so warm that everyone had cutoff shorts and flip-flops and bare arms that glowed in the moonlight. Afterward, Annette and I walked home together, arm in arm, stopping to kiss under the oak tree next to the school playground, leaning into the trunk together. She tasted like salt and fudge and the full moon, and everything was perfect.

The moon high, we walked together to Annette's house. We were sneaking through the door and laughing when the voice came at us.

"You're late," Shannon hissed, making both of us jump. I let go of Annette's hand just in time, because a second later, Shannon turned on the floor lamp next to her chair. I squinted in the light, trying to get my eyes to adjust while she rose to her feet and weaved toward us.

"What do you think you're doing sneaking around in the middle of the night?" Her green eyes were narrow slits. Shannon seemed to hate that her daughter had friends, had a social life. Like she didn't want Annette to be loved.

"We were at the Full Moon Party," Annette said. "Dad knew where we . . ."

"Don't lie to me!" Shannon raised a hand and Annette ducked, forcing her mother's arm to swing hard through nothing but air. She lost her balance and careened into the armoire.

"Mama!" Annette said, reaching out a hand to break her fall.

"Don't touch me!" Shannon hissed. Annette inched away from me and toward her mother, which seemed counterintuitive even though I understood why—Shannon hated any reminder that we were a couple.

It was like being split in two. Half of me wanted to get the heck out of there, especially because my presence was probably making things worse for Annette. But I also couldn't leave until I knew Annette was safe.

You should go, Annette mouthed.

I gave her an "are you sure?" look, and she nodded.

"Let's go upstairs," Annette told her mother. "I could use a good night's sleep."

Shannon deflated then, like a little bit of air had been let out of her. "All right," she said wearily as Annette took her by the arm. I watched the two of them walk up the stairs, Shannon leaning heavily on her daughter, and I marveled at how quickly the situation had taken a turn. As I walked to the door I made a silent wish that it wouldn't turn again.

The bark of the elm tree felt cool and rough against my face, and I pressed my cheek into it, taking a breath. I liked it up here. I felt sort of separate from everything below, as though I was watching life at Brookwood instead of participating in it. Maybe I could stay up here. Maybe I could have some sort of satellite existence at boarding school.

The couple on the baseball field got up off the ground and walked away, arm in arm, laughing. It made me ache for Annette, and I wanted to climb down the tree just as suddenly as I'd wanted to climb up. I needed to see her, to talk to her.

I was about to hoist myself to my feet when I heard a creaking sound behind me—a window opening. I held my breath, wanting to turn around but willing myself not to.

"Doing a little extracurricular spying, Subzero?"

No way, I thought. *No freaking way*. I turned around and found myself just a few feet from Penn, who was half hanging out of the window, his shoulders practically filling the opening.

"Or are you just opposed to stairs?" He leaned forward and grinned, and I could see over his head into the room, which was large and, besides him, occupied by a pair of boys sitting around a table covered in cards and poker chips. I recognized Hank, and a boy named Sam Moon from English class.

"Is that Josie?" Hank said, rubbing his eyes like Toby used to do when he'd just woken up from a nap.

"The one and only," Penn replied. And then, quieter, "Don't ask me why, Subzero, but I'm not entirely surprised to find you sitting in a tree outside my window."

"I wouldn't let it go to your head," I told him. "I had no idea this was even your dorm, much less your room. And it's not my fault the best climbing tree stands right outside your domicile—I certainly didn't plant it."

"Domicile," he echoed, opening the window wide in invitation. "I don't suppose you know how to play Texas Hold'em? We need a fourth."

I considered telling him I'd never heard of it, but that would've been a bald-faced lie since I'd actually played more than a few hands—my dad had a standing poker night and had taught me the game. "Isn't gambling against the Brookwood Code of Behavior?" I asked, deflecting the question altogether.

"That would be the smaller infraction, actually," he explained. "Climbing through a window into a boy's dormitory room is, according to the code, a bigger offense."

Somehow, breaking the rules made climbing into Penn's room that much more appealing, especially since I wasn't the slightest bit interested in doing the thing that the rule was undoubtedly made for—fooling around with a boy.

"Well, in that case . . ." I scooched myself toward the window, then stood on the (thankfully) wide branch below me. Clutching every branch that seemed viable, I kept my head straight while I walked toward the building, grabbed the edge of the open window, and swung a leg over the windowsill as if I were wearing leggings instead of a vintage knit minidress. A short hop onto my Converse and I landed squarely in a very large, very messy room full of boys.

CHAPTER 12

♥

Well, this is interesting, I thought, wondering what exactly I should do now that I'd broken a major school rule and was surrounded by several students of the opposite sex. Not that I hadn't hung out with boys before, of course. My house was absurdly full of them. But these guys were not my brothers—I hardly knew them, even Penn.

There was an awkward silence during which Hank and Sam looked to Penn as if he were holding a clipboard and a list of instructions for what to do when a tree-climbing girl lands unexpectedly in your dorm room during a Saturday night, all-boy poker game. I took that opportunity to check out the table, which was covered with playing cards, colored chips, and what appeared to be a whole lot of Doritos crumbs. From the looks of things, Hank was not having a good night, Penn was holding his own, and Sam was raking it in.

"Who's dealing?" I asked, breaking the silence and sitting down in the only empty seat—a ratty armchair between Hank and Sam and across from Penn. *Just pretend they* are *your brothers*, I told myself. *That ought to be easy enough.* The room actually bore a striking resemblance to Ben's, but with different posters— musicians, mostly—and more stuff. The desks and bookshelves were crammed—one with comic books—and there was a lot of furniture. Like the ancient coffee table with the faded leather top, the treacherous-looking sofa, the armchair I occupied with its lopsided, mismatched cushions, and the mini fridge covered in stickers.

"You are," Penn replied, watching me amusedly from the other end of the table. I noticed for the first time that his smile was crooked—the left side of his mouth drooped a tiny bit. "Do you know how to play?"

"I've held a hand or two," I fibbed.

"What's your buy-in?" Penn asked. "The usual is twenty."

Crap, I thought. *I knew this was too easy.* "Um, I don't have any cash. I wasn't exactly planning on having to buy anything."

The boys exchanged glances and a second awkward silence stretched over us like plastic wrap.

"I'll spot you," Penn said. "Twenty?"

Twenty was more than I had in mind—back home we played with pennies and nickels. And my weekly allowance wasn't exactly hefty. But when in Rome . . . "Twenty is great."

Penn counted out several chips in four different colors. "These are twenty-five, fifty, a dollar, and two," he said, pushing them across the table.

I picked up the deck of cards. "Clean?"

"Sparkling," Hank replied. I held the already-shuffled deck out to him. He cut, then put a green chip on the table—the small blind. Penn slid two chips across the leather for the big. I burned a card and dealt two to everyone.

I glanced at my hand. Pocket aces—a spade and a heart. Nice, but it was never smart to get cocky.

Everyone matched the big blind on the first round. "All in," I said, burning a card and laying the three-card flop in the center of the table. King of hearts, eight of hearts, two of spades. I had two aces and three hearts. A tiny improvement, but I'd need two more hearts for a flush.

Hank tossed three dollars' worth of chips onto the table. He had something. Penn and Sam called but didn't raise. The bet was at four. I raised by a dollar.

"And she raises," Penn said, pressing his lips together and nodding slightly.

Hank stroked his square chin and slid two more chips across the leather, meeting the bet. I burned a card and revealed the turn, the fourth, faceup card. It was a three of hearts.

"Lotta hearts," Penn said.

With all but one final card on the table, I had exactly what I started with—a pair of aces. Another ace would give me three of a kind; a heart would give me a flush.

Hank raised another two dollars.

"Too rich for my blood," Penn said, tossing his cards to me. Or was it at me? One of them landed face-up . . . the ace of diamonds.

Damn, I thought. My odds of getting three aces had just dropped, fast.

Sam was in with a call but no raise.

Oh, what the hell. I shoved another two dollars' worth of chips across the table. If I was in, I was in.

I placed the final card faceup on the table. A ten of hearts.

I willed my face to remain a mask. I had a flush of hearts: the king, the ten, the nine, and the three on the table, and the ace in my hand.

How ironic, I thought abruptly. I held a handful of hearts while Annette was breaking my real one.

It was down to me and Hank, who pushed another two dollars across the table.

"I'll see you and raise you a dollar," I said, pushing my chips to the center and trying not to notice how much I was betting.

Penn let out a low whistle. "Subzero does not mess around."

Hank dropped another dollar's worth of chips—the last he had—into the pile. He'd matched my bet and was all in.

Sam rubbed his hands together excitedly. "Let's see 'em, folks."

Hank flipped his cards first, and I blinked in surprise. He had a flush of hearts, too. For some reason, I hadn't been expecting that. He also had, overall, higher hearts than I did—the cards on the table plus the queen and the jack. If he'd had my nine, he would have had a flush *and* a straight. But he didn't.

I flipped my cards, and Hank groaned. My high-card ace beat his slew of face cards. I won the hand.

"Gentlemen, I believe we have a competitor," Sam announced.

"Beginner's luck," Hank groaned.

"I'm not so sure." Penn's crooked smile was back. "But either way, it's the end of the game for you, my friend."

"Tell me something I don't already know," he groused. "And hand me the bottle."

"Drowning your sorrows?" Penn asked as he opened some sort of compartment under the end of the table and pulled out a bottle of Absolut and several shot glasses—the same ones I'd used in Annette's room—and lined them up on the table.

"Does everyone around here have matching shot glasses?"

"Of course," Sam replied with a shrug. "They sell them in the Brookwood store, so we can charge them to our parents."

"You're kidding me."

Sam shook his head, his almond-shaped eyes solemn. "Dead serious. The receipt says *glasses*, so they have no idea. Or at least they never ask."

That was crazy, but somehow totally believable.

Penn set four glasses on the table and filled three. "You in, Subzero?"

"Do I look like I'm out?"

He shot me a hurt look, but I couldn't tell if he was teasing. "Just checking. I wasn't sure if they did shots in Minnesota."

Penn handed out the glasses and we clinked above the giant pile of chips I'd just won. "To Saturday night visitors," Penn said. "Take Sam out next so he can get back to his comic books, okay?"

"Hey," Sam protested.

"That's how you used to spend your Saturday nights, isn't it?" Hank asked. "Reading about the Green Lantern?"

"It's just Green Lantern, there's no *the*," Sam said. "And taking me out is never going to happen."

Hank raised a glass. "Bottoms up," he said.

We drank. The vodka was icy cold, which I wasn't expecting. *There must be a freezer in that secret compartment*, I thought as the viscous liquid slid down my throat.

"Make it a double," Hank said, holding his glass out for a refill. I wasn't sure if there was one in every group—someone who always wanted more—or if Hank was simply making a show of his loss to an interloper. Regardless, he got the refill he asked for, along with the rest of us, and drank it down in single gulps.

Slamming his glass down on the table, Hank turned to me. "Did they teach you to play like that at Red Lobster?"

"You betcha," I replied, slipping into my Minnesota accent. "They have poker and seafood smorgasbord every Sunday night."

"Poker and seafood what?" Sam asked.

"Buffet, Midwestern style. Picture a long, long serving station filled with wilting vegetables, mediocre seafood, and about ten different kinds of Jell-O salad. My grandmother could make an entire meal out of Jell-O salad, especially if she forgot her dentures."

All three boys cracked up, and I hoped I wasn't revealing too much about myself, about where I came from. There definitely weren't any Jell-O salads in the Brookwood servery.

"I love Jell-O salad," Sam said with a nostalgic sigh. "My aunt makes an awesome cranberry one every Thanksgiving."

We were all silent as the Absolut seeped in and we pondered the glories of Jell-O. Then Penn put the vodka away, closing the compartment door with a soft thud, and pulled out a roll of Pep O Mint Life Savers. Unwrapping several at once, he handed them out.

"Are you going to shuffle those cards, Subzero?" he asked. "Hank's the dealer from here on out. If we don't give him something to do, he'll drink all the booze."

"Dude," Hank protested. His blue eyes were slightly bloodshot, which made him seem a tiny bit vulnerable.

Sam laughed. "It's true."

I handed over my shot glass and got to work shuffling the cards. I folded early on the next hand, and the hand after that. If there was one thing I'd learned from my dad when it came to poker, it was better safe than sorry. Unless you were feeling devious and tried to bluff—in that case all bets were off.

Which is what happened on the hand after that. I went all in with nothing but a pair of eights and bluffed the boys out of another huge pot, nearly taking Penn out of the game and making a very big dent in Sam's earlier winnings. As I organized my hoard of chips into neat little piles, I felt excited for the first time since I'd arrived at Brookwood. And it wasn't just the winning, or having some extra cash. It was having fun and being myself. It was feeling comfortable. It was nobody in the room thinking I was detrimentally weird. Or if they did, they didn't seem to mind.

On the next hand, I miraculously got a full house before I even saw the last card, and bet heavily. That marked the end of the game for Penn, and almost the end for Sam.

"Well, gentlemen, I believe it's time to move on to the next event of the evening."

A sharp silence descended over the room, and Hank and Sam looked to Penn, who blatantly ignored them as he opened a drawer in the coffee table and pulled out some sort of map.

Hank turned his back to me and leaned toward Penn. "Dude, what are you doing?"

"Getting out the map."

"Not cool."

I fidgeted, not quite understanding what was going on, but that it was uncomfortable and clearly had something to do with me. My gaze landed on a small, shabby stuffed animal—a rhino, I guessed, on a shelf above one of the desks. It was old, and quite adorable.

Penn lifted a corner of the map and gestured with his chin to the table. "Do you see the chips sitting in front of her?"

"I'm not blind," Hank replied. "But she's—"

I stood, whacking my shin on the coffee table. "Hey, guys, I think it's time for me to head back to my dorm," I said. I didn't want to go, but things were suddenly tense and I *really* didn't want to contribute to that. The last hour and a half had been way too fun.

Penn raised a finger in my direction. "Hold on a sec." Whether to me or to the guys, I had no idea, but I dutifully sat back down in the weary armchair.

"Yes, Subzero is, quite obviously, a girl. But I would like to suggest that she is not your typical Brookwood female."

Thank goodness for that.

"Let's consider the facts. She climbed up to Horace Brookwood Tower alone, in a tree, with no prodding whatsoever. She made it through the window in a dress with no fuss and subsequently whupped our asses in Hold'em."

"Speak for yourself," Sam objected.

"A technicality," Penn maintained. "Not to mention the two shots of Absolut she consumed, which appeared to go down like water and, as far as we can tell, had no effect on her cardplaying whatsoever. If you ask me, there is no question regarding her worthiness."

"Four is too many," Sam said.

"*Three* was too many," Penn replied. "You were the third."

Hank leaned back on the sofa, crossing his arms across his chest. "Sam's your roommate. And he's a geek," he added. "No offense, Sam."

"None taken."

Penn ran a finger across the map.

"A fourth person would only add thirty-three percent additional mass," Sam calculated.

"Less, actually," Penn said. "She's small. And we know she can climb. She might actually come in handy."

I bristled. What was I, a Leatherman?

Hank sighed and ran a hand through his dusty-blond hair. "This isn't right."

"Do we need to review the code?" Penn asked quietly.

"No!" Sam and Hank chorused.

Code? What code? I was feeling very confused. Maybe Penn was wrong when he said that the vodka'd had no effect on me.

"I'm good," Sam said.

Hank rubbed his bloodshot eyes and exhaled in resigned disgust. "Fine. She's in."

CHAPTER 13

♥

The next thing I knew, I was following three boys down the HBT dormitory hallway to the stairs. Hank went in front and made sure there were no faculty around, signaling when it was safe to proceed. We passed a couple of boys I'd seen on campus but didn't really know, and they waved casually. Apparently, girls in the boys' dorms without permission were as commonplace as vodka shots.

The stairs dumped us in the basement at the end of a long hall, and the trio of boys turned en masse and moved effortlessly to the far end, where they rounded a corner and stopped just outside an institutional metal door with a large lock and no handle. "Okay, Sammy," Penn murmured. "Work your magic."

Penn and Hank strolled away from the door as if they had decided to head back in the other direction, a pair of casual strollers. I trailed behind, forcing myself not to peer at whatever Sam was doing. It wasn't like me to follow a bunch of boys around like a puppy, but I was seriously curious and also having a good time. If I was going to follow anyone at Brookwood, the boys seemed a lot more fun than the girls.

I heard a soft click behind me, like a latch coming undone. "All clear," Hank whispered as Sam swung the door open. I peered beyond him and saw a long tunnel with giant pipes running along one side at eye level, disappearing into the darkness. A wave of stale, dry, but slightly sweet heat whooshed out to greet us.

All at once I understood. Sam had just unlocked a door to the steam tunnels, and we were going in.

"In we go." Penn made an "after you" gesture with his hands. I stepped back slightly, trying to ignore the opening's resemblance to a giant black maw. "Um, quickly," he added.

I felt a little woozy as I stepped into the hissing darkness, instantly swathed in a dank heat.

"Incoming!" Hank whispered, hurtling himself into the tunnel and practically crashing into me.

Sam grabbed the edge of the door, closing it behind us just as the chatty voices of passing students reached our ears.

"That was close," Penn said. His voice sounded muffled and echoey all at once, thanks to the concrete surroundings and close quarters.

And then the latch clicked shut.

"Whooooooo," Hank said creepily, sending shivers up my spine.

"Cut it out," Penn chided while someone got whacked on the arm.

"Hey," Sam objected.

"Missed." Hank laughed.

"Whatever. Cut it out," Penn said. I heard something rustle and a beam of light illuminated his face. "Take this." He handed me a headlamp before pulling two more out of his backpack and giving one to Sam.

"You're shorting me?" Hank said in clear complaint.

"Josie's new. She needs a light."

"So give her yours." Even in the near dark, I could see Hank's annoyed expression, the challenge in his raised chin.

"I can't. I go first."

"She can have mine," Sam said. "I only need light when I'm picking locks."

Sam handed over the headlamp while his words sank in. There would be more lock picking, evidently. I shivered in the steam, unable to ignore that I had somehow gone from homesick mess to brokenhearted, rule-breaking hooligan in the space of a few hours.

Penn started to move along the tunnel, making a right turn after about twenty yards. "Be careful, Subzero," he said. "The steam in some of these pipes is over two hundred and fifty degrees, and there's no way to tell which ones are hot and which are cold. And you don't want to get tangled up in the electric cables, either."

He didn't need to tell me twice. I could feel the heat emanating from the giant steam pipe several inches from my head, and the snakelike mass of cables on the floor didn't leave much room to walk. A vintage knit dress was clearly not the attire of choice for this sort of thing, but at least I was wearing sneakers. I focused on not weaving while Penn moved like a speed-walker, chasing the beam of light that stretched out of the darkness in front of us.

"Almost there."

Almost where? I wondered. I was trying not to notice the trickle of sweat running down my back and just put one foot in front of the other when Penn halted abruptly and I careened into his back, losing my balance.

"Watch it!" Hank steadied me just before my bare arm grazed a pipe.

"Total fail, Penn," Hank said. "You didn't give her any warning about the junction. She's a freakin' newbie, remember?"

He lingered on the word *newbie*, and I rankled. *I* wasn't the one who'd stopped short in the tunnel.

Penn didn't seem to be listening—selective hearing was clearly one of his well-honed skills. He'd pulled out the map and was consulting it in the beam of his headlamp. I'd barely gotten a gander back in the dorm, so I leaned in to get a closer look. It was a map of Brookwood. I recognized several dorms, the science building, the library, and the main hall—but that clearly wasn't the point. The point was what was *under* the buildings. The point was the tunnels.

"It's this way," Penn said, raising his head to throw light into a tunnel leading off to the right. It was narrower than the one we were in, with two rows of steam pipes instead of one.

"Are you sure?" Hank questioned, blinding me with his beam. I shielded my eyes and watched Penn fold the map and stuff it into his back pocket before forging ahead.

As I followed along behind, it occurred to me that we seemed to have a destination in mind—this wasn't some general exploration adventure. "What's this way?"

"The library," Sam's voice replied from behind me.

"We're having a study session?"

Sam chuckled. "The library basement," he clarified. "The vault."

"Dude," Hank said.

"What?" Sam replied. "She's gonna know anyway. She's *here*, isn't she?"

"No kidding." Was it me Hank didn't like, or girls in general?

Penn made a left-hand turn and climbed a short ladder. I hoisted myself up behind him, the rusty steel hot against the skin on the insides of my fingers. Up here the tunnel was wide—almost like a long, narrow room—and the floor was covered in cables. "Electricity," Penn explained. "It's insulated, but watch your step."

As we moved forward, a loud clanking erupted in the darkness, making me jump and tangle my feet in the thick wires.

"It's just the steam," Penn consoled as he steadied me.

"The two-hundred-and-eighty-degree steam," Hank clarified.

"I thought it was two fifty." I swiped at my damp forehead with my arm. My entire body was covered in a layer of perspiration and another layer of grit, and I was dying of thirst.

"It would be higher if the school would finish the system upgrade down here," Penn said. "Some of these pipes are ancient. It's a miracle they don't explode."

"How reassuring," I replied. The passage widened and we seemed to be going up. Then, all at once, it ended at a small metal door.

"This isn't right," Hank said, ducking around me and plucking the map out of Penn's back pocket. "Can I see the map?"

Penn looked up and his headlamp beam flashed across Hank's

sweaty, squinting face. "Sure," he said sarcastically. Hank had already unfolded it and was tracing his finger across several buildings.

"This can't be the library."

Our tunnel-traveling line became a lopsided circle as we gathered around the map.

"We could be over here," Hank offered, pointing to the tunnel that approached the library from the other side.

"Don't think so," Sam said. "We didn't take enough turns."

"Maybe the map is wrong," Hank said. "We don't know how old it is."

Ignoring them, Penn put his hand against the crack in the hatch door. "No draft," he said. "Question is, are we going to pick the lock and see what's on the other side, or not?"

"I'm game," Sam said.

Hank shifted his weight and lowered the map to his side. "It's not the library."

"I agree," Sam said quietly. "But we wouldn't be down here if we didn't like exploring." He held up his pick. "Ready and willing."

"Josie? What do you think?"

Surprised to have a say, I shrugged. "I'm with you guys."

"All right, then," Penn said. He took his headlamp off and slid it onto Sam's head. "Pick away."

About twenty seconds later, Sam slowly pushed open the mini door, peeking around its edge. "Utility room," he informed us in a low voice. "Medium size." He was quiet for a minute, investigating, while we huddled behind him. A waft of cooler air hit my face and I suppressed the urge to dive through the opening. I was sweating like a pig. "And it's empty," he finally said, swinging the hatch wide. The room wasn't that different from the tunnels, with a row of old furnaces, steam and water pipes, and cables along one wall. But it *was* bigger and, thankfully, cooler. At the far end, a staircase led up.

The furnaces hummed quietly, a welcome sound after the hissing, clanking pipes.

"Going up?" Hank asked.

Penn stashed the headlamps in his backpack while my eyes adjusted to the dimly lit room. Looking down, I saw that Annette's grandmother's dress was covered in black smudges, and trails of spiderwebs crisscrossed over the front. *Oh shit.*

I was still gaping at my filth when Penn started for the stairs. Swiping at a couple of webs, I followed.

The concrete stairs zigzagged up to a higher level. A closed metal door—complete with handle—greeted us at the top. Penn put his ear to the door and turned his grin to us. "And behind door number three?" he asked playfully.

"No idea," I offered, my heart pounding with too many things to keep track of. I looked down at Grandma Ruby's dress again, wondering how I would ever get it clean.

"Science building," Sam guessed.

"Just open the door," Hank gruffed from behind me.

"All right, then." Stepping back, he pulled open the door with a flourish, and I raised my head.

Oh. My. God.

CHAPTER 14

♥

Standing approximately fifteen feet from me was the infamous Lola No. Who, for whatever reason, I'd never had a face-to-face encounter with. I wasn't even sure she knew my name.

We could have been anywhere on campus but had ended up in my dorm, where Lola No was not only on duty but front and center. And staring right at me. What were the odds of that?

I stepped forward fast, letting the door close behind me and praying that the boys had ducked behind it quickly enough to go unnoticed.

Lola No looked me up and down, her blue eyes glinting. She was unusually short, I suddenly noticed. Under five feet for sure.

"Ms. Little," she said. "Are you going to tell me what you were doing in the boiler room, or should we make our way to Dean Austin's office so you can tell *him* instead?"

I kept as much distance between us as possible and tried not to squint in the bright light. *The boiler room*, I thought, relieved. *She thinks I was in the boiler room.* Then I realized that being in the boiler room was apparently enough of a crime to warrant a trip to the dean's office, on top of which I was suddenly overcome with wooziness and utter stupidity. I had absolutely no idea what to say or do.

I was standing there like a filthy mute idiot when Roxanne appeared out of nowhere, dressed in a pair of paint-splattered jeans and a T-shirt. It appeared she had skipped the dance and spent the evening working on her art.

"Josie!" she singsonged, stepping up to us with a meaningful look I didn't understand. "I've been searching for you *every-where*." She planted herself next to me and slung an arm around my shoulder like we were best friends. "You won the round for sure," she said. "Nobody could find you."

Trying to look casual and grasp what was happening proved nearly impossible, but at least Roxanne was propping me up. *Find me*, I repeated in my befuddled head. *Find me . . .*

"She was hiding," Roxanne explained when I didn't.

"Yes," I seconded. "I was hiding . . . in the boiler room. Not a very bright idea, obviously. The place is filthy."

Lola No wasn't listening. Like a cheetah stalking its prey, she slinked over to the basement door and threw it open.

"Shit," I whispered, feeling a wave of sticky panic. But the landing at the top of the stairs was empty—no boys in sight. Lola No switched on the light and peered over the railing to the lower level, which required tiptoes despite her two-inch clogs.

She is really *short*, I thought as she flicked off the switch and marched back to us like a miniature general. "And would you care to tell me where the other hide-and-go-seek players might be?" Her question was punctuated by the slam of the door behind her.

"Still searching," Roxanne said boldly.

Lola No turned to my roommate. "I don't believe I was speaking to you, Ms. Wylde."

"I'm not sure," I said, trying to sound appropriately submissive and half hating myself at the same time. I didn't want to provoke Lola No, but I wasn't the kind of person who rolled over, either. Plus, there was my breath to worry about, Life Savers aside. (Roxanne was right: Altoids worked better.) "Still searching for me?"

Lola No nodded and turned to look at the clock at the end of the hall. "Let's hope they're finished with their search in the next seven minutes, shall we? We wouldn't want anyone to be late for curfew."

"Of course not." I was feeling dirtier and more idiotic by the second. "I'm sure they'll be here any moment."

Lola No's gaze didn't falter as she wrinkled her nose, suddenly smelling something foul (me). "I suggest you shower and change your clothes, Ms. Little. They're rather . . ." Her voice trailed off as Becca, Annette, and Marina sauntered through the front door, their arms linked together and their heads tilted back in laughter. I remembered our moments of perfect after the Full Moon Party—the feel of Annette's arm linked through mine, the slight stick of her skin from the warm night. Now her arms were linked with Marina on one side and Becca on the other.

Becca spotted us first. I saw her turquoise eyes take in everything and judge it, saw her make a split-second decision to keep on walking. Marina was less astute.

Oh crap, I thought with a jolt. Did Marina tell everyone about the kiss? Had Annette and I been outed? *Actually, that might be something to hope for,* I considered as Marina sauntered up to me. *That might make things easier.*

"Josie, you're a mess!" Marina said. "Where have you been?"

"Hiding," I said quietly. I glanced at Annette, tried to get a read. Were we broken up or not?

Guilt flashed across Annette's face, quickly replaced by shock when she noticed her grandmother's beloved dress. Her eyes narrowed in anger for precisely two seconds before they widened with sadness and disappointment. I wanted to rip off the orange knit right there and leave it in a pile on the Cortland floor, a pathetic impulse to distance myself from the evidence. It was oh so too late.

"She's been found," Lola No said. "By me." She ran a palm over her wavy hair as if to smooth it and turned to the newly arrived trio, who were nodding in unison. "And duly informed that the boiler room is off-limits now and forever. I trust you ladies had a nice evening?"

"It was excellent," Marina cooed as Roxanne squeezed my arm in annoyance.

"Good. Now I suggest you find your rooms—curfew is in four minutes."

"All righty, Coach," Becca said with a casualness that surprised me. I expected Lola No to rebuke her, but she just nodded as Becca nudged Marina and Annette forward. They glided down the hall, a single unit of legs and arms and torsos moving forward like figure skaters, disappearing into Becca and Annette's room. I watched them go, feeling strangely numb as my legs followed involuntarily . . .

Roxanne tugged on my arm. "Let's go," she said, pulling me toward the stairs. Her grip was firm, and I was too tired to resist as my roommate led me up the three flights and down the corridor to room 316, which looked nothing like it usually did. The floor was covered with giant, brightly painted pieces of paper the size of bath towels. "Sorry," Roxanne said. "I'm working on a project, and the art room isn't open late on Saturdays. Some of the pieces are still wet."

I made my way gingerly across the room and slumped onto Roxanne's bed.

"No rest for the weary," Roxanne said, stacking the dry pieces of paper next to the wall. She held out a hand to pull me up. "You need a shower." She shoved me through the bathroom door. "Use soap!" she added, slamming the door.

I smiled in spite of myself—I'd heard my mother use that refrain for years on my brothers—especially Toby, who had a tendency to collect dirt. *First things first*, I told myself as I plugged the sink and turned on the water. I took off the dress, wincing again at the black streaks that dotted it. Toby and I obviously had filth in common.

A section of the chenille trim had been torn from the hem and was missing. From the tree, probably. Was that really just a few hours ago? My second Saturday night at Brookwood was a lot like the first—totally bizarre. I was about to shove the dress into the sink full of water when I stopped myself. I did not possess my mother's stain-eliminating magic, and this was not some T-shirt I had spilled catsup on.

I hung the dress on a hook, turned on the faucets, and stepped into the steamy shower, facing the spray and catching the water in my tender palms. I'd narrowly escaped getting busted by Lola No, thanks to the smart thinking of my roommate. But what about everything else? Had Marina blabbed about the kiss? And what had happened to the boys after I walked through door number three to face Lola No? Had they gone straight back to their dorm or taken a detour?

I didn't have answers to any of these questions, nor would I tonight. So I turned around and let the warm water run down my back and eventually, remembering Roxanne's advice, reached a grubby hand for the soap.

CHAPTER 15

♥

Sunday brunch was different from any other meal at Brookwood. The buffet was open from ten to one, which meant the tables in the dining room were never completely full—people ambled in and out as they pleased (and some, especially the PG jocks, students who had already finished high school and came to Brookwood for a gap year of sports, came more than once). There were no classes or practices or games, and students and faculty alike seemed to treasure this little bit of freedom. It was the one day that allowed you to determine your own schedule, a schedule that invariably started with brunch.

Roxanne and I were silently wolfing down our Nutella and strawberry crepes that Steve had made for us. I hadn't offered any explanation about the night before and she hadn't asked, which was weird. Weirder still was the fact that it *didn't* feel weird to just let it sit there between us. Maybe because we didn't know each other well enough for it to really be between us? I wasn't sure.

"Good Sunday morning, ladies," Penn said, pulling out the chair across from me with his foot. He and Hank had appeared out of nowhere, their plates heaped so high I wondered how the stuff on top didn't slide off. I tried to read their faces, eager to know how their journey back to HBT had gone, but they revealed nothing and I knew better than to ask.

Roxanne looked decidedly irritated by their arrival. "Who are you calling a lady?" she huffed.

"Josie," Penn replied. "Just Josie."

Since when did he call me Josie?

"*Ladies* is plural."

"I was just trying to be efficient. Would you rather I ignore you completely?"

"Maybe."

Penn unwrapped his fork and set his napkin on his lap. "All right, then. Consider yourself invisible."

"Being ignored and being invisible are not the same thing," Roxanne pointed out.

Hank sighed and shoved a giant bite of scrambled eggs into his mouth, chewing madly. "Dude, give up," he said, his mouth half-full. "You're not gonna win. She's merciless."

Roxanne shot Hank a look of death. Whoa, what was that about?

"Who's competing?" Penn wanted to know. "I'm just here for food." He rolled up a pancake and ate half of it in one bite.

I was wondering what was going on when Becca showed up with her fruit, yogurt, and egg-white omelet, Marina and Cynthia and Annette right behind her. Annette's tray matched Becca's exactly, right down to the color of their coffees, but Marina had a giant bowl of fruit and some cornflakes. Her eyes met mine as she sat down.

Had she said anything to Annette about the argument, or the kiss? I wondered yet again. Maybe she'd been too drunk to remember, though it seemed unlikely. She'd shown no signs of being out-of-control wasted.

Maybe girls kiss girls all the time here, I mused while I sipped my juice. Though from what I could tell, that seemed even more unlikely. There had to be at least a handful of lesbians here, but nobody appeared to be out.

"Mind moving over?" Becca asked, setting her tray down before anyone could answer. Maybe the question wasn't actually a question. Maybe it was rhetorical.

The word *rhetorical* reverberated in my brain, and I remembered the English essay, a compare and contrast of Shakespearean sonnets, that was due at seven forty-five the next morning. Just remembering the assignment, along with the dozen math equations I had to solve and my anthropology reading, made me a little sick to my stomach. Or maybe it was sitting with but clearly *not* sitting with Annette. Or the half cup of Nutella I'd just consumed. Regardless, it wasn't pretty.

"Invisible and ignored," Penn said. "What's the difference?"

"They're the same." Becca poked a fork into a strawberry.

"I don't know," Marina offered. "If you could choose to be invisible, that might be good. But feeling invisible sucks. And being ignored is no fun, either."

Surprisingly thoughtful. And it was not lost on me that Annette was ignoring *me* as she busily picked apart her mushroom-and-egg-white omelet.

"I could use some invisible," Hank said.

"You were invisible all summer." Roxanne's voice was sharp, but her eyes were sad. It was becoming apparent that I wasn't the only one at the table with a wounded heart.

"Does believing you're being ignored make it true?" Marina asked.

"Ah, truth versus belief," Penn said in perfect imitation of Professor Mannering. He twirled his fork in the air absently, dropping bits of scrambled egg onto the table. "They are two separate things . . . until so many people *believe* something that it becomes a *truth*. The earth was flat once, was it not?"

In anthropology, we'd been talking about how beliefs shape our actions, and this was one of Mannering's examples.

"Of course not," Roxanne huffed.

"Exactly. Of course not," Penn said in his regular voice. "But everyone believed it was, since proving otherwise could mean falling off the edge. And until that ship didn't actually fall off the end of the earth, a flat earth was a truth because everyone believed it. An accepted belief in practice is the same as a truth."

"A truth is a fact," Hank said. "A belief is something a person can *consider* fact. Not the same thing."

"Only it doesn't always matter," Marina added.

"Of course it matters." Becca cradled her coffee cup in her hands protectively. "When doesn't it?"

"When the believing becomes more important than the truth?" I suggested. I could totally hear Professor Mannering saying that, and had learned it firsthand when Annette and I were outed. We were still the same people we'd been the day before—that was a fact. But people perceived us completely differently because of their beliefs . . . and not in a good way.

"Or when the truth has yet to be discovered," Penn added.

Becca rolled her eyes. "We've only had one week of classes and you're already talking Mannering nonsense," she said. "Why doesn't that man retire already? He gets crazier every year."

"Professor Mannering is awesome," Marina said. "I'm trying to get into that class. I hear you learn all about the Amazonian peoples, like those crazy Jivaro, who shrink heads and wear them around their necks!"

"You mean the Shuar," Hank corrected. "The term *Jivaro* lumps several clans together, which none of them really appreciate."

Marina picked a soggy cornflake off the edge of her bowl and ate it. "I don't care what they're called as long as they're the ones I've heard about. Who doesn't want to take a class about spiritualism, hallucinogens, and shrunken heads?" She leaned forward. "I've heard that the kids who took his class in the sixties used to drop acid to find out what Jivaro ceremonies were like."

"Shuar," Hank repeated.

Cynthia stared hard at Marina across the table. "Are you *still* obsessing about Edward Hunter?" she asked. Her words dripped with displeasure.

"Who's Edward Hunter?" Annette asked, speaking up for the first time.

"Some kid who died like half a century ago," Becca grumbled.

"*Exactly* half a century ago, in fact," Marina said.

"Here we go again." Cynthia tossed her napkin onto her plate.

"What?" Marina said. "It's *true*."

"Is it true?" Penn asked. "Or just a belief?"

"It's true," Marina said, scrunching up her face. "I think."

"Would someone please explain what you're talking about?" Annette asked. "I'm a little lost."

"Of course." Becca's smile was wide and self-important as she set down her fork and straightened. All it took was an audience for the girl to get interested. "Fifty years ago, when Brookwood was in its boys-only heyday, there was a terrible accident and a student named Edward Hunter—Hunt—died. He was supposedly some sort of genius—a science whiz—and a major legacy, but also a bit of a . . ."

"Dork," Marina finished.

Becca took a sip of juice and sat back, fingering her pearls. God, she was annoying. "He supposedly had an authentic shrunken head that his grandfather had traded with the Jivaro Indians in Ecuador."

"Shuar," Hank corrected.

"Whatever," Becca said dismissively. "The point is the head itself, not who he got it from. Anyway, Hunt was a dork, but also a scientific genius. A bunch of boys wanted him to make LSD in the chemistry lab so they could have a hallucinogenic Jivaro ceremony, but Hunt refused, saying it was too dangerous."

"Which didn't go over well," Marina said.

Becca gave Marina a little kick under the table, and Marina scowled.

"Right," Becca said. "The boys were furious. They told everyone his shrunken head was a fake, and then stole it to prove they were right. Hunt went to get it back, but died mysteriously that night—in the tunnels."

"What tunnels?" I asked, all innocence.

"The steam tunnels," Becca explained with a slightly pity-ing look.

I tried to appear befuddled.

"The administration demanded that the head be returned to the family. Hunt's grandfather had verified that it was not only authentic but also a family treasure. But the boys who'd stolen it claimed that Hunt got it back before he died."

"So where is it?" Annette asked.

"Nobody knows," Hank said. "We're not sure it's here at all, or even if it ever existed."

"Is it a truth or a belief?" Penn asked yet again, this time with exaggerated mysteriousness.

"I think the kid was misunderstood," Hank said.

"How generous of you," Roxanne sniffed.

"Well, the poor kid really died," Marina said. "That much is true."

"Right, but like forever ago," Penn put in, still waving his fork around. But I had the sense that he was bluffing, that prowl-ing around the steam tunnels was directly tied to Edward Hunter and his supposed shrunken head.

His shrunken head. I had to let that sink in. It was one thing to talk about this stuff in anthropology, where you could keep the weirdness several thousand miles away in the Amazon. It was quite another to find out that there might be an actual shrunken head right here, at Brookwood Academy.

On the other hand, a lot of things at Brookwood were pretty bizarre. The perfectly groomed campus. The crazy intensity of the academics. The matching shot glasses, apparently owned by all, filled with expensive vodka. And even Sunday brunch. I mean, here I was with Annette—and yet not with Annette—and six other people we'd met only a week ago—people I'd so far gone to class, danced, partied, eaten, played poker, steam tunneled, and almost gotten busted with.

I repeat: people I'd known for seven days.

Everything was so much closer together here. As if we weren't people at all but tiny microbes swimming around in a petri dish. Which was, in a way, more terrifying than a missing shrunken head. Because although I'd been here for only a week, I already understood that getting *out* of the petri dish was impossible, that now that we were here, there was no escaping Brookwood.

"Enough banter," Penn said as he shoved his chair back, the heavy wooden legs scraping across the tile floor. "I've got to get to it. My English essay calls, and I haven't even finished the poems."

The English essay—something else I couldn't get out of.

I expected Hank to follow suit, but he just sat back and sipped his OJ, obviously lingering. What was he waiting for?

Roxanne turned her back to him. "I've got some French Impressionists to study. Are you finished, Josie?"

Hank's eyes flickered with remorse. I glanced over at Annette, who had shaped her uneaten omelet into a smiley face. The mushroom slice made an awesome nose. I waited for her to acknowledge my presence, but she didn't, and when I looked up, Marina was watching me.

I stood and picked up my tray. "Yeah, I'm ready," I said. "Let's go."

CHAPTER 16

♥

It wasn't until Monday after classes, on the way back to the dorm, that I found Annette alone.

"Hey, you," I said, coming up behind her.

She turned. "Josie, hey." I tried to read the expression in her eyes, but they were as elusive as morning mist on a lake. "I was going to come find you yesterday, but I had a ton of schoolwork," she said as we kept walking. (They didn't call it homework at Brookwood—probably because we never got to go home.)

"Yeah, me too. They really load it on here." We reached the turnoff for the dorm but kept going, our footsteps hitting the pavement in perfect rhythm as we moved up the path and found a little bench.

"Did we break up on Saturday?" I asked as soon as our butts hit the seat, the question refusing to stay inside a moment longer.

"What?" Annette said, blinking. "No!" Then she was quiet. "Josie, no. That wasn't what I was trying to say. I just, I don't know. I guess I just wanted to keep dancing."

Relief flooded through me, giddy and light.

Annette looked out at the field for a long moment, then turned to me. "I love you, Josie, like always. But I still need to be just me in front of people."

So much for giddy and light. "Why?"

Her shoulders fell slightly. "I thought I explained this already."

"Apparently I'm a little slow on the upload," I admitted.

Annette shoved some crimson- and mustard-colored leaves aside with the sole of her shoe. "Because for the first time ever, I'm in a new place, with a clean slate. And I just want a little time to be myself first, before I'm with you."

"Do you want to be with me?"

"Yes, of course. Why wouldn't I?"

I shrugged as a crow swooped into a nearby tree. "Okay, how much longer?"

Annette shook her head slightly. "I'm not sure."

"That's not very reassuring."

"Did you just hear me tell you that I love you, and that I want to be with you?" Annette asked, as if I were an impetuous child. "Nothing has changed between us."

Nothing has changed between us. I tried to absorb those words, to feel them in my bones. But things didn't seem to fit the way they used to. *We* didn't seem to fit the way we used to.

Annette read my expression like an open book with large print. "Stop overthinking, Josie. It just makes everything worse."

I did overthink, I knew. And I certainly couldn't say it made things *better.*

She smiled at me and stood, reaching for my hand. "Everything is fine, I promise."

But a week, and then two and then three, went by. September became October and we were still a secret. Meanwhile, I seemed to be surviving my Brookwood life, if often hanging on by what felt like an unraveling thread. My essays for Professor Drake had intelligent-sounding titles and used as much *logic* and *rhetoric* as I could muster. They were, to the best of my ability, *authentic*. And I didn't think they totally sucked. Whether Professor Drake thought they totally sucked was unclear, because every essay was covered in red ink when returned to its author, and he didn't give grades. "You should know how you are doing without my having to tell you," he liked to tell us over the top of his tortoiseshell glasses.

Math was another story. I managed to get the schoolwork done and tried to pay attention in class but usually got lost and had to ask Cynthia for help. I was surprised when she always seemed willing. Professor Roth called tests and quizzes "demon-strations." Only she pronounced them "dem-un-STRAY-shuns," which was annoying because it felt like she was pointing out just how far I could *stray* from the material she was trying to teach. I failed the first quiz and so far hadn't gotten anything higher than a C.

Anthropology was the best class by far, and not just because Marina had transferred in, though she was definitely a lively addi-tion to the discussions. We *were* in fact learning about the tribal peoples of the Amazon, all of whom fascinated me. Professor Mannering followed his syllabus to the letter, too, because he asked us over and over what things *meant*.

"This is the most important thing we can ask ourselves," he croaked, pacing back and forth among his artifacts and skulls. "Thinking about what our experiences mean is the best way to figure out who we are, to explore our essential humanity."

"As individuals, or as a society?" a girl named Ingrid asked.

"Class?" Professor Mannering asked.

"Both," we replied.

So I was fascinated by anthropology, distraught about algebra, and had essentially no idea how I was doing in English. I also had no idea what was going on with Annette, though I couldn't exactly ignore the fact that she was spending more and more time running and less and less time with me. Or that we were still in the closet. And though I regularly crossed paths with and found myself at the table with them, I knew that, with the possible exception of Marina, I hadn't really been accepted by Annette's new posse of friends—the Soleets.

"That's a good thing," Roxanne insisted one Saturday afternoon in October. We were sitting in a booth at Mike's Diner in town, eating glazed doughnuts—heated in the microwave with melted butter.

"My brother August told me about these," she said, sliding a fork through the doughy ring and adding, "He and his friends used to get stoned in the woods on the way here." The butter dripped onto the Formica table as she raised the fork to her mouth, closing her eyes for a moment to savor. "There used to be a lot more drugs at Brookwood, but they had a big crackdown a few years ago. That's why everyone drinks."

Everyone *definitely* drank, including me and Roxanne. We split the cost of our vodka fifty-fifty and kept it in the back of our closet, carrying it across the field to our bench in the woods once or twice a week. We always kept to Roxanne's two-shot limit as if it were a mandate, though. Roxanne knew what she was doing and I didn't question her.

I took a bite of my own doughnut, which tasted like heaven and sin at the same time. "Are the Soleets really that bad?" Correction. I didn't *usually* question her.

Roxanne eyed me over her bite of doughnut. "Absolutely. And Becca and her posse are even worse."

"What kind of worse?"

She dropped her fork to the table, her dark eyes clouding as if there were a storm brewing behind her forehead. "The bitchy, popular, entitled kind of worse," she said, taking an exasperated sip of water. "The 'we are the only people who matter' kind of worse. The—"

"All right, all right," I said. "I get it." I believed her, and yet somehow didn't want to. I wanted to believe that there was something good there, something worthwhile to attach to, because otherwise Annette spending so much time with them was seriously depressing.

Roxanne finished her doughnut and started rifling through her bag. "I've got a bunch of errands to do," she said as she opened her wallet. "You want to come?"

I looked at her guiltily.

"Let me rephrase that," she said. "Is your essay for Monday done?"

Sometimes Roxanne was worse than my mother.

"That's what I thought," she said. "So I guess you'll be heading back to our room."

"I guess," I agreed.

"I'll pick up the ill-fated carrot dress for you."

It took me a second to realize that carrot was the color. "That would be awesome. Thanks."

We checked the bill and left our money on the table. "You sure you don't want me to come?" I asked as we pushed through the door.

"Positive. I'll see you on campus."

I sighed at her retreating back moving up the sidewalk and wondered how Roxanne got her work done. From what I could tell, she spent most of her time on her art, and yet she pretty much pulled straight As.

The walk back to Brookwood was short, and fifteen minutes later, I was back in our room. The giant pieces of painted paper were gone, but now the carpet was littered with confetti-like scraps of pink, red, orange, yellow, and blue. Roxanne had spent hours cutting out colored shapes, and these were the leftovers. It looked like someone had barfed up a rainbow on our floor.

Roxanne was crazy talented—she got it from her mother, who owned a gallery and had occasional shows at small museums around the country—and spent all of her free time on her art. Which, at the moment, involved a zillion colored shapes cut out of painted paper, à la Henri Matisse's cutout phase.

"Matisse became chair- and bed-bound after he got abdominal cancer in his seventies," she'd told me. "He couldn't paint or sculpt anymore, so he turned to paper. With the help of his assistants, he started cutting shapes out of painted pieces of paper, putting them together to create collages."

She'd flashed a picture of a Matisse cutout at me, called *Blue Nude*. "The man was a genius," she'd declared, clicking to another image, one of his dining room in Nice. The walls were lined with cut out figures—swimmers, divers, and sea creatures.

"You can't see it here because the picture is black and white, but the figures were a gorgeous, aquamarine blue," Roxanne told me. "He created his own swimming pool when it was too hot outside to get to a real one."

I knew nothing about art, but I believed her.

Leaving the scattered confetti where it was, I grabbed my twelve-hundred-page *Norton Anthology of Short Fiction* off my desk. This weekend's assignment was to read Shirley Jackson's "The Lottery," choose a theme, and write an essay about the chosen theme's major components. I climbed up to my bunk, propped myself against the wall with pillows, and hunched over the book, pencil poised for margin note-taking.

I was three pages into the story, which was getting creepier than life in the warring Amazon, when I heard a knock on the door. Nobody ever knocked on our door, and I looked up, curious. "Come in."

The door opened and Annette appeared, wearing her cross-country uniform and a Giovanni's tee. It sounds totally stupid, but my heart actually skipped a beat. I hadn't been alone with Annette in what seemed like forever—it was almost as if a beautiful stranger had walked in.

"Hey," she said a little breathlessly.

"Hey."

She glanced down at the carpet.

"Piñata party," I joked a little nervously.

She raised an eyebrow. "Really?"

"No. Roxanne's working on an art project."

"Huh. Looks messy."

Silence.

"Where is Roxanne?"

"She went to town."

Click. Annette locked the door, and I felt the blood rush in my ears. How many times had Annette locked my bedroom door at home? A hundred? A thousand?

Annette slipped off her shoes and climbed the ladder to my bed. I had several questions, starting with "Where have you been lately?" But she was pulling my *Norton Anthology* off my lap and crouching over me, and then stretching herself out on my comforter. She leaned in and kissed me, soft and slow, with a gentleness that made my heart feel like it was made of lead and was going to fly away, all at once.

"You smell good," she murmured.

She ran her fingers along my back while her lips and tongue searched for mine. Her hand slid under my shirt and found my breast. I'd longed for her and now here she was, smelling like salt and autumn and herself. Like Annette.

"I've missed you," she said, sitting up to lift her jersey and sports bra over her head. The sight of her nakedness, of her pale, barely damp skin, made my breath catch and I pulled her back to me, inhaling her, kissing her mouth, her neck, her shoulder, her belly. My body tingled with longing as we touched each other, as her fingers touched me the way no one else could until everything else seemed to slide away, until there was nothing but Annette.

Later, we curved into each other like spoons in the window-filtered sunlight, just lying there, breathing and content. Almost perfect. Almost, but not quite.

"I talked to my mom yesterday," Annette said, running a thumb over my opal pendant. "It was five thirty and she was already sloppy."

I turned so I could see her face.

"I wasn't even listening to what she was rambling about. I just kept thinking how happy I was not to be there—to be so far away," she said. "And then she got all emotional, saying she couldn't believe her only daughter had left her, and I felt awful."

I felt a flash of anger. That was so Shannon. "She wants you to feel guilty, Annette. She's manipulating you."

Annette sighed. "Probably."

"Probably?"

"Okay, yes. She's manipulating me. But she's also my mom."

"She was also hurting you when you lived at home."

She nodded, biting her lower lip. "I know. But now that I'm here, my dad has to deal with her by himself."

"Your dad is an adult."

She let out her air in a whoosh. "Yeah." She moved the clasp of my opal necklace to the back of my neck and wrapped one of my curls around her pinky.

"Annette?"

"Yeah?"

"What are we doing?"

"Lying on your bed?"

That wasn't what I meant, of course—she wasn't answering my question. Part of me wanted to push her—get us out of the closet, into the open, where we could shine in the sun. But for some reason, I couldn't get the words out.

"Some of the girls are ordering pizza on Friday, after lights," Annette said, totally switching gears. "You should join us."

I tried not to let disappointment seep in—the last hour had been too perfect. But I wanted more of this intimacy—a lot more—not a pizza party with the Soleets.

"You need to give these girls a chance, Josie. You had a good time with us on Dress to Impress night before you ran off and ruined my grandmother's dress."

That felt a little snide, but I couldn't deny that I did run off. And even though she was trying to sound lighthearted about the dress, I *had*, probably, ruined it. And we both knew how much she loved it.

"I'm having it cleaned," I told her. "Roxanne says that Royal Cleaners can work miracles—"

The door handle turned and Annette bolted upright, instantly searching among the covers for her shirt. "Josie?" Roxanne called.

I was pulling on my own clothes when I heard the key turn in the lock. A moment later, the door opened and Roxanne appeared, loaded down by shopping bags. "What's with the locked doo—" She stopped mid-sentence. "Oh, sorry."

Annette's jersey had just cleared her shoulders and she yanked it down but still looked utterly exposed, and a lot like the first time Shannon almost caught us fooling around in her room.

We were twelve. "What was that?" Annette whispered, sitting up fast. Her ponytail was lopsided, her shirt untucked.

"I didn't hear anything," I replied, smooching her on the lips and knocking her math textbook to the floor. We'd been studying for a math quiz in her room, and had gotten a little distracted.

"It sounded like a car door." Her eyes darted toward the hall.

We sat perfectly still for several long moments, listening, hearing silence.

Annette picked up the math textbook and flipped to the right page. She scanned it for a second, then slammed the book shut. "Done!" She smirked. Then she pounced on me, pinning my arms to the bedspread and attacking me with kisses (not a bad way to be attacked).

Annette and I had been doing a lot of kissing. Not in public, of course, but whenever we were alone. Her ponytail tickled my neck and she lay down next to me and put her hand on my belly under my shirt, brushing her fingers over my skin.

My heart pounded as butterflies took flight in my stomach, their delicate wings flapping wildly. We were heading into uncharted territory. I put my hands on either side of her face and opened my mouth just a little, my tongue tenuously venturing forth. We had just started to French kiss and I had no idea what I was doing. The only advice I'd gotten was from my older brother, Ben, and as far as I could tell, he was no expert. Though we did, at least, both like girls.

Annette sighed as our tongues tentatively mingled, and she slid her hand to my waist, pinching it.

"Hey!" I said in protest.

"Hay is for horses," she replied, leaning back in. I was inhaling the chocolate and butterscotch cookies we'd stolen from the kitchen, when I heard footsteps coming down the hall. I bolted upright, hitting Annette's chin with the top of my head.

"Ow!"

"Door!" I whispered frantically. Annette pulled my shirt down over my stomach and undid her ponytail holder, shaking her hair free.

"What are you—"

"Annette?" The door handle turned.

Annette leaped to her feet and bent over, letting her golden hair touch the ground before running her fingers through it like a comb.

"Yes?" she replied as she righted herself, pulling her hair through the elastic band into an impressively neat ponytail. The girl was as sly as a fox.

Shannon's tall frame appeared in the open doorway, the corners of her mouth dropping the moment she saw me. "Do you have any *other* friends, Annette?" she asked, the disgust in her voice lingering over the rim of her gin and tonic.

I was too freaked to take offense—my heart thudded in my chest like Josh's drum machine. "We're doing math," I offered. "Decimals."

"Well, it's getting late, and Annette needs to start dinner." Her eyes glinted and I noticed for the hundredth time that they were just like Annette's, only two shades darker and a zillion shades meaner.

I pulled my cell out of my pocket. "My mom just texted that she wants me home by six."

"You'd better get out of here, then." She took another swallow and pushed off the doorframe. "You wouldn't want to be late."

"The cleaners in town are still working on the dress," Roxanne said while Annette busily swept her hair back into a ponytail. I wasn't sure what she was so stressed about—Roxanne had found us in the bathroom the day we arrived and obviously didn't care that we were a couple.

Shooting me a "what gives?" look, Roxanne tipped the bags, dumping her goods on the floor and sending colored scraps of paper flying. There were bottles of shampoo, conditioner, lotion, a huge jar of bath salts, and a paper bag with some kind of large bottle.

"What's in the bag?" I asked.

Roxanne reached in and pulled out a magnum of vodka.

"You carried that giant bottle across campus in broad daylight?" Annette was aghast.

"It's an old trick my brother taught me." Roxanne had one older brother, August, who'd graduated from Brookwood two years ago. He was at Harvard now. "They don't expect students to be brazen enough to tote bottles of booze around during the day, so they never check. Plus, they don't actually want to bust you. They want to turn us into überprofessionals who will go out and rule the world." She brandished the bottle like a cowboy with a shotgun. The girl was freakishly strong.

Annette regarded Roxanne with a look of skepticism, as if she were a species of girl she'd never seen before.

"What?" Roxanne asked. "I'm not kidding."

"I believe you," Annette said quickly, hopping down from the top bunk and turning back to me. "Ten thirty, Friday," she said in invitation. "Think about it at least." Stepping gingerly over the array of stuff on the carpet, she disappeared through the door.

Roxanne shoved the bottle of vodka back into the paper bag and stashed it in the bowels of our closet. When she reemerged, she picked up her toiletry stash, flicking the wayward bits of colored confetti off the bottle of shampoo. She stood there for a second, her dark eyes on the bottle of Pantene. I could tell she was thinking about something.

"What?" I asked.

Roxanne half shook her head. "I hate to admit it, but she's not totally wrong to be skittish. I mean, I'm totally cool with girls who like girls. Who cares? But the thing is, some people around here *do* care, and they judge." She walked into the bathroom and dumped her stuff into the sink.

I considered that for a minute, remembering how people at home had judged, too. Even after Annette had sweetened everything with her smile and her fudge, people still talked. Some pretended they didn't know. Others pretended they didn't know *us*. But most people eventually got over it. Would it be the same here?

"Marina saw us kiss the night of Dress to Impress."

"And she didn't say anything?"

"I don't think so."

She set the shampoo and conditioner next to the tub. "That girl has more going on than she wants us to know." She sat on the edge and arranged the bottles in a row. "Josie?"

"Yeah?"

"Is it simpler when you're both the same sex? Like, do you get stuff about each other because you've got the same hormones?"

"Does it seem simpler?" I asked.

Roxanne shook her dark head slowly. "No," she admitted as she got to her feet and picked up the broom, ready to attack the floor. "It seems like relationships eat you up no matter who they're with."

CHAPTER 17

♥

"I'll take a pepperoni," Marina said, handing over a flimsy paper plate. Two pizzas had just been delivered to the dorm, and we were piled into Annette and Becca's room, buzzing around the cheesy, crusty, tomato-saucy pies like starved flies.

"Save me one!" Cynthia protested, waving her own plate in the air. Becca snatched the paper disc and hastily slid a greasy piece onto it before handing it back.

I bit into my own piece of cheese and chewed. It wasn't great pizza—far from it. The crust was underdone and too thick, and the sauce tasted like tomato paste. But as I pulverized the mediocre combination of carbs, fat, and salt between my teeth, I felt unexpectedly okay. Pigging out on pizza was something I knew how to do—something all five of us seemed to have in common.

"Pass me a cheese," Annette said. Her plate was grease-stained and bent dangerously when Becca topped it with a second slice. Annette lifted it to her mouth and caught the greasy tip of pizza between her teeth, mumbling her thanks between chews.

Marina flipped open the lid to the pizza box and grabbed her third piece of pepperoni. "Thank God this is calorie-free." She took a huge bite and chewed it like cud.

Cynthia nodded, nibbling the last of her crust.

"Since when?" I asked. "Last time I checked, grease and carbs were pretty damn caloric."

Becca smiled at me—the smile she reserved for those who just didn't get it. I willed myself to let that smile go right through me, to vaporize into thin air, but the word *Soleet* swam in my brain like a minnow in a pond.

"You're going to eat pizza with who?" Roxanne's voice swam right along with it—she'd been unable to hide her disdain when I told her where I was going. "Why, exactly?" she'd asked.

"Because Annette asked me to," I'd replied, knowing my answer wouldn't satisfy my roommate. For some reason, I really cared about what she thought. There was something about Roxanne that rang true—she didn't seem to do things unless she wanted to, as if peer pressure didn't exist for her.

Cynthia leaned against Annette's bed, her palm cradling her stomach. "I think I'm going to be sick."

"Perfect timing!" Marina chortled. Why didn't *she* get the pitying smiles from the Soleet in charge? Was it the wardrobe? The money? Both?

Becca had gotten to her feet and was rifling through a drawer. Moments later, she produced a multipack of toothbrushes—five, to be exact. She ripped the package open and handed one to each of us. Baffled, I took the green plastic wand with bristles, noting with surprise that it was a no-name brand. Apparently, Soleets could be rich, popular, *and* cheap. "I've got my own upstairs," I said.

"This is different." Marina jiggled with laughter.

"We'll use the bathroom at the end of the hall so we can each have a stall," Becca instructed. "Cynthia can keep watch."

Watch? "What are we watching for?" I asked.

"Intruders," Becca replied, as if that explained everything.

The other girls were on their feet, clutching their toothbrushes and looking exhilarated. It seemed we were all going into the bathroom across the hall. I followed the other girls through the door, noting that we were practically in formation—probably the result of Becca and Annette spending so much time with Lola No.

Cynthia dutifully took her post at the door. As Becca and Marina disappeared into a pair of stalls, the purpose of our mission began to unfold in the back of my brain. My mouth dropped open as the words *calorie-free* echoed in my mind. *Wait, really?* Half a second later, I heard the first gag—Becca's, I think— followed by the sound of liquefied pizza surging into the toilet.

I clutched Annette's sleeve. "You're not actually goi—"

The defiance in her eyes silenced me, clearly saying "yes, I am," and I watched as she tugged the fabric loose from my fingers and stepped into an empty stall. I heard Marina retch and heave a mass of pizza puke, heard the spatter of regurgitated crust and sauce and cheese hit the water, and found myself wondering when the toilets were last scrubbed.

Annette gagged and retched, tricking her body into sending the partially digested food back up. A second later, the contents of her stomach splattered into the toilet, sending a fresh waft of pizza puke to my nose. *This is so messed up on so many levels*, I thought. Was this really what she'd been doing on Friday nights? The thing she wanted me to be a part of?

Someone flushed a toilet, and I heard a bolt unlatch. A moment later, Becca appeared—pink cheeked, a little sweaty, and extremely pleased with herself. As if she'd just done something impressive, something I should admire. She saw me standing there next to an empty stall with a fresh toothbrush and a clean toilet and her eyes narrowed as if to say "I knew you didn't have it in you."

I had absolutely no idea what to do with that, or even where to begin. So I silently turned and left the bathroom, walking past Cynthia and taking the stairs two at a time.

CHAPTER 18

♥

I rushed up the stairs, flustered and wondering what was wrong with this place. With Becca. With Annette. I practically ran right into Roxanne, who was at the top and heading down. "How was it?" Her voice had an edge of fake cheerfulness.

"You don't want to know," I replied.

"Let me guess—the pizza was calorie-free."

I gaped. "How did you know?"

She half rolled her dark eyes. "Ritualistic barfing isn't exactly original around here."

"What, it's like a thing people do? Like play field hockey?" She looked so calm just standing there, as if she were telling me that there was a new glee club starting up.

"Sort of, yeah."

"Sort of?" I echoed. The pizza was becoming a mean wad in my stomach, and for a second I thought I might need to throw up for real. I threw a glance over the edge of the railing. If I aimed right, I might even be able to hit the first floor—a little gift for Becca.

"People do it all the time," Roxanne said, nonplussed. "Welcome to boarding school."

I gaped at my roommate, not sure what I expected from her,

what I wanted her to say. Giving up, I changed the subject. "Where are you going?"

"Laundry," she said, a little grumpily. "I'm out of underwear."

Roxanne disliked doing laundry almost as much as she disliked the Soleets, and had well over two dozen pairs of underwear so she wouldn't have to wash her clothes very often.

"You want help?"

"Not with my clothes," she said. "But I could use help cutting pieces for my next project." I watched her face shift into excitement. "I have a new idea, and I think it could be brilliant!"

"Whoa, did you just use the *B* word?" Roxanne *never* said anything close to brilliant about her art. She was her own worst critic.

"I did!" She was practically gleeful.

I peered at her. "Who are you, and what did you do with my roommate?"

She laughed. "Will you help?"

I nodded.

"Great." She dashed down the stairs, and I headed to our room, which was half-covered with new cutouts in blues, grays, and greens—all traces of the rainbow confetti were gone.

In the bathroom, I turned on the hot water and slathered my hands with soap, as if I could wash the barfing scene off. I wanted to figure out why the group vomiting was so shocking. It was no secret that Sara Kinsley binged and barfed her way through freshman year back home. But Sara was a mess—she did it because she had a problem. Becca and her posse seemed to be doing it for fun.

I rinsed my hands and studied my reflection in the mirror—my unruly auburn hair, my pale skin, my smattering of freckles and amber eyes. I looked exactly like the girl who'd come here six weeks ago, but didn't feel the same at all. And what about Annette? She clearly needed to be accepted by these new girls, by Becca. How far would she go to be one of the pack?

Something on my desk beeped—something that sounded like my phone. That made no sense, though—my phone had been destroyed by Brookwood's high-end watering system.

I dried my hands, then heard it again. My desk was piled with books, papers, and a bunch of other crap I wasn't sure what to do with, so it took a good fifteen seconds to find the thing, which had been plugged in, presumably by Roxanne. It beeped a third time, and there was a text on the screen.

Meet us under the T at 11:45. –PM

PM. Was that the time, or was that . . . Penn McCarthy? Or both? It had to be Penn, but how did he get my number? And what was going on with my phone? (Not that I could complain about having a functioning cell.)

I checked the time. 11:22. Could I make it to the T in twenty-three minutes? Did I know how to get there? But even as I considered these details, I was pulling a long-sleeve shirt over my head and changing into sneakers. Rummaging through my desk, I slipped a tiny flashlight into my pants pocket and walked out the door, leaving the barf party behind.

I padded down to the laundry room to tell Roxanne where I was going, but she wasn't there. "Roxanne?" I called quietly. The dorm was completely silent—apparently the barfers had gone to sleep on their empty stomachs. I stood there for several seconds, wondering where Roxanne was, and then decided I needed to go—I was short on time as it was.

Walking to the end of the hall, I silently opened the door to the basement. I was greeted by semidarkness and the hum of the furnace.

Heart thudding and half-certain someone was about to barge into the utility room and haul my ass to the dean's office, I quickly got myself through the hatch and pulled it closed. Stale blackness engulfed me as I retrieved my flashlight from my pocket. I shined the beam down the long, cramped tunnel. My skin was already damp.

This is seriously creepy, I thought, shivering. Part of me wanted to hurl myself against the hatch and land with a thud in my dormitory boiler room, where I could breathe normally and turn on a light. The tunnel was already way creepier than it had been the last time I was in it—probably because I was dead sober, and alone. Without a map or another person to guide me. I shined my light back at the door I'd come through longingly. *Get going, chicken.*

I took my first step, and then a second and a third. I tried to walk at an almost normal pace, bending my head and willing myself to be narrower than I actually was. *You've been here before—it's the same tunnel.* The seemingly endless hiss of traveling steam filled my ears.

Within minutes, I came to the wider section where tunnels branched out in several directions. I shined my flashlight down one tunnel, then another. This was where we'd figured out that we weren't heading toward the library, I remembered. But where was the T?

I pointed my beam of light back down the tunnel I'd come through. It looked much narrower than it had felt when I was in it, and I wondered if I was mistaken. Maybe I'd come out of the passage next to it? I shined my light into that tunnel. It was practically identical.

Oh crap, I thought. *I'm not sure.*

Panic rose in my throat, tasting almost exactly like the barfy bathroom had smelled. But I couldn't freak out now—I had to keep going. And to do that, I had to get a grip. I envisioned the Brookwood buildings above my head. I'd come from my dorm, which was on the edge of campus—the only thing beyond it was the athletic center. I'd traveled straight, then left, and then straight some more. I should be under the main building by now, maybe the dining hall . . . was that the smell of dinner?

I shined the light down the tunnel I thought I'd come from a second time. Was that it? I peered into the semidarkness, willing the answer to come to me. Instead, the shaft of light dimmed, flickered, and disappeared altogether.

I stood stock-still in the darkness, trying to remain calm. I whacked the flashlight against my leg and pushed the power switch. I lifted it to my face even though I couldn't see a thing.

"Come on!" I shouted, arms flailing. I felt the flashlight slip between my fingers, but my brain took too long to react. By the time I understood what was happening, the slender metal torch had already clattered to the floor.

CHAPTER 19

♥

Oh shit. The tunnel was pitch-black. Sweat trickled down my back like rows of ants marching downward, following the flashlight to the floor. I couldn't believe I hadn't brought my phone. I wasn't used to carrying it around—you weren't allowed to have it in public—and it had been broken since the day I arrived. Still, totally stupid.

I thought I'd heard the flashlight land just to my right, but I forced myself not to lunge after it. I had to keep my bearings to have any hope of finding it.

I *really* needed to find it.

The pipe behind me clanged, then went quiet. I could hear the steam hissing in the tunnel to my left. I dropped to my butt and scooched forward slowly, hoping my shoes would protect me from anything that was too hot to touch. The big pipes were behind me, but there were cables all over the place. My hands scraped across the dirty cement floor as I inched my feet forward, lifting the toes and swinging them downward so they could "eat" my flashlight like a video game monster.

I rotated in circles, counting how many turns I made and creeping outward to enlarge the circumference. My foot touched something, but it was just a cable.

Be grateful it didn't shock you, I thought, fighting back tears. What was stupider, barfing up pizza on purpose or compulsively heading into the steam tunnels without a reliable light source . . . alone?

Quit whining and keep searching. I wiped my cheek with my hand, then realized I'd just smeared dirt across my face. I turned slightly and got back to feet waving. I was wondering just how foolish and desperate I looked when my foot touched something.

Reaching out, I sank my fingers into something oozy and soft. "Ahhhhh!" I recoiled, bumping a pipe and boomeranging right back toward whatever it was. Only it wasn't oozy and soft any-more—it was round and hard. My flashlight. Snatching it up, I said a silent thank-you to the tunnel gods, adding a silent please. Finding the flashlight was only half the battle—I needed it to work.

I whapped the metal casing against my palm. Nothing. I bit my lip and tried not to follow my worst-case scenario thoughts. I was unsuccessful.

With no light, there was no way I'd find my way out of here. I'd probably pass out from the heat and die in the tunnels like Edward Hunter, only nobody would even remember me because I so obviously wasn't some kind of genius, nor was I in possession of some valuable archeological artifact. I was just stupid, compul-sive me.

I could feel the grit on my cheeks mixing with tears. God, I was pathetic. Unbelievably, undeniably pathetic. I'd gotten myself into this mess and now here I was, sitting on the filthy tunnel floor doing absolutely nothing but feeling sorry for myself.

The flashlight was warm from the heat in the tunnel, and I caressed the on/off button with my thumb, feeling the smoothness of the metal. I pressed it one last time and (miracle!) a faint beam of light illuminated my small section of tunnel, including a mass of matted hair and two sunken eyes on the floor right next to me. The head!

I screamed, crab-crawling backward into a steam pipe. The fabric covering my thigh sizzled and a searing heat burned my leg, but I barely felt it. I'd just found the shrunken head! I cautiously shined the beam over the thing on the floor, and was immediately grossed out and disappointed. It wasn't the head at all but a decomposing dead rat. Its shriveled eyes had pulled back into its skull and clumps of matted fur stuck to its rib cage—fur and a rib cage I'd just touched. I wiped my hand on my pants. Yuck.

I was still staring at the thing when I heard a noise. Voices? *Please let it be voices*, I prayed silently. The pipe behind me groaned, and I willed it to be quiet so I could hear. Then I saw a beam of light around a corner, off to the right. Someone was coming. The groaner chose that moment to go silent, and I could make out footsteps shuffling along the dirty floor. A second later, the beam flashed in my eyes, momentarily blinding me.

"Fancy meeting you here."

The relief that washed over me was so strong I only barely resisted the urge to rush forward and throw my arms around the boy leading the pack. Penn dropped the light away from my eyes and came up next to me, just in front of Hank and Sam. "We thought maybe you weren't coming."

"I was waylaid," I explained, my voice scratchy from heat and only recently subsided panic. "Technical difficulties." I didn't want to get any further into that subject, so I added, "Who's navigating?"

"Is that an insult, Subzero?" Penn sounded a little wounded.

"Perhaps I should rephrase. Who's got the map?"

Hank chuckled, and Sam waved a large piece of paper in the air. "I do," he said. He raised his head, shining his headlamp into one of the subtunnels. "We're going that way."

I noted that it was the direction I thought I'd come from, but chose not to mention it. None of us were expert underground navigators, and I put myself at the back of the class. "Don't step on the dead rat," I warned as Penn started off. I passed my beam right over the decomposing bugger, thinking it was strange that I couldn't smell him.

Penn jumped back, nearly tripping on a line of cables. "Holy crap!"

I gave him a little shove forward. "Nothing to panic about— just a decaying rodent."

"Gross."

Um, yeah.

We started to move. I was so happy to have company and multiple light sources that I practically floated through the tunnel. We jagged left, then right. The passage widened and sloped downward.

"Where are we going?" I asked.

"The athletic center."

"Because . . ."

"Just because."

I didn't buy the "just because" story—I was figuring out that Penn wasn't really a "just because" kind of person. But I let it slide.

The tunnel leveled off, and we came to a hatch. Penn and I stepped aside so Sam could get to work. Thirty seconds later, we were on the other side, in a room humming with electricity. I breathed in the cooler air, smelling bleach. There was a whooshing noise, too . . .

"That's water," Hank explained, reading my expression. "We're in the pool pump room."

We switched off our various lights and stashed them in our pockets. "What happened there?"

Sam was pointing to the burn hole in my pants, and the angry swelling on my thigh.

"Pipe contact due to a close encounter with dead steam-tunnel rodent."

"Would you stop talking about the dead rat?" Penn asked, his nose wrinkled.

"Don't be such a baby," Sam chided. "You okay, Josie?"

I ran a finger across the welt on my thigh. It was a good two inches long, and now that I was paying attention, it throbbed like a mother. "Yeah."

"Shhh," Penn said, raising a finger to his lips. "I think I hear something."

It was hard to hear anything other than water rushing through the pump system, but there *was* something else . . . voices.

"Someone's in the pool," Hank stated.

I turned. "After lights?"

Penn looked mischievous. "If you know how to get in without being detected, it's the best time to swim."

We headed through the pump room door onto the pool deck, hiding ourselves behind the bleachers that ran the length of the pool. I hadn't even gotten a look when I heard Hank gasp.

"Mother lode," he said.

I peeked around the edge of the bleachers and involuntarily sucked in my breath. At the far end of the pool, Annette stood on the diving board, wearing nothing but a bra and underwear and poised to dive. Moonlight streamed through the wall of eight-foot windows, reflecting off the water droplets that clung to her skin. She looked like a freaking moon goddess.

"Go for it, girl!" Marina was in the gray-blue water, her breasts bobbing on the surface.

"Isn't that . . ."

Splash! Annette disappeared into the pool.

"My girlfriend," I said, just like that. Only the words didn't feel quite right as they came out of my mouth, and there was bitterness in my voice.

"Some sort of water goddess," Hank corrected breathlessly.

"Annette, that was fantastic!"

I could feel Penn watching me. "Your girlfriend?"

Becca was on the board now, getting ready to dive.

"Yes." I didn't bother to explain that things were actually a lot more complicated than that.

Penn shook his head as if to clear it, his hazel eyes filled with something I didn't recognize.

Becca took two lunging steps, bounced, and leaped, tilting her head and arching in a perfect swan.

"Josie . . ."

"What," I snapped. I really didn't need a reaction, especially not from Penn. "Are you homophobic or something?"

Penn winced, his eyebrows clashing together behind his tousled hair. He raised his hands a little and took a step back. "No, Subzero. I'm not homophobic."

Over his shoulder I could see Marina climbing the ladder. Sam and Hank were dumbstruck as she strode to the end of the board and bounced once, twice, three times . . .

"That's gotta hurt," Hank's hands instinctively covered his chest.

Splash! When she surfaced, she was giggling madly. You had to hand it to her—Marina had game—and something told me that Roxanne was right. There was a lot going on with that girl.

All three girls were in the water now (where was Cynthia?), diving and goofing around. For a fleeting moment, I considered stripping down and joining them. Why the heck not?

Because you weren't invited, I reminded myself, remembering the barfing party. Was that really just a couple of hours ago?

"Did you know they were coming here?" Penn asked.

I shook my head, then realized I could ask him the same question. The boys hadn't said *why* we'd come to the athletic center. "Did you?" I couldn't keep the accusation out of my voice.

"Hey, who's there?" Marina called out, her voice echoing off the tiled walls.

We froze, and waited.

"Penn McCarthy, is that you?" Becca's voice rang out, clear as anything.

"In our dreams," Marina said.

"I swear I heard something."

"I heard it, too," Annette agreed.

Behind the bleachers, Sam, Penn, and I were standing stock-still. Hank, though, was unbuckling his belt, a giant smirk on his face. He dropped his pants to the floor, revealing plaid boxer shorts. "You said it yourself," he told Penn. "It's the best time to swim."

Before we could stop him, he'd pulled his shirt over his head and stepped out from behind the bleachers.

"Hank Jeffrey!" Marina chortled. "Who else are you hiding back there?"

Penn looked at me, as if he needed permission. I shrugged noncommittally at first, then thought, for a second time, *Why the hell not?*

Sam pulled his Green Lantern T-shirt over his head and dropped it onto the lowest bleacher. "May as well join the party," he said with a small smile.

I was about to pull off my sweatpants when I realized that showing myself would basically announce that I was hanging out with these boys after lights, and something told me I didn't want to do that. I dropped my hands to my sides.

"You go," I said. "I'm going to sit this one out."

"You sure?" Penn asked. "I can skip . . ."

"Penn McCarthy, we know you're behind there!" Becca called. I heard someone get out at the shallow end—heard footsteps coming toward us. I ducked farther behind the bleachers just as Annette appeared. Water dripped off her light blue bra.

"Don't be shy," she said, tugging Penn's arm. "The more, the merrier!"

Penn took a step sideways to block me while I crouched lower, half under the bleachers. My heart was thudding like a freight train. He hesitated for the smallest of moments before walking onto the pool deck behind Annette and stripping down to his boxer shorts, leaving his clothes on the bleachers.

"Last one in's a rotten egg," Marina called as Annette slipped back into the water. Penn dove in and swam a few easy strokes to the far end and got back out, heading for the diving board and the other guys.

I felt a little like a Peeping Tom, crouched behind the bleachers, watching. But I was riveted.

Hank did a cannonball from the diving board, sending up a giant wave of water in the deep end. Penn followed with a double.

"Show-off!" Becca reprimanded, but she sidled closer to him as the water settled, smiling. All three girls did, actually. Penn appeared to be some sort of water-activated magnet.

Sam was an elegant diver, and took several turns on the board while everyone else was in the pool. Then, suddenly, Becca was out of the water and walking toward the ladder, her lacy turquoise thong grabbing everyone's attention.

She climbed quickly, then marched straight to the end and did a cannonball, mimicking the boys. Before I knew it, there was a full-fledged cannonball contest going on, including Penn and Hank off the board at once, which sent waves of water onto the deck and under the bleachers, soaking my sneakers. As I felt the water seep into my socks, my mind flashed back to my first night at Brookwood, and I wished Roxanne would appear out of nowhere with an invitation and a bottle of vodka. I suddenly realized that right then, I was *out* of the petri dish. And, to tell you the truth, I wasn't sure I liked it any more than being *in* it. It felt a little lonely.

After the boys had proven their cannonball supremacy, the group got back to splashing around. But not for long.

"We'd better get out," Penn said. "The guards will be on soon."

Annette put on a little pouty face and then leaned back until she was fully horizontal, floating and looking up at the ceiling.

"Yeah, we'd better," Becca agreed. They swam to the edge of the pool and climbed out, little rivers of water running down their bodies and dripping on the tile. The girls had towels and dried off first, handing them to the boys before getting dressed. I watched Annette slip into a pair of jeans and one of her favorite sweaters, a soft gray with a boatneck collar.

"Are you gentlemen going to escort us back to our dorm?" Marina asked as she slipped on her shoes.

"Not a good idea," Sam said. "Traveling in a large group after lights is never smart."

None of the girls successfully hid their disappointment, but I knew they weren't going to argue. Nobody wanted to get busted.

"Oh, all right," Becca said for all of them. "We'll just have to forge ahead on our own, then." She raised her chin a little in mock offense. "Let's go, girls."

The girls stuffed their towels into a backpack and left the natatorium through a door across from the bleachers marked GIRLS LOCKER ROOM.

The moment the door clicked shut, Penn was crouched next to the bleachers. "You okay under there?"

"Yeah, I'm fine." I stood and stretched. "Nice cannonballs," I added, cracking a smile.

"Dude, we rocked it!" Hank said, slipping his shirt over his head and giving Penn a fist bump. I could see his erection through his boxers, and turned away with a chuckle—it reminded me of the pup tent my brothers used for campouts in the backyard.

Sam checked his watch. "Do we still have time?"

"If we're crazy quick," Penn replied.

"Time for what?" I asked.

"For the thing we came here for in the first place," Sam said.

"Which is . . . ?"

"A little redecorating in the display cases in the hall." Penn opened his backpack to reveal a stash of tacky, carnival-style stuffed animals. "Our embellishments," he explained, and pushed open a door to a wide hallway lined with display cases. I followed, eyeing the stuffed animal legs sticking out of his partially zipped backpack. "Are we replacing the trophies?"

"No, adding," he said, a hint of deviousness in his voice. "We're adding one rhino to each case." He dumped the stuffed animals on the floor. "For comic effect."

Sam picked the lock on the first case and slid the door open while I considered possible placements. This was clearly the lacrosse case, with quite a few First Places and a giant New England Championship towering over everything. But where to put my fuzzy friend? Top corner? Smack in the middle?

"You should hurry," Sam said as he picked the next lock. "Security comes by on the half hour, starting at midnight."

I shoved the rhino into the cup with its stumpy front feet dangling over the edge and slid the glass door closed. Penn had already put two rhinos on display—one clinging for dear life to the edge of a trophy cup like a fallen alpinist, and another flying above the top shelf, hang-glider style.

I picked up a small, brownish rhino with extra stitching across the back. "This guy is super cute," I said, noting that he seemed older than the others. He looked familiar, too. "Did he come from your room?"

"Damn it, Hank," Penn muttered, taking the rhino from me and distractedly stroking the worn fur on top of the little guy's head before stuffing him back into his pack. "He's not supposed to be in here." He took a different rhino and helped him into a perfect spread-eagle between a pair of matching wrestling trophies.

"Why are they all rhinos?" I asked.

"Sutton," Penn said.

"Sutton?"

Penn gave me a "wow, you are a total newbie" look, reminding me of the way my brothers gave me crap about not knowing game stats. They couldn't quite comprehend why I didn't have them all memorized, but didn't hold it against me, either. "The Sutton School is our archrival, and the rhino is their mascot."

I had a fleeting memory of Becca mentioning a track meet against Sutton, only, come to think of it, I hadn't seen a whole lot of girls' cross-country trophies in the cases. "Right," I said distractedly. Were there *any* girls' cross-country trophies around here?

Penn handed me the last rhino and checked his watch. "Make it quick," he instructed.

I carried the rhino over to the last case and eyed the array of football trophies warily. "Any ideas?" I asked Sam just as the door opened and Hank appeared.

"Dude, XYZ," Penn said.

Hank fumbled for his zipper and pulled it closed, and a wave of sadness washed over me. I wished I'd gone swimming, that I'd chosen to dive in instead of watching from the sidelines. But it was too late now.

Squeezing my hands together, I realized that I was still holding the rhino. I shoved it into the display case, perching him atop a giant football, and slid the door closed.

"Can we get out of here?" I asked, trying to sound normal.

"Mission complete." Sam stuffed the lock pick into his back pocket and quietly opened the door to the pool. All was quiet, and we were heading back to the dorms. *Well, that's something,* I thought grimly as I followed the boys back into the pump room and through the hatch. The dark, stale air was comfortingly familiar. *And I'll take what I can get.*

CHAPTER 20

♥

By the time I got back to my room, it was 12:52 a.m. Not wanting to disturb Roxanne, I slipped into the bathroom and closed the door behind me before flipping the light switch. I turned on the hot water and pulled off my filthy clothes.

The swelling on my thigh burned on water contact—the welt was raised and blistered. Extending my leg as best I could to protect it, I crookedly washed my body, letting the liquid warmth run down my shoulders and back. I could have slept right there.

Willing myself to keep moving, I turned off the tap and toweled down. After gingerly blotting the wound on my thigh, I pawed through the shelves of hair products, multivitamins, and laxatives until I found a tube of antibiotic ointment. I slathered a bunch on my burn, then stuck a not-quite-big-enough Band-Aid over it.

You can redo it in the morning, I told myself as I slipped into my pajamas. *Right now you need to sleep.* Sneaking out of the bathroom, I climbed the ladder to the top bunk.

"What took you so long?" a voice whispered. The covers lifted and I saw Annette's long, slender form in my bed, more naked than she'd been on the diving board.

In my head, I froze. I didn't slide in next to her and put my mouth across hers. I didn't remove my pajamas in the darkness, my heart pounding with anticipation. I didn't wrap a hand around her narrow waist and cup her breast with another. I was too full of questions and doubts and confusion to melt into her, to let her envelop me.

My body, however, had a mind of its own.

CHAPTER 21

♥

"Pass the salt," Becca said, wagging her hand in the air expectantly. It was seven thirty a.m. and we were rushing through breakfast to get to class. As I burned the roof of my mouth on my coffee, I couldn't help but notice that everyone seemed a little bleary, an adjective that didn't even begin to authentically describe my own state.

Annette had stayed in my bed until five o'clock, nestled up against me. I was still dozing when she slipped away, and I had no idea whether Roxanne knew she'd been there, since she, too, was gone when I woke up.

So many things had happened in the last twenty-four hours that I could barely keep track, much less sort out what they meant. Part of me loved having Annette spend the night—the first time since we'd arrived at Brookwood. But I was also feeling more and more unsettled about us, more and more bothered by the choices she was making.

I took another sip of coffee just as Roxanne appeared with a giant bowl of Lucky Charms. I scooched over so she could get by and she sat down next to me, her back less than twelve inches from Hank at the next table over.

So here we were again, the lot of us, together in the dining hall. Our lives at Brookwood were so entangled that escaping one another was almost as impossible as escaping ourselves. We really *were* like microbes in a petri dish—microbes that collided and smashed together and sometimes lost their individual shapes, becoming a single mass of mold. I cradled my mug in my hands and told myself that I wanted nothing to do with the moldy mass, that keeping my distance from the Soleets was the right choice. But somehow, I wasn't entirely convinced. And when Annette's eyes locked on mine over the top of her juice glass and she smiled—the sly, secret smile we'd shared at many breakfasts before—I was even *less* convinced. I was that easy.

"Hey," I said to Roxanne, feeling sheepish about Annette spending the night. I knew it was bad form to fool around when someone was right below you, and was pretty dang sure Annette didn't ask for permission before climbing up to my bunk, either. Should I apologize? If Roxanne had no idea she was even there, would that just make things worse?

"Hey, yourself," she replied coolly.

I felt my stomach drop. She knew.

"Anyone want to take my algebra quiz this morning?" Marina asked, flipping through her math text in a last-minute attempt to prepare. "I'm hopeless with exponents and logarithms."

My stomach dropped again. I'd completely forgotten about my *own* algebra quiz. I'd planned to study the night before but had gotten wrapped up in barfgate and then the tunneling-turned-swim-party . . .

I'd been struggling in algebra and knew I needed to ask for help but hadn't quite gotten around to it. Professor Roth wasn't exactly the most approachable teacher.

Cynthia shook her head. "Stressing about my Latin test. Why do you think I skipped the pool?"

Roxanne's head shot up.

"Because you never swim with us after lights," Marina replied a little sulkily.

Hank turned. "You ladies want a bullhorn so you can announce it to the whole room?" he asked.

Roxanne's eyes searched my face. *Pool?* they asked accusingly.

I felt a flash of guilt, and then resentment. I didn't even get *into* the pool!

"Did you go swimming last night?" she asked quietly.

I shook my head. It was the truth, but she didn't look like she believed me.

"You said you'd help me with my project."

I felt my face flush with shame. "You meant right then—last night?" But even as I asked, I knew that was what she'd meant. It seemed so obvious now.

"I didn't mean next week," she said, her dark eyes cloudy. Roxanne was extremely adept at hiding her feelings, except for her eyes. And as they locked on my face, I could see that she was really hurt.

"I didn't—"

"I know you didn't," she said, cutting me off. "That part is clear." She got up from the table, leaving half her bowl of cereal—even the marshmallows, which she always saved for last—floating on top of the pale pink milk.

My stomach sank all the way to the floor as I watched her walk away. I'd definitely blown it. Pushing my plate aside, I turned back to Becca, who was still on Cynthia and her Latin roots. Nobody even seemed to notice Roxanne's departure.

"Oh, please, Wu." Becca set down her mug, sloshing the cream-and-sugar-laden coffee dangerously close to the rim. "The whole school knows you're fluent in practically every language *except* Latin—it's only a matter of time before you master that, too."

Cynthia didn't flinch. "All the more reason for me to memorize the conjugation of this week's thirty roots."

"Can I have a few drops of your overachieving blood?" Marina asked. "My parents are threatening to yank me out of here if I don't get my grades up."

I could relate to that problem, except I didn't feel pressure from my parents. I felt it from the school.

"I thought you didn't like it here," I said without thinking. "Or did you mean 'embrace the horror' as a compliment?"

Cynthia looked up from her Latin, her eyes defensive. Marina leaned toward her unfinished French toast. "Horror is everywhere, and relative," she explained, "because Mummy is a bit of a bitch with a fondness for prescription drugs, and Daddy has fidelity issues—he spends more money on his mistress than he does on my tuition. Way more."

Becca rolled her eyes and plunked another sugar cube into her coffee while Marina pulled her cardigan around her and returned her attention to algebra, but not quickly enough to completely hide the sadness on her face.

"I'm sorry," I mumbled.

Annette was leaning over the side of her chair, avoiding the entire scene with remarkable aptitude. Had she even been listening? I waited for her head to surface, but she just kept fiddling with her book bag. Her coffee was gone, but she'd barely touched her food.

"Time for class," Becca announced. Cynthia closed her notebook and got to her feet, ready for the thirty roots. I tried to make eye contact, to let her know I felt bad about upsetting her roommate, but she didn't give me the chance.

"Ready, Marina?" she asked gently as Annette slung her reorganized bag over her shoulder.

"Ready as I'll ever be," Marina replied with a sigh. She slammed her book shut, shoved it into her bag, and followed Cynthia to the window, where Steve was rinsing dishes.

I waited while the other girls dropped off their trays, and tried to muster a smile.

"That good?" Steve asked, grabbing a stack of bowls.

"Better," I said drily.

His gloved hand rested gingerly on the soggy piece of toast on the top plate. "Don't let the turkeys get you down," he offered.

"Thanks," I replied, setting my dishes on the stainless steel counter with a grimace. I wanted to decide once and for all that these girls were turkeys—every one of them. Becca still didn't appear to give a crap about anyone but herself, but Marina couldn't be written off that easily—she'd kept the kiss she'd seen under wraps and overall seemed pretty damned human. And Cynthia had just defended her roommate (without even speaking).

I wanted to hate them, to not care at all about my flub. But I couldn't.

And then there was Roxanne.

I dumped my tray into the pile, feeling like total crap. "Right," I mumbled. "Except I'm beginning to think that I'm the biggest turkey of all."

CHAPTER 22

♥

The best part of English class, hands down, was listening to the other kids snicker about the rhinos we'd left in the trophy cases. Professor Drake actually stopped teaching for a few minutes. "I can see that we need to spend a few moments reacting to the embellished trophy cases discovered in the athletic center this morning," he said, turning from the whiteboard with a sigh. "Go ahead, get on with it."

"All rhinos."

"Had to be Sutton."

"How'd they get in?"

I felt a tingle of pride as the banter spread throughout the room. Sam sat very straight, pretending to wait for the lesson to begin, but a small smile tugged at the corners of Penn's lips. Becca, who was sitting next to Penn, gave him a sideways look of suspicion, then beamed at him.

"Are we finished?" Professor Drake asked as his eyes traveled the room, momentarily settling on each of us in turn. This is actually possible when there are only eleven students in class. "Because I'd like to move on to helping you learn how to write coherent, thoughtful essays." The rest of the class was spent on coming up with themes for "The Lottery," which I found depressing. First of all, the story itself was depressing. Sure, it started out with sunshine and blue skies and the anticipation of an annual event. But it *ended* with a person getting stoned to death. And it was hard to get excited about hypocrisy, mob mentality, and human cruelty, especially when all three things only reminded me that I'd totally blown it with Roxanne the night before. How did I not get that she meant right then? She'd used the word *brilliant*!

Maybe you didn't want *to get it*, I thought miserably.

After English, I went straight to my own kind of doom: my algebra quiz. Which I failed. After another lesson on linear equations that I barely understood, I headed to anthropology, determined to put my woes behind me.

Professor Mannering was in rare form. Particularly rare form, actually, because he *always* reminded me of the rare and unusual artifacts in his classroom. There was something about his birdlike movements and the intensity of his eyes—I'd never had a teacher anything like him.

"Peoples," he began. He put an *s* on *people*, he told us, because we weren't all from the same tribe. Tribes were not limited to rural places but were in fact everywhere on earth, complete with beliefs and traditions and patterns of behavior. The Soleets were, for example, a tribe. And, I supposed, the poker-playing tunnelers were, too. "Today we shall examine the cultural anthropology paradox." He scrawled the words on the board. "Can anyone tell me what this means?"

"Well, a paradox is a contradiction," Penn said.

"Exactly." Mannering beamed. "It is a thing that contradicts itself. Now, how could cultural anthropology be a contradiction?"

The room got quiet. Professor Mannering took a sip from one of three coffee mugs on his desk and made a face. "Ack, Wednesdays," he muttered, swallowing with a grimace.

Marina raised her hand. "Well, on the one hand, anthropologists are supposed to study other cultures for the sake of understanding different human behaviors. On the other, didn't it all start when Europeans decided to conquer the world? Isn't anthropology directly linked to colonialism?"

Professor Mannering nodded. "Indeed, the roots of cultural anthropology spread deep and wide when European thinkers became interested in the differences between 'civilized' and 'primitive' cultures. Even today, anthropological research is funded by schools and governments and institutions, all of which have interests that undermine the very cultures and lives they are studying." He paused. "Land, oil, medicines . . ." He trailed off, returning to the board to write: *Who is the anthropologist ultimately loyal to?*

A boy named Damon raised his hand. "The institution funding him, of course," he said derisively. "They're the ones paying the salary."

"But that's just more colonialism," Marina objected. "I say she should be loyal to the culture she is studying. Otherwise, the people won't trust her."

"Or him," Damon shot back.

"Can't the anthropologist be loyal to both?" Penn asked.

I found myself shaking my head as things came into focus. "She can't win," I blurted.

Professor Mannering's eyebrows shot upward. "Ms. Little?"

I felt my face flush as everyone turned in my direction. "Well, by definition, the anthropologist is part of the colony—she is a Westerner. So even if she can't stand colonialism, she is still a part of it. Being an anthropologist puts her smack-dab in the middle of colonialism itself."

Professor Mannering's eyes flashed, and he nodded as the bell rang. "That, peoples, is precisely the anthropologist's paradox. An extremely sticky situation, anthropology." He smiled at us, as if this were good news. "Read the next chapter in *A Companion to Latin American Anthropology*, and be prepared to discuss your essential humanity!"

"Whatever that is," Damon muttered.

I closed my notebook, feeling both embarrassed and proud for my exclamation—another paradox. They were everywhere, it seemed. Shoving all my stuff into my bag, I wished that, for just a little while, I could take a break from my humanity altogether.

CHAPTER 23

♥

After classes, I headed up to the fields to watch Annette run—my first visit to the competitive sports madness at Brookwood. I'd noticed week after week that, in the space of an hour, the school transformed from a place of higher learning into an athletic circus. Most of the student body suited up in Brookwood red and gold and headed out to the fields for an aggressive match of something or other. Teams from myriad other schools descended upon us right after lunch, dressed in their school colors and ready to tromp us (which, as it turned out, was often the case).

Thanks to (1) my general dislike for team sports and (2) the fact that Roxanne liked to spend her Saturday afternoons either in town eating doughnuts or working on her art, I had thus far avoided the sports scene.

Thanks to my screwup, I wouldn't be spending the afternoon with Roxanne, which worked out in a weird way because Annette had asked me to come see her race. I'd quickly agreed. My essential humanity was telling me to be *loyal*, and I was also curious about this running business, especially after listening to Becca pep-talk Annette at breakfast and lunch all week about her 10,000-meter race—a longer distance for Annette—in their match against Brewster.

As I followed the pathway to the athletic center, I noted wryly that the field Roxanne and I sometimes crossed in pursuit of consuming alcohol and where I inadvertently drenched myself on my first day was now overrun with boys in uniform, chasing a soccer ball. At Brookwood, alcoholic and athletic events took place on the same stage (a tidbit that could not be found in the glossy pages of the school's catalog). At the moment, Hank was in goal and Penn was playing striker. The few Brookwoodies who didn't play sports stood on the sidelines, cheering, while a kid dressed as a wolverine, Brookwood's mascot—those little animals on the Vespers ties weren't bears after all—attempted to rile everyone up.

On the field, Penn was *everywhere*. I'd been on the sidelines of enough games to know which players were worth watching. A great player had a palpable relationship with the ball—seemed to know where it was headed before it had even been kicked, was there to greet it, and handled it as if it were an extension of his or her body. Penn was one of those players. I watched him, amazed, while he charged the opposing forward, stole the ball, took it upfield, faked a pass, and scored with a powerful kick to the corner—all as if he were strolling down the sidewalk. Impressive. I watched the other team's goalie send the ball up the field before I spotted a cluster of female cross-country runners making their way through the 10,000-meter course. Oh crap, I was late. I stood on tiptoe, zeroing in on a pair of girls from Brewster, followed by Becca and . . .

"Go, Annette!" I shouted as her head came into view behind the crest of a grassy hill. She was running several body lengths behind Becca, who was stepping up her pace in a bid for the lead. Becca's lips were pursed in a straight line, her face set with determination. Annette looked plain miserable.

"Go go go!" I cheered as the runners closed the gap between themselves and the finish line. I jogged toward them, panting within fifteen seconds and wondering for the hundredth time why Annette had chosen to do this.

Thirty yards from the finish, Becca sprinted past the girl from Brewster to win the race. I watched Annette try to muster up a strong finish, but it was all she could do to stumble across the line.

Jeez, I thought as I headed over with the water I'd brought for her. Annette was bent over, her hands on her knees, gasping.

"Are you okay?" Up close, she sounded a little like Darth Vader. "Water?" I held out the bottle I'd filled with water and ice back in the dorm.

"Ugh, no," she said, pushing it away. "Too cold."

Since when? I thought as she straightened. Her entire face was the color of cooked shrimp, her usual floaty ponytail stragglers superglued to the sides of her face.

"Here you go, runner girl," Becca said, appearing behind us and handing Annette a water bottle filled with a pink liquid. She wiped her forehead on a towel and took a swig from her own. "Electrolytes are our friends."

Still breathing hard, Annette took a long, gulping drink. She wiped her mouth with the back of her hand and smiled weakly—she appeared to be recovering. But a second later, her face buckled and she doubled over again, puking all over the grass. Her teammates stepped back with remarkable speed, as if expecting it. Me? I just stood there stupidly while vomit cascaded onto my Converse. I noticed little pieces of chewed-up lettuce and sunflower seeds in the pile of slop (no pizza remnants in sight).

"Bummer," a teammate said, wrinkling her nose.

"Nice." Becca took another swig of electrolytes-are-our-friends. "You obviously pushed yourself to the limit."

Seriously? Was the goal to barf your way through Brookwood? I pulled Annette's ponytail away from her vomit-covered chin, wiping it on the edge of my shirt. "Are you all right?" I asked again.

Her eyes met mine and I was shocked to see that they were full of annoyance. She tugged her ponytail away before straightening and toweling her chin. "I'm totally fine," she said, trying to laugh—the strange, high-pitched laugh I heard the night of Dress to Impress. "Just a little post-race puke."

Lola No appeared at Annette's side. "Decent race, Anderson," she said, all business. "Ten thousand might be the distance for you. We need to work on pacing, though. You went out too fast."

She glanced down at the patch of barf she was standing in. "And maybe go easy at the lunch buffet on race day," she added, lifting her foot out of the glop with a little shake.

This is amazing coaching? I thought, remembering Becca's soliloquy about Lola No's cross-country leadership. But Annette's expression was full of reverence, and aside from the pile of vomit on the grass, you'd never have known that she'd just tossed her cookies onto the field. "Thanks, Coach," she replied. "I'll do better next time."

Meaning what, exactly? You'll run until you fall down and can't get up? Until you pass out?

Lola No nodded. "Excellent. Team meeting in five." She wiped her shoe on a clean patch of grass.

Becca clinked her water bottle against Annette's. "A one-three finish," she noted. "Not too shabby." She turned to me, her eyes gleaming with audacity. "And you said Annette doesn't like to run."

I held her gaze, dying to retaliate with *She doesn't*. But regardless of whether or not that was true, it was becoming painfully clear that it wasn't my place. My relationship with Annette had changed dramatically. She was no longer someone I was supposed to help, to stand up for.

She'd somehow become someone I was merely supposed to watch.

CHAPTER 24

♥

"The key to the what?" I asked, staring at the gold key in Sam's hand. We were in Penn's room at the tail end of a Saturday night poker match. I'd held my own but hadn't raked it in—the cards weren't there for me. Too busy being there for Sam, apparently.

"The vault," Hank repeated. "In the library basement."

"The one we tried to find the first week of school?"

"Yes, exactly," Penn confirmed.

"And how did we get the key?"

"Sometimes it comes in handy to be the geeky rule-follower," Sam said with a laugh, his eyes gleaming in the lamplight. "They never suspect you of anything."

I looked out the window toward the library, which was, as usual, lit up like a beacon. *The touchstone of the Brookwood campus*, the catalog said. *A place where students gather to study, research, read, and write.*

And commit trespassing crimes, I added in my mind. But having a key was a little different. Having a key meant we had access, that we wouldn't have to sneak through filthy, dead-rat-infested steam tunnels.

"We still need to take the tunnels, though." Penn dashed my hopes in an instant. "Sometimes the doors are guarded, and the exterior door to the library has a trip-wired alarm system."

I fingered my burn through my jeans. It had broken open and oozed before it scabbed over, despite my attempts at first aid. "Are you sure we can find it?"

"Ye of little faith," Penn protested, counting out chips.

"We went wrong the last time we tried to find the library, and my run-in with Lola No wasn't exactly my idea of a good time. I didn't convince my parents to let me come here so I could get busted and shipped back home."

"Relax," Penn said. "Nobody is getting shipped home. We're going to be careful. Besides, kicking students out is the last thing the administration wants to do."

I pictured Lola No's interrogating face. "Are you sure about that? It seems like that's *exactly* what they want to do."

"*Seems* is the operative word," Penn replied. "They want to appear as though they're out to bust us, to keep us in line. But student success is essential; it guarantees the respect, gratitude, and financial support of our parents—the continuation of the elite way of life."

"Why *did* you come here?" Hank asked me, changing the subject as he slipped a deck of cards into its case.

If the question had come from one of the girls in my dorm, I might have been taken aback. But Hank's expression revealed his curiosity—he actually wanted to know.

"To get away," I replied honestly.

"I hear that," Penn said. "The more distance between me and my parents, the better."

"For us, it was Annette's mother," I told them. I hesitated, searching for the right words. "And I also thought Annette and I would be different here."

Hank's jaw momentarily opened before he pulled it closed, and Sam busied himself with his own money counting. They knew who Annette was, of course—they'd all been at the pool when I'd blurted out the word *girlfriend*. But I had no idea whether they'd talked about it, and they obviously weren't comfortable talking about it with me. I wasn't totally sure I felt comfortable talking about it with them, either, but had never been very good at holding back.

Penn's elbows rested easily on his knees. "And are you?" he asked, studying my face with a boldness I didn't expect.

I almost looked away, but didn't. I almost didn't answer, but thought that would be a cop-out. And I wasn't ashamed of myself, or Annette, or why we'd come here. I was just, it seemed, perpetually confused. I'd thought that coming here, getting away from Shannon and Virginia Falls, would strengthen us. Instead, it seemed to be our undoing. "Yes," I said, trying to keep the sadness out of my voice. *Only not in the ways I'd hoped.*

Sam counted out one- and five-dollar bills and handed over a small stack. "Your original twenty, plus seven fifty in winnings for tonight."

Penn groaned and eyed his measly pile of bills. "There's nothing little about her."

I tucked the money into my pocket, searching for some resolve and knowing that I'd at least be able to contribute to the vodka kitty for room 316. I steered the conversation back to the steam tunnels. "Why, exactly, are we so bent on breaking into the library?"

The three boys exchanged glances, the room's silence broken by a posse of dorm mates having a mini wrestling match in the hall.

"We're looking for something," Penn said.

I paused, then said it. "Something like a shrunken head?"

Sam clucked his tongue and shook *his* head, making his straight dark bangs swing from side to side.

"Yes, we are looking for the shrunken head," Penn admitted.

"So you think it's real."

He shrugged. "I think looking is a lot more entertaining than not looking." He leaned back in his chair. "Being at Brookwood isn't exactly a picnic. We spend most of our time trying to meet expectations, many of which are impossible. We can't ace every test and win every game. We can't spend every minute studying or training or competing. We can't win at all costs and always be decent human beings."

"You make this place sound *so* inviting."

Penn shrugged. "Sorry," he said. "I guess I'm a little jaded."

"I thought we were looking because you can only do so many vodka shots and deal so many hands of poker on a Saturday night," Hank said, stretching his legs across the coffee table.

"That, too," Penn agreed.

I watched Penn's face, watched the corners of his eyes pinch together. He'd just summed up his Brookwood existence so easily, so simply. And yet we all knew that life at Brookwood *wasn't* simple. Not for me, not for Annette, not for Penn. Not for anyone.

Penn stared blankly at the bottom of Hank's shoes, but I could tell he wasn't really with us—it was almost as though he'd gotten up from his chair and walked out the door. But then he was back, on his feet and pulling open the door to his closet, revealing a massive heap of clothes on the floor, above which hung three blazers (two navy blue and one brown herringbone) and several dress shirts in an impressively neat row. Half a dozen ties hung next to the shirts and jackets like towels on a rack, their V-tips aligning perfectly. Penn grabbed his tunnel pack from a hook and dug a long-sleeve shirt out of the pile.

"Is that your laundry?" I asked, noting the striking difference between the clothes on hangers and the giant jumble on the floor.

"My wardrobe," Penn corrected, slinging the pack. "Are we ready, people?"

Five minutes later, Sam swung open the metal door in the basement, and the four of us stepped into the tunnels. The black maw of several weeks ago now seemed like a welcoming darkness, one in which I could disappear from everything that felt so complicated above. Somehow, when I was in the tunnels, it was as though I was no longer at Brookwood—all I had to do was follow the passageways and be careful not to trip or get burned.

"Hawkins Memorial Library, here we come," Hank said, casting his headlamp beam beyond Sam into the blackened tunnel. Our order was reversed this time, with Sam in front, Hank second, me third, and Penn bringing up the rear. From the first steps away from the hatch, I could tell we were in a hurry. We didn't actually move very fast, but there was an intent to this mission, some kind of purposeful reverence. We also branched off in a new direction fairly quickly.

"Lights are in less than an hour, so we've got to keep moving," Penn said, reading my thoughts.

"Yes, General McCarthy," Hank quipped.

"Somebody's got to keep us on sched—"

"Shhh," Sam said. I could hear voices above us—girls, it sounded like. Or a coed mix. "We're under the café, which means we're almost at the second junction." Sam started forward again, slowly, his headlamp illuminating the darkness and bouncing off the cracked concrete walls. The pipes were on both sides in this section, and the usual cables lined one side. I was eyeing the floor warily when my nose collided with Hank's shoulder blade. Half a second later, Penn's chin bonked me in the back of the head.

"Junction," Sam said.

"A little late there, Sammy," Penn said in my ear as he clutched my arm for balance.

"Shit!" Hank howled. "Burn!"

"Sorry," Sam said regretfully.

"You all right?" I asked.

"Think so." I could tell Hank was wincing. I shined my light on his arm and saw an angry red slash just below his elbow.

"That's gotta hurt." I remembered the throb of my own blistered skin.

"Does, a little," he admitted.

"Forty-eight minutes," came the time toll from Penn.

Sam's light fell on a plank that crossed a three-foot chasm in the floor, and a double-wide pipe covered with a web of smaller pipes and cables.

"That's the junction?" I asked.

"See the tunnel behind it?" Sam asked.

"Um, yes," I said. "But I also see several obstacles *in front*."

"M'lady doesn't want to walk the plank, boys," Hank quipped.

"Watch it, Hanky," I warned. "I'm not entirely above pelting an injured man."

"Hanky," Sam echoed. "I like it. We can call you Hanky-Panky."

Hank whacked Sam on the shoulder. "Hey," Sam objected. "No attacking the leader."

"You can't say it's not appropriate, Hanky," I pointed out.

"I have no idea what you're talking about," Hank objected halfheartedly as Penn's guffaws filled the tunnel, dying in the dank.

Sam straightened and cleared his throat. "Dudes, we've got business to attend to," he said. "Like getting behind that giant pipe."

"Who are you calling a dude?"

"Fine. Dudes and Josie, we've got business to attend to."

"What business?" Hank asked. "We're just going to have to cram ourselves through."

He squeezed past Sam and shined his light on the plank, walking across without hesitating. It teetered a tiny bit but seemed sturdy enough, and I crossed before I could psych myself out. While the other two followed, Hank and I studied the possible paths around the pipe.

"Looks pretty gnarly," he said. On one side, the cables were thickly clustered, leaving almost no room. On the other, the pipe was dangerously close to the wall.

"I can get through there," I announced, dropping to the ground. I wasn't sure what had come over me, but I suddenly wanted to get to the library. I pulled my jacket over my face for protection and started to shimmy, feetfirst, under the pipe.

"Holy shit, Subzero," Penn said as my thighs cleared the pipe. I raised the sweatshirt off my face. "Don't distract the guinea pig," I said, still scooting. "We wouldn't want her to erupt into a ball of flames." The pipe was coming closer and closer to my chin, but the truth was that getting under it wasn't going to be as sketchy as it looked—so far, I had several inches of clearance.

Once my head was clear, I got to my feet and shined my flashlight around. The tunnel was pretty open up ahead, with only a single pipe running along the side. "Come on over, boys," I said. "The tunnel's fine."

Apparently, it is harder for boys to shimmy under things than it is for girls, because they hemmed and hawed the whole time, and Hank declared twice that he couldn't do it. By the time everyone was through, Penn was tapping his watch. "Thirty-one minutes," he reported gravely.

We scurried like lemmings to the end of the tunnel, our beams of light directed intently at the floor. Sam had his lock pick ready when we got to the massive metal door at the end. He stood for several long moments, silent and still, listening.

"What gives?" Hank asked.

Sam held up a hand. "I think I saw someone, and we don't want to be stupid," he whispered. "Josie can't fast-talk her way out of *everything*."

Too true, I thought. "Do we know where we'll come out?" I asked in a low voice.

"The library basement, right across from . . ." The lock clicked, and a moment later the door cracked open.

". . . The vault."

"What's the vault for, anyway?" I asked in a low voice. "Brookwood's stash of gold?"

"No, its shrunken head!" Hank said, adding, "That's what we're hoping for, anyway."

"Shhhhh!" Sam was all business. He pulled the door inward, peering around the edge.

We waited for what seemed like forever, mute, in the darkness. I half expected Penn to prod us onward with a time announcement.

"Clear," Sam finally said.

I let my breath out in a quiet whoosh, unaware until that moment that I'd been holding it, and followed the boys into the library basement. Getting into the vault was absurdly easy—Sam just stuck the key in the lock and turned. "They really oughta upgrade security," Hank said as we stepped inside.

"What the . . ."

Sitting in the middle of the room was a long, heavy oak table, on top of which sat a row of perfectly aligned, bright orange plastic . . .

"Pumpkins?" Sam pronounced.

"Maybe Hunter left us a little flock of enlarged plastic heads instead of a single shrunken one," I suggested.

"Who cares about the actual pumpkins?" Hank asked. "Look what's in them!" The eight smirking jack-o'-lanterns were filled to the brim with an array of miniature candy bars. Hank snatched up a handful.

"Hold on," Penn said.

Hank dropped the candy, jutting out his bottom lip as if a bully had just stolen his entire trick-or-treating haul. "Hold on for what?"

"Maybe we should deliver these," Penn said, thinking, "to various administrators . . ."

Hank's face flashed with mischievousness. "As a sort of gag," he said, catching on.

Sam turned from a file cabinet where he was trying to pick a lock. Aside from the table and (at the moment) the pumpkins, the vault was nothing more than a small room with safe deposit–like boxes lining the walls. "Too risky. If we take our pumpkin friends out, the administration will know we got in, and that's not something we want to broadcast. Thornfeld wouldn't take it lightly, especially with the board breathing down his neck. He's supposed to be tightening the ship."

"That's running a tighter ship," Penn corrected.

Sam shrugged. "Whatever. You get what I mean." He went back to lock picking.

Hank was staring longingly at the candy, and the Snickers bar at the top of jack-o'-lantern number four had started to call my name.

"Just a few," I heard myself saying.

Penn clucked his tongue. "You're a mess, Subzero," he said, rubbing a smudge off my chin. "Have you been playing with boys again, young lady?"

I caught my reflection in a shiny gold lockbox. I *was* a mess, but didn't really care. "Who are you calling a lady?"

"Bad news, people," Sam interrupted. "I can't get in—these locks are too small for my pick."

"Maybe security is tighter than we think," I suggested. "Do we even know if the head is in here?"

"No. It's just a guess," Penn admitted, his voice full of disappointment. He ran a hand through his cobwebby curls.

"Guess we'd better drown our sorrows, then." Hank grabbed a Kit Kat.

Penn snatched up the Snickers I'd been eyeing, ripped it open, and checked his watch. "Fourteen minutes," he said around a mouthful of nougaty peanuts and chocolate.

We wolfed down our favorite fun sizes and stashed extras in our pockets for the road. Then we exited the vault, closing and locking the door behind us.

The tunnels felt hotter than I remembered on the way back, and we moved fast. I was the first one under the pipe, but the boys increased their speed impressively. Before I knew it, we were back at our entrance point, and Sam was opening the door.

I was about to follow Hank into the hall when Penn grabbed my hand and spun me around. "There's just one little thing, Josephine," he said. His voice was low and intense, and in the dim light, I didn't see him duck his head. The next thing I knew, his lips were brushing against mine, warm and insistent.

CHAPTER 25

♥

Josephine? I thought as my head swam. *Did he just call me Josephine?* And then, *Hey, this isn't as gross as I thought it would be.* Penn's lips were surprisingly soft, and he tasted like peanuts and chocolate. His hands rested on the small of my back, and I couldn't help but notice their strength. *How stupidly cliché,* I thought, followed by *Holy shit, am I really kissing a boy?* I had never kissed a boy. Had never been the slightest bit interested in kissing a boy.

And then, just like that, Penn pulled away and sort of cleared his throat. The shaft of light from the hall reflected off his face, but I couldn't read his expression. "Okay, maybe not so little," he admitted. "But I couldn't pretend anymore."

"Pretend?" I echoed stupidly. Pretend? *Oh my God. Josie, you are such an idiot!* I had totally, completely missed it. Of course, I wasn't exactly accustomed to boys swooning over me. For one thing, I was out. Well, at home I was out. For another, I basically considered myself to *be* one of the guys—not the girl guys fell for.

Ugh. Was this really happening?

"Um . . . are you going to say something?" Penn asked.

I looked up at him, totally unclear about what to say while possible responses flashed in my head: (1) *I love Snickers,* (2) *Your lips are a lot softer than I expected,* (3) *I've never kissed a boy.*

None of those seemed the slightest bit reasonable, so I went with (4) "That wasn't too terrible." Because it *wasn't* too terrible—just totally alien.

Penn sort of winced and looked away, and I felt a weird combination of relief—he didn't look like he was going to kiss me again—and guilt—I'd just hurt his feelings. He was quiet for a solid thirty seconds.

"Josie," he finally said, his voice faltering. He cleared his throat. "Josie, you have to know I wasn't trying to fall for you. I mean, you don't even *like* guys. But from the moment I saw that crazy mass of curls, you sort of floored me. Then you fell asleep at first Vespers and laughed about it. You showed up in a tree outside my dorm room and crawled through the window like it was nothing. You play poker like a pro, but not quite like anyone I've held a hand with. You're smart and outspoken and funny and beautiful. Only you don't even know you're beautiful, which not only makes you more beautiful but different from practically every other girl in this place, maybe every other girl, period."

What was he talking about? *Who* was he talking about?

"You make everything more fun, more interesting, more . . ."

He trailed off while I stood there, as if the oxygen had been sucked out of the tunnel—hardly any was reaching my brain. I couldn't form a coherent thought, much less put thoughts into words or say them out loud.

Thankfully, Penn was *really* moving on. He stepped back and wiped my face with a corner of his T-shirt, then pulled my hood up. He'd reverted to familiar territory for us—brotherly friendship.

"I'd take the back entrance into your dorm," he advised. "The fewer people who see you, the better."

I nodded mutely while he pushed open the hatch.

"Dude, what gives?" Hank asked, pointing to the clock that hung in the basement hall. "Lights are in three."

"See you later," I said, quickly brushing off my pants and heading for the door at the end of the hall. I felt woozy, like I'd just downed three shots of Absolut. Whether it was from the heat in the steam tunnels, Penn's kiss, or his soliloquy was impossible to figure out.

By the time I stepped through the back door to my dorm, I was certain I had the words JUST KISSED PENN MCCARTHY plastered across my forehead. I kept my head low as I darted up to the third floor.

"Digging in the dirt, Josie?" a voice called as I passed the second floor. The voice was vaguely familiar, but I didn't bother trying to see who it was. I could hear footsteps coming up the stairs behind me and they sounded distinctly authoritative. I hit the top stair and made a beeline for my room.

"What happened to you?" Roxanne said as I shoved open the door.

"Nothing," I lied, slipping into the bathroom. The latch had just closed, when I heard Lola No's voice.

"Was that Josie?" she asked. "In a black sweatshirt?"

Maybe the words were plastered across my back, I thought bleakly.

"Yes, ma'am," Roxanne replied. "She's been spending a fair

amount of time in the bathroom lately, what with her, um, digestive issues."

I pulled back my hood, surprised that Roxanne was covering for me. She'd been essentially invisible all week, spending extra time in the art studio on her new project but not saying a word. My reflection revealed a huge black smudge smearing my cheek and a netting of cobwebs glued to my head just above my ear. I swiped at the sticky threads and turned on the hot water.

"Josie, I need to see you," Lola No said. "Now." What made Penn think the administration didn't want to bust us? *She* certainly seemed determined.

Trying to breathe normally, I scrubbed at the black spot with a washcloth and watched it fade. "You do?" I called as I toweled my face dry. I opened the door and stuck my head through the crack, keeping my clothing hidden. "I'm really not that attractive."

She squinted at my face. "Not amusing. Where have you been?"

The scabby burn on my leg started to throb anxiously. "I was in the main building," I half lied.

Lola No folded her arms across her chest and waited for me to crack. My automatic response was to pretend I was having a staring contest with Josh, which I always won. After a good fifteen-plus seconds, Lola No blinked and raised her chin. "I hope that was an honest answer, Josie," she said, equally enunciating both syllables of my name. "For your sake." She disappeared out the door.

The moment she was gone, I half collapsed onto the toilet. My palms were sweaty and I felt sick.

"I was actually kidding about the diarrhea," Roxanne said. She picked at an orange-painted fingernail and lobbed a sideways glance. "Even though you'd deserve it."

I looked up and saw that the hurt from the pool party was still there, just not as fresh. "Roxanne, I—" All kinds of things to say flooded into my brain—excuses, justifications, reasons. I closed my mouth and thought for a second. "I know I do," I agreed. "I totally blew it."

"Good. I'm glad we agree and I don't have to beat you up." She smiled wryly. "And lucky for you I used the *B* word prematurely—I've been making improvements all week."

"I'm ready to help when you say the word," I vowed.

"Excellent," she said. "I'll be holding you to that. But you still haven't answered my original question. What happened to you?"

I leaned forward until my forehead was resting against the pedestal sink, my skin absorbing its cool porcelain whiteness. I turned and looked at her with one eye. "Penn McCarthy," I said. "Penn McCarthy happened to me."

Roxanne squinted her response in my direction, her dark eyes so narrow they seemed to disappear into her face. She exhaled very, very slowly. "You didn't."

I sat up. "No!" I squirmed. "Well, sort of."

Roxanne disappeared through the door and returned with our bottle of vodka. "Maybe this'll help." She handed it over.

I started to unscrew the top, then reconsidered. I didn't want it. "No, thanks."

"That bad?"

"Possibly."

She filled a glass of water instead and sat down on the bathroom floor, drawing her knees up to her chest and wrapping her arms around them. We sat there in silence for several minutes. "Wanna start at the beginning?" she finally asked.

"Not really," I said. "What I want to do is hit DELETE."

Another long exhale. "A delete button would be nice," she agreed. "I can think of several things I'd like to erase from my record."

"As in school record?" She'd piqued my curiosity and comforted me with a single sentence.

"Any record." Roxanne lowered her knees, her legs stretching flat across the tiny hexagonal tile. "Sometimes I feel like the world is keeping a record, keeping constant track, and I just want to fall off the radar. But we were talking about you."

I put my forehead back against the cool sink, my opal pendant clanking against the porcelain, and let out a tiny groan. I knew I was about to spill it, because if I didn't let some of this stuff out, I was going to explode. And also because Roxanne appeared to actually give a crap.

"I've been playing poker and exploring the steam tunnels with Penn and his posse, and as we were coming out tonight, Penn whirled me around and kissed me."

Roxanne was focusing on a plaster crack above the toilet, but I could tell she was paying close attention. "How romantic."

I was tempted to take a sip from the vodka bottle, but resisted. "Which part?"

Roxanne laughed. "All of it?" Her cadence was covered with question marks. "But seriously. Hank plays poker with Penn, and it has always been clear: No Girls Allowed. Same with the pranks and the tunneling."

"You know about the tunneling?"

She took a sip of water. "Josie, I dated Hank for most of last year, before he went to France and decided it was his job to hook up with some girl named Babette. Of course I know about the tunneling. I just never knew the details."

So that's the story between her and Hank. I considered telling her that boys were assholes, but what did I know? Were they any worse than girls? "They go in through hatches, and pick locks when they need to. Oh, and they have a key to the vault."

Roxanne practically sprayed water all over the bathroom floor, and it took a while for her to regain composure. "They have a key to the vault?"

I nodded.

"A vault key in the hands of the peanut gallery," she murmured with a devilish smirk. "That could really turn the administration on its derriere. But we digress from the heart of the matter, which is, of course, Penn McCarthy kissing you."

Penn McCarthy kissing me, I thought. Only that *wasn't* in fact the heart of the matter. At all. It was what he told me afterward, about how he fell for me. It was the risk he took. Penn McCarthy saw me, really saw me, and wanted me anyway. And now, as I considered those few moments in the steam tunnel, it occurred to me that nobody, not even Annette, saw me that clearly.

"Josie?" Roxanne said. "You in there?"

I blinked and turned my head. "Yes," I said. "I'm here."

"Well?"

"Well, what?"

"Well, how was it?"

The porcelain was warm now, no longer offering respite, and I sighed with disappointment. The answer was a single word.

"Confusing."

Roxanne watched me carefully. "Confusing?" she repeated, letting the word roll around her tongue. "That doesn't sound good."

I moved my forehead to a cooler patch of porcelain and closed my eyes. "No, it doesn't."

CHAPTER 26

♥

I had absolutely no idea what to say to or how to act around Penn, so I just sort of . . . ignored him. Which turned out to be surprisingly easy, given that we had two classes together and generally hung out with the same people. Unfortunately, pretending Penn didn't exist left a pretty big void, because except for Roxanne, Penn was the person I talked to most. Or maybe the person whose opinion I valued most.

Besides Annette, I reminded myself, ignoring the little voice that questioned whether that was still true.

Penn didn't appear eager to talk to me, either. He seemed to be keeping a distance. I missed his banter and his antics, which he'd toned down, too. In class he didn't have much to say.

Professor Mannering was just the opposite—he had *plenty* to say. We'd further discussed the anthropologist's paradox but hadn't really come to a consensus about what it meant regarding anthropology itself. Everyone had their opinion, it seemed. This didn't bother Professor Mannering, though. He seemed to like it.

Now we were starting to talk about indigenous cultures of the Amazon, some of whom had very unusual beliefs. At times the subject seemed to transform Professor Mannering into a little kid telling ghost stories around a campfire, while at others he seemed overcome with guilt about having been a colonist himself. Starting when he was nine years old, he'd spent two years in Ecuador with his explorer father.

"We visited many cultures, but the one my father was most interested in was the Shuar," he explained, his eyes a surprisingly bright blue behind his glasses. He'd actually cleaned them! "The Shuar were technically under Quito government, but they lived so deep in the Amazon jungle that they governed themselves. Seeing a non-tribesman was unusual—seeing a white man was *really* unusual . . . unless of course the white man was a hallucination."

Professor Mannering went on to explain that the Shuar believed that the regular "waking" life wasn't real. "The forces that determined events were supernatural, and could be witnessed, understood, and manipulated with the help of their ancestors and natema, a brew made from an Amazonian vine." He paused for a moment. "A strong hallucinogen."

"Oh, come on," Damon said. "That's crazy."

"Not to the Shuar, it isn't." Professor Mannering's face was dead serious. "Appropriate ceremonial use of natema helps a Shuar warrior find out who he is bound to kill."

The class erupted into guffaws, but Professor Mannering pulled us back. "Peoples," he said, "who are we to say that another's beliefs are wrong? Who is anyone?" He was perched on the edge of his desk like a vulture on a fence. "The Shuar are loyal to their beliefs. They don't believe in death by natural causes—they believe it to be the result of invisible enemy attack. Under the influence of natema, they discover who is responsible, and once that is known, they have little choice but to gather forces, plan an attack, and kill them."

"Of course they have a choice. Everyone has a choice," a girl named Maxine said.

Professor Mannering's face darkened. "Technically, yes. But such things are not always so simple. Revenge is deeply rooted in the Shuar culture, as is ancestral loyalty. Without the blessing of those who came before them, they believe, their culture will not survive. Not exacting revenge for a death will bring the wrath of their ancestors and, indeed, their own demise.

"It often took weeks or months to plan an attack, and several days of difficult travel on foot to complete it."

Marina raised her hand. "What about the shrunken head business?"

Professor Mannering blinked, and hesitated, as if he wasn't sure he'd heard her correctly. "The shrunken head?"

"Wasn't it normal practice for the Shuar to shrink the heads of their victims?"

"Oh yes, you mean the tsantsa," Professor Mannering replied, his face relaxing a little. "I was getting to that. After the enemy is slain, his head is cut off, and a meticulous process of skinning and shrinking begins, often during the journey home."

He paused for a sip of coffee. "During the headshrinking process, various rules must be strictly upheld. Warriors must abstain from sex, and certain foods and other activities must be avoided. This is to help keep certain spirits away—not doing so is extremely dangerous."

"This is all sounding like hocus-pocus," Damon said.

"Not to a Shuar, it doesn't," Marina said.

"To them, this is life . . . or death." Professor Mannering

dropped his gaze to the floor, as if he suddenly wanted to hide his eyes for a moment, and cleared his throat before continuing. "I will not go over every little detail of headshrinking—this is not a neurosurgical class. But I *will* tell you that a skilled headshrinker can remove the skin, hair, and cartilage from the head and skull in just fifteen minutes."

The classroom grew completely silent.

"The entire shrinking process takes nearly a week and involves boiling the head and the use of hot sand and pebbles to cure the skin. The eyes and lips are sewn shut so that the spirit of the victim cannot see, or cry for revenge. The skin is blackened to keep the spirit from escaping altogether."

His blue eyes looked right at me and I realized I was holding my pencil in a death grip. I put it down.

"Europeans saw the tsantsa as mere trophies," he said. "But to the Shuar, they were the souls of their enemies. The *trapped* and *powerless* souls of their enemies," he added. "A tsantsa would be worn for approximately one year, during which time three important ceremonies were held to show the ancestors that revenge had been accomplished. After the third ceremony, the head was discarded."

"Discarded?" Penn repeated. It was the first time he'd spoken during the entire class. "Like, thrown away?"

"Not exactly. They were sometimes given to children, or sold to Europeans."

"Sold?"

"Traded is more accurate, I suppose. The Shuar traditions went unchanged for hundreds of years, but by the end of the twentieth century, white men's intrusion and fascination with shrunken heads created a commercial demand. The Shuar were amenable to trade, and the rate of exchange was simple: a gun for a head."

A gun for a head. The words swirled.

"Demand for tsantsa led to an increase in tribal warfare, however, while at the same time the white man's diseases caused many Shuar deaths . . . deaths that, naturally, had to be avenged."

"So the white man killed the Shuar with their germs, which made Shuar kill more Shuar, and in the end the Europeans got the heads." Marina looked more than a little horrified.

"That is precisely correct, I'm afraid," Professor Mannering agreed. "And perhaps even worse was when a white man came in contact with a tsantsa before the ceremonies had been completed, when it still carried the soul of the victim. I myself know of cases in which a Shuar warrior was forced to abandon his sacred tsantsa before completing his obligation to his ancestors."

"Abandon? Like just leave it somewhere?" I asked.

Professor Mannering nodded solemnly. "Yes, Ms. Little, I'm afraid so."

"But where?"

"Wherever seemed safest at the time, I suppose. In the river, or the jungle . . ." Professor Mannering's voice faltered. "But certainly the location matters less than the actual abandonment. Imagine killing someone, shrinking his head, and then just leaving it somewhere, knowing that your ancestors will exact horrible revenge for not fulfilling your sacred obligation, but that handing over a sacred tsantsa to a white man would make the ancestral revenge even worse."

"Between a rock and a hard place," Maxine murmured.

"Between ancestors and aggressive, colonizing Westerners," Professor Mannering said as the bell rang. I blinked at the clock, surprised that forty-five minutes had already passed.

I glanced down at my notes and shuddered. While I'd been sitting in anthropology, a skilled Shuar warrior could have removed my head from my skull three times.

CHAPTER 27

♥

"What do you think, my child?" Roxanne asked, emerging from the bathroom with her hands pressed together, as if in prayer. Her face was a mask of empathetic calm. "Tell me your sins."

"Too many to list!" I grinned and adjusted my habit. It was Halloween and we were going as a pair—priest and nun. I pulled my black robe over my head and added one of the cross necklaces we'd made out of cardboard, black string, and metallic gold paint from the art studio.

Roxanne bowed slightly and pulled a bottle of Grey Goose from the folds of her robe; we'd splurged with my recent poker winnings. "Let us bow our heads together in drink," she said in monotone. She poured two shots and handed one to me. "To the sinners of the world, and therefore, job security."

I chuckled as we clinked, and drank.

Roxanne wiped her mouth with the back of her hand. "Speaking of sins, maybe you can find Penn and pucker up—cause a little scandal in the church," she teased in her regular voice.

I whacked her on the arm before screwing the top back on and stashing it in the closet. "That's just what we need," I said as I reemerged. "Scandal."

We dutifully popped our Altoids into our mouths, shoved our pockets full of the fun-size candies my mom had sent in a care package, and checked our side-by-side reflections, making final adjustments. Roxanne pulled two small prayer books out of a desk drawer.

"You have prayer books?" I asked, unable to keep the incredulity out of my voice.

She shook her head and handed one over. "I stole them from the chapel."

"Another sin!"

Laughing, we left the room, our robes swirling behind us as we descended the dormitory stairs. When we hit the first floor, my laughter halted. I hadn't talked to Annette or Penn since the kissing incident and was, secretly, grateful. What was I supposed to say to Penn? And, more important, to Annette? I had no desire to kiss Penn again, that much was clear to me. But untangling how I felt about being so adored by someone—even a boy—wasn't so easy. And Penn's affection cast a sallow light on my relationship with Annette. So much had happened between us in the last two months—so much pulling apart. What was left to hold us together?

You should tell her about Penn's kiss, said a voice.

No, don't, said another.

What do I owe her? they both wondered.

The door to Annette's room was closed. Was she behind it? Already dressed? She hadn't decided what she was going to be as of lunch the day before, and Becca had been full of suggestions. Becca was always full of suggestions, suggestions Annette seemed to accept as if they were gospel.

"Coming?" Roxanne called from the exit door, looking very serious in her priestly attire. I hurried to catch up with her and we left the dorm, skirting the main building to the other side of campus and perusing every costumed figure we passed. I was particularly impressed with the outhouse and the gaggle of boys dressed as showgirls.

"Nice legs!" Roxanne hooted.

"Thank you, Reverend."

Normally, students weren't allowed off campus on Friday nights—it wasn't considered the weekend since we had classes on Saturday—but Halloween was an exception. Away from campus, the streets grew more and more boisterous with every passing block. Little kids clutched their candy bags and rushed from house to house, ringing doorbells and stuffing candy into their mouths. By the time we got to the House of Horrors, an old gabled Victorian covered in fake spiderwebs, we were in a swarm of costumed individuals, young and old. The line was fifty people long.

I scoped out the scene, pretending not to have my eyes peeled for Annette. I couldn't help it, really—we'd spent every Halloween together since we were six, and she was usually my costume partner.

"I hate lines," Roxanne complained, falling in behind giant bottles of catsup and mustard.

"So use your position with the church to cut, then," an approaching voice suggested. It was Hank.

"That's more your style than mine," Roxanne retorted, eyeing his outfit. He was dressed as the Flash, complete with yellow boots and foam lightning bolts instead of ears. "And who will you be flashing tonight, I wonder?"

"Not me," Penn said, tugging his fur-lined hood over his head. Was he trying to avoid making eye contact with me? He was the Flash's nemesis, Captain Cold, and had on a blue-and-white ski parka and a pair of white fur boots. Coming up behind them was the Green Lantern . . . Sam.

"Mr. Moon was in charge of costumes, I presume?" I said. Penn was right next to me, and though it wasn't the first time I'd seen him since the kiss, it was as close as I'd gotten.

Hank tugged at his red unitard near his crotch. "I certainly didn't come up with this madness."

"I think you look pretty good," I said, smirking. "Not everyone is willing to attempt the red-hot superhero look."

Roxanne glared at me, her eyes clearly saying "now you're calling this jerk a superhero?"

"Can't you just freeze this guy out?" she asked Penn.

Penn shook his head. "Afraid not. He's too fast."

"You can say that again," Roxanne agreed while I continued to scan the crowd. The line was moving pretty quickly and we were almost at the entrance.

"Say what again?" Dorothy from *The Wizard of Oz* asked. Only it wasn't really Dorothy—it was Becca. And Marina, dressed as the same barmaid she'd been at Dress to Impress, with a few alterations. I half wondered why she'd repeated the costume—I knew for a fact that she had way more creativity than that.

"Becca should really be the Wicked Witch of the West," I whispered to Roxanne as someone in the crowd let out a low whistle.

"Hell-o, Ariel," someone hooted.

"You wanna swim over here, princess?"

I turned and saw Annette teetering up the sidewalk. *Uff-da*, I thought as I tried to take in what I was seeing. She was wearing a costume she'd worn before—Ariel—only this version was different. This version was . . .

My brain searched helplessly for the right word.

"Doesn't she look incredible?" Becca fingered a Dorothy braid and grinned like a Cheshire cat while Annette wobbled up to us, hastily trying to adjust her flap of a tail with the help of Cat-in-the-Hat Cynthia.

Ariel-Annette's metallic green tail was skintight, the filmy purple bodice totally sheer except for the shell-shaped cups, studded with pearls, that covered her breasts. Her hair had been dyed a hideous orangey red.

"Hi, everyone," she said breathlessly while I tried to get a handle on her purple eyelids and fire-red lips. And then, to me, "I'm Ariel again. Remember when I was Ariel?" She giggled. "This time I got to dye my hair."

Of course I remembered. We were eight and had gone as a duo—Ariel and Ursula, from *The Little Mermaid*. Shannon had refused to let Annette dye her hair, and as I watched her fiddle with her bodice, I found myself thinking that, against all odds, Shannon had been right.

"I hope the color is temporary," I murmured. It was hard to look at her, and I could tell she'd been drinking by the way her words sort of slid together. Not slurred, exactly, but slippery. Not that I really had the right to judge. We'd *all* been drinking. It was the Brookwood norm.

Annette leaned into Penn, who was clearly trying not to look too closely at her costume (unlike Hank, who seemed unable to help himself). Becca tugged her upright, and I found myself wanting to take Annette by the elbow and walk her up the hill to our dorm, to see her safely home. Or at least put Penn's Captain Cold parka on her—she was shivering. But taking care of Annette wasn't my job anymore. Hadn't she made it clear that she didn't want my input, or help?

"Nice shells," I finally said. I was momentarily tempted to knock on one, to see what they were made of, but we had arrived at the door of the decorated Victorian—it was time for the House of Horrors.

"No cutting," Roxanne said to the others, sounding fed up. She handed our tickets to a familiar-looking Dracula while everyone else moved away.

"Hey," Dracula greeted me. I had the vague feeling I was supposed to know him, but didn't, so I crammed a Milky Way in my mouth and stepped into the haunted house. Which, it turned out, was not nearly as scary as a tipsy Annette with fake red hair, bad makeup, and a skintight costume. Still, the spooky sound track was unnervingly loud and the whole place smelled like latex and fake smoke. I was more than a little relieved when we finally exited the side door into the night.

As if on autopilot, I rushed around to the front of the gabled house, my eyes adjusting to the light as I scanned for the rest of our crowd, for Ariel-Annette. I tried to remember how long the line had been when we'd gone in but had no recollection whatsoever.

"Are we going to stand here and wait?" Roxanne asked. "Because I can think of about a hundred other things I'd rather do." She waved her prayer book.

"Really? A hundred?" I unwrapped a Kit Kat.

"All right, five."

I bit off the top layer of crispy wafer. Roxanne was right. What was I waiting for? Annette was clearly having her own Halloween, without me. "One is enough," I said between chews. "Let's go."

We headed up a narrow road with massive, decked-out-with-skeletons-and-fake-gravestones houses, and cut through the woods into a church parking lot, emerging next to a small grave-yard (a real one) flanked by forest.

"A cemetery?" Until that moment I'd had no idea it was even there.

"Yeah, and famously old. Some of the people in here died in the Civil War." She pulled a flask from the folds of her robe. "How about a little Communion?"

"Vodka, tombstones, and fun-size chocolates," I said with a hollow laugh. "What a combination." Part of me was still back at the House of Horrors with Annette and the others—a bigger part than I wanted to admit. Seeing her in that sleazy Disney mermaid costume had been crazily unnerving. What made her dress up like that? Did she know what she looked like? Could she see herself, or was she too smashed together with the other microbes in the Brookwood petri dish? She'd told me she wanted people to see her as an individual before we told them we were a couple, but as the weeks passed, she seemed less and less herself. *Is that true? I wondered. Or is it just that she's becoming less and less of who you want her to be?*

Roxanne led the way along the row of stone crypts, peering at the engravings on the tombstones. "Eleanor Bradshaw, loyal wife, mother, and friend, 1868 to 1952. Calvin Northrop, civil leader and loving father, 1898 to 1967."

Our feet crunched over the fallen leaves as she read inscriptions aloud, searching for the right dead person to sit with. "Frances Stone, 1893 to 1993. Now With Her Creator."

I shook my head slightly. "Too religious, even for you and your prayer book."

"It's not mine!" Roxanne unscrewed the top of the flask and took a sip. "Frank Mathison, 1902 to 1919."

"A teenager," I noted. "All right if we sit with you, Frankie?" The only response was wind rustling the trees and distant hoots of Halloween laughter.

"We'll take that as a yes," Roxanne said, plopping down.

I followed suit, inhaling the rich, decaying smell of autumn as I cleared away the leaves and spread my candy on the grass. Snickers, Reese's, Kit Kats, M&M's, Baby Ruth, Skittles, and my favorite, Almond Joy. I greedily unwrapped one and devoured the super-sweet chocolaty coconut. Roxanne opened a small package of M&M's, which contained a grand total of eleven colorful candies, and handed me six. "Have you talked to Penn?"

I shoved the M&M's into my mouth and crunched on the candy shells. "Who?"

"Penn McCarthy. Captain Cold. The boy you made out with in the steam tunnels."

"I did not make out with him!" I half shouted, shoving her sideways. "It was one kiss, and he kissed me."

"Uh-huh," she said, handing me the flask and unwrapping a Reese's. "And you showed your utter disapproval by biting his tongue off."

"He took me by surprise."

"Good surprise?"

"Holy crap, Roxanne. Hank is right—you *are* merciless." But I forced myself to consider the question, because the part that came *after* the kiss, the part that revealed how well he understood me, how much he liked me was, in some ways, good.

"Do you want to kiss him again?"

"No. But I can't say I don't like being adored." I sighed. "Sometimes I wish I *did* want to kiss him. Or that I could just pretend that I did."

"I so hear that." Roxanne leaned back on the grass. "Sometimes I want to ignore that Hank went off to Paris and hooked up with some smoky-eyed French female. He says it was a fling, that it has nothing to do with how he feels about me. And it would be so easy to just get back together.

"But I can't," she said, her voice quiet. I could hear loneliness in it, and heartache. "I can't pretend I don't care, that I'm not totally pissed."

"We shouldn't pretend," I agreed. "It just isn't the way to go."

Silence, and then, "Aren't you sort of pretending with Annette?"

"What?" I asked, feeling my face flush. But I remembered that Penn had used the word *pretend*, too, right after he kissed me. He said he couldn't pretend anymore. Was I pretending with Annette, or just fooling myself? Or both?

"Forget it," Roxanne said. "I shouldn't have said anything. We both know it's a jungle out there." She unwrapped a Baby Ruth and ate the whole thing in one bite.

"It's a jungle, all right," I echoed, chewing on a wad of Milk Duds. I lay back and looked up at the stars, listening to the hoots of Halloween while the word *jungle* lingered in my head. My thoughts drifted to the Shuar and their unshakable belief in the spirit world. It seemed totally nuts, but Professor Mannering had a point. Who was I to tell them what was real? Who was anyone?

When all our candy and vodka were gone and the cold got the best of us, Roxanne hauled me to my feet, and we headed across Route 6 and hopped the low rock wall. We were on the far side of campus, next to the baseball field and the boys' dorms.

Here again, I thought as we passed first base. I found myself eyeing the elm tree outside Penn's window, and was instantly frustrated. Maybe it was seeing Annette in that sleazy getup. Maybe it was the comment that Roxanne had made about our relationship. Or maybe it was that Penn and I had been acting like the kiss had never happened. It had happened, all right. My lips sort of burned, thinking about it happening—although to be fair, it was probably the tangy mixture of Altoids, vodka, and chocolate I kept burping up.

It didn't matter. I was done stewing. Done avoiding Penn, avoiding Annette. I was ready to talk. I *needed* to talk, to both of them.

"I'll meet you in our room," I told Roxanne. "I've got something to do." I could feel my resolve solidifying. I'd start with Penn and talk to Annette back at the dorm.

Roxanne turned to me, suspicious. "Are you sure?" she asked, throwing a glance toward Penn's window.

I squared my shoulders as best I could, being a little drunk and in a full-length robe, and nodded.

"Lights is in half an hour," she said. "Lola No is on."

"I'll be there in twenty."

"You want me to wait?"

I waved her off. "No, please don't. I just have to take care of this. I'll be fine."

She watched me from first base, looking very priestly in her robe and cross. "Twenty minutes," she said warningly. "Or I'll come back and get you myself."

As my roommate disappeared into the shadow of the main building, I glanced up at Penn's window. A dim glow emanated from the tower room. A hazy memory reminded me that climbing the tree to his window required a running start, so I rushed forward and jumped, throwing my arms around the lowest branch and inching my fingers up the sides. I felt like my shoulders were being ripped out of their sockets as I linked my fingers together and walked up the trunk, being careful not to get snagged on my robe. Finally, I was upright. Vaguely nauseous, but upright.

This is crazy, I told myself. *Go back to your dorm.* But I added that getting into the tree was the hardest part, and it was done. Plus, I really needed to talk to Penn.

I got to my feet and steadied myself against the trunk while I peered at the branches overhead. I had no idea which route I'd taken before, but there seemed to be several options. I chose one before I could change my mind, and got moving.

Up I went, capitalizing on my momentum and practicing what I would say when I was face-to-face with Penn. I put my foot in a crook next to the trunk and pulled myself up with a vengeance, but my robe caught and I practically choked on the collar. I sat down fast, clinging to the surrounding branches, and yanked the heavy fabric away from my throat.

Christ, Josie. Get a freaking grip. I wrapped my arms around the trunk, giving it a scratchy hug. The ground was farther away than I'd thought, and spinning a little. Clearly the stairs would have been the wiser choice. The stairs, and taking off the robe before I'd started to climb.

Better late than never, I thought as I unbuttoned the robe. I wobbled slightly, but managed to pull it over my head, getting lost for only a moment in the heavy folds. I balled the robe up and shoved it between a couple of branches.

That's better, I thought, getting back to my feet. I was now dressed in black leggings and a T-shirt, and could climb much more easily. I swung my leg up to a higher branch, ignoring my queasy stomach, my sights set on the dimly lit top floor. Within a minute I was outside Penn's window. I peered through the leaded glass, trying to see if anyone was inside. The only light came from the desk lamp in the corner, and the chairs around the coffee table were empty. It appeared I had climbed the tree for nothing—nobody was home.

And why would Penn be in his room? I chided myself. *It's Friday night, and Halloween!*

I was lowering my leg to a branch below me when the door to Penn's room opened and he came in, still dressed as Captain Cold minus the jacket. I steeled myself and reached forward to open the window, then pulled back. Someone was coming in behind him— someone wearing the parka.

I squinted, trying to see, and blinked. Shimmery fabric. A tail. Fire-red hair.

Oh. My. God.

Annette slipped into the room and out of the parka, dropping it onto the rickety armchair along with her shoes. She looked like she did the night of Dress to Impress, relaxed and exhilarated. While Penn shoved his dirty clothes into the closet, she adjusted her pearl-studded cups, and when he turned back, she took his hand and pulled him toward the sofa.

He didn't resist.

Don't look! a voice said, as if that were possible. I felt nausea crawl up from my stomach as Annette leaned into him and they started to kiss. The desk light cast its beam on them like a soft spotlight, and I could see everything in unfortunate detail—their mouths, their tongues, their hands. And Penn's erection.

Annette pulled back a bit and laughed, wrapping one of his curls around her fingers and pulling him back in.

I leaned forward, bile officially in my throat. Were they drunk? Annette seemed tipsy, but also decidedly in control of what she was doing . . . and the situation.

Does it even matter? I asked myself as Annette stretched herself next to him, the way she'd done with me countless times. I leaned in closer, loosening my grasp on the tree trunk, horrified but unable to stop myself. I leaned farther and farther forward until . . .

"Shit!" I was falling, flailing my arms in an attempt to grab anything that might break my fall. My arm twisted behind me and the jagged end of a broken limb scraped across my calf. I let out a yelp and half landed on a thick branch, wrapping a leg around it, clutching at the bark with both hands. I wasn't exactly stable, but I wasn't moving anymore.

Above me, the window opened. Silence. And then, "Josie?" Penn's voice called, sounding shocked and a little bit slurry. "Are you all right?" God, I hated the sound of his voice. I hated everything about Penn McCarthy.

"Now you're talking to me?" I shouted. "Now?"

I wondered if Annette was still sprawled across his sofa, if she was waiting for him to return to her arms. I was too low to see, though, and certainly wasn't going to look up at him.

"Josie, I—"

"Go fuck yourself!" I shouted as I started to climb. Down, as fast as I could. "No, wait. I have better idea. Go fuck Annette!"

CHAPTER 28

♥

"Josie, wake up!"

I rolled over and opened a single sticky, sugar-and-vodka-hungover eye, which revealed a very fuzzy Becca.

"Annette is missing. Josie, can you hear me?"

Of course I could hear her. She was practically screaming in my ear, for Christ's sake. I willed both eyelids open and sat up, my body aching and bruised, and remembered. The climb. Penn and Annette. The fall.

"Annette is missing," Becca repeated.

Good, I thought, falling back onto my pillow. *I hope she stays that way.*

"Josie!"

I turned to face her. "What do you mean, missing? She probably went for a run or something." I gazed up at the Turtle Lake crack, since closing my eyes again would undoubtedly take me back to the horror movie from the night before.

"I need your help!" Becca shrieked.

Her high-pitched squeal made my head hurt, and I suddenly noticed that her usually superior-sounding voice didn't sound the slightest bit superior. It sounded panicked.

I sat up again. "I'm listening."

"After we saw you at the House of Horrors, we did a little trick-or-treating, and then she went off with Penn. A bunch of us were in the common room at lights, and I assumed she'd come in. I thought she must have been in our room, or Lola No would've gone ballistic. But she wasn't there when I went to bed, or when I woke up."

"Dining room?"

"Not there." Pause. "Nobody has seen her."

I don't want *to see her,* I thought. *Ever.* But even as I had these thoughts, I knew they were ridiculous. Of course I wanted to see her again. I wanted to see her so I could kill her.

"Josie!" Becca was losing it.

I checked the clock. It was 7:04—our first class was in forty-one minutes. Could we figure this out in forty-one minutes?

I threw off the covers and jumped to the floor, landing hard. Ouch, my leg really hurt. I was not in good shape.

"Thank you," Becca breathed, her face relaxing a little. "Where would she go?"

To Penn's room? I thought. She definitely could've spent the night there. But Annette never overslept in the morning—she was always gone before daybreak, so she wouldn't still be there. I had no idea where she'd be, I realized. I'd barely talked to her in days.

I was searching for some shoes when Lola No appeared at my door. "Headmaster Thornfeld would like to see the two of you," she said. "Immediately." I searched her face for her usual hard expression, but it wasn't there. She looked agitated, worried. "As in *now,*" she added before she disappeared.

"Shit," Becca said, her eyes flickering with fear. She moved fast—down the stairs, across the circle drive, and into the main building. I followed and waited for her to say something, to give me some advice about what to do or say in Thornfeld's presence, but she kept her mouth clamped shut and her feet moving forward. Where was Roxanne when I needed her?

The first thing I saw when I walked into Thornfeld's office (besides the headmaster himself) was an orange plastic pumpkin filled with candy. Its wide, toothy grin mocked me as I sat down in one of two Windsor chairs that faced his desk. I peered at the diplomas on his wall from Cornell and Yale and ran my tongue over my fuzzy, needed-to-be-brushed teeth. They were disgusting.

"I'm afraid you are not here for good news," Thornfeld said. He took off his reading glasses, carefully folded in the temples, and set them on his desk. He seemed to be stalling, and he looked tired. Exhausted, even.

"Miss Anderson is in the hospital, recovering from alcohol poisoning."

Becca inhaled sharply and without sound, but I was not so discreet. "Oh my God," I exclaimed. Becca shot me a venomous look, which I didn't understand, and pretended not to see. "Is she all right?"

"Not yet, but I believe she will be. She was found on a bathroom floor in Cortland Dormitory by Professor Franke, at two o'clock in the morning."

I gazed at him, trying to absorb what he was saying. Why would she be on the bathroom floor in the middle of the night?

"There was also an empty bottle of Skyy vodka and, from what I understand, a large pool of vomit. She was unconscious." His eyes bored into me, then Becca, all signs of fatigue gone. "Would either of you like to tell me how she got there?"

It took me a couple more seconds to register that Professor Franke was Lola No. I imagined her tiny frame crouched over Annette on the tiled floor. Annette with her mermaid tail, fake red hair, and purple eye shadow. With the smell of Penn McCarthy and vodka and barf all over her. Unconscious.

My whole body got hot with alarm, and I fleetingly understood why Becca had been glowering at me a moment before. We weren't supposed to panic in front of the administration—especially when rule breaking was involved. We were supposed to remain aloof and, if necessary, calmly but firmly declare our innocence (Roxanne had drilled that much into my head). Only right here, right now, not panicking was not possible. Annette wasn't some random student who'd blown it by having a few too many—she was Annette.

I forced myself to look directly at the headmaster while images from the night before flashed in my head. Annette at the House of Horrors, flushed and tipsy and leaning into Penn. Annette dropping her shoes onto a chair. Annette pulling Penn toward her . . .

I looked away from Thornfeld, wriggling uncomfortably in my seat. I reached for my opal pendant, for something solid to touch, but felt nothing around my neck. It was gone. And worse, I had no idea when or where I'd lost it.

"Josie? Do you have something to say?"

I dropped my hands into my lap. "No," I replied, grateful that I could tell the truth. I'd laid eyes on Annette twice the night before, for a total of ten minutes, and barely got close enough to touch her. I honestly had no idea how the events of her Halloween had played out. (Except for fooling around with Penn, of course.)

"Miss Ryder?"

Becca seemed frozen in her chair, her face an impressive mask of detachment. "I'm so sorry, Headmaster Thornfeld, I don't. I was with Annette during the early part of the evening—she came with a group of us to the House of Horrors in town. Afterward the group dismantled and I lost track of her."

Dismantled? What were we talking about, a bomb? *Ugh. In a way, yes.*

"You didn't see her at lights?" Thornfeld asked pointedly. "She is your roommate, is she not?"

"Yes. But I was in the common room cleaning up after our Halloween party. She wasn't in our room when I went to bed, but I assumed she was in the bathroom or something."

Thornfeld leveled his gaze at her. "I believe she was," he replied severely.

Becca's face turned bright red as she realized what she'd just said. "I meant getting ready for bed in the bathroom," she corrected.

"You have a lavatory attached to your room, do you not?"

"Yes, but with four girls, it sometimes gets crowded."

Thornfeld looked like he wanted to leap over his desk and yank her by her pearl necklace. But what could he do? He clearly had no proof of anything—just a girl in the hospital, and probably a fair amount of fallout. Shannon was a force to be reckoned with, and there was the board I'd heard rumblings about.

"You are dismissed for now, Miss Ryder, though this is certainly not the end of our conversation. Miss Little, you will remain for a few moments."

Remain? I watched Becca get up to leave, and tried not to let panic overtake me. I was about to be alone in the headmaster's office, and Annette had been rushed to the hospital. Plus I certainly hadn't been following the rules.

"Please close the door behind you." The pumpkin jeered in my direction while the headmaster tapped a finger on his desk, and I noticed a little orange card hanging off one side. "Happy Halloween, from Linus."

The headmaster was watching me carefully. "I don't know anything," I said, blinking fast. "I wish I did, but I don't."

"I believe you," he said with surprising kindness. "That's not why I asked you to stay."

Did he ask? I wondered. I'd certainly considered it an order.

"I wanted to tell you that Annette is at Eden General Hospital and has asked to see you. Because she has been suspended and will not be returning to Brookwood right away after she is released, the administration has decided to grant her wish." He paused, probably to let this information sink in. "Mr. and Mrs. Anderson are flying in this afternoon to take her home when she is well enough. Dean Austin will drive you to the hospital when your classes are finished for the day." His expression was unfaltering, but the tiredness at the corners of his eyes was back. "I am sure I do not need to impress upon you the gravity of this situation. Blemishes like this do not recede quickly."

Blemishes? As in zits?

I swallowed and fought to maintain a bland expression despite my internal cascade of emotions. This was so screwed up. What had made Annette drink herself into such a stupor? Into unconsciousness? Everyone drank at Brookwood, but not like that. And yet, in many ways, Annette was only doing what everyone else did.

Why are you defending her? an incredulous voice asked. *She ditched you, strung you along, and screwed around with Penn.*

I had to fight to keep my body upright and my expression neutral as the answer came screaming into my head like a freight train: *Because you, Josie Little, brought her here in the first place.*

CHAPTER 29

♥

Most of the time I considered myself lucky to have double anthropology on Saturday mornings, but that day I would've sat through a dozen algebra classes to avoid seeing Penn. Because of my meeting with Thornfeld, I wasn't at breakfast—thus far he'd been invisible. Which was good, because I literally had no idea what I would do with his body after I killed him.

I walked quickly by the pond and into the science building, then lingered awkwardly in the hall. I was a little early for class, and Headmaster Thornfeld was in the classroom with Professor Mannering. The man was all over the place.

"I'm sorry, Linus," I heard him say, surprised that I could hear anything through the closed door. Looking up, I noticed that the transom above it was wide open. I stepped out of view, my back against the wall, and listened. "It is out of my hands, I'm afraid. The board has made a final decision."

"I can't say I'm entirely surprised," Professor Mannering said, his voice resigned. "Though I had hoped they'd let me stay through the end of the semester. It will be a bit awkward to leave my students mid-discussion . . . some of them are extremely insightful."

"They will miss you, no doubt, as will I."

"I appreciate that, Percy," Professor Mannering said. "As well as your coming to tell me immediately. It will give me a little time to get things in order."

"I assumed you'd want to know as soon as possible."

"I'm not quite sure what I will do with myself," Professor Mannering said amusedly, "but life has a way of keeping things interesting."

"You can say that again," Thornfeld agreed.

"Life has a way of keeping things interesting," Professor Mannering said again, and both men laughed before the room fell to silence.

"I am grateful for your work here," Thornfeld said.

"And I am grateful for the many years of support."

Several more seconds of silence, and then footsteps. A moment later the door opened and Thornfeld appeared, walking right past me as if I were invisible.

The significance of the conversation was sinking in when Marina approached. I almost blurted out what I'd just heard, but managed to keep my mouth closed. It wasn't really my news to tell.

"May as well bite the bullet," Marina said, nudging me forward as students filed through the door. Another nudge and I was in the classroom, which was, thankfully, Penn-less.

"Let's sit on the other side," Marina suggested. "That way we can glare at him as he comes in the door."

"You're glaring, too?" I asked, feeling sick to my empty stomach. On top of everything else, my favorite teacher was apparently leaving the school, and pronto.

Marina half shrugged. "I'm definitely not smiling at the boy."

"Take some seats, please!" Professor Mannering said from his desk, sounding remarkably like himself. Wasn't he upset? "We have business to attend to."

Marina and I made our way through the maze of desks and sat down by the window. The dog-eared *National Geographic* magazine in front of us gave off a musty smell, and I blinked at the date under the title: October 1921. Almost a hundred years ago.

"Holy old thing," Marina said.

"Yeah," I agreed. The magazine smelled of moldy paper, and the steel staples that held it together were rusted. The table of contents was right on the cover and there were only four articles in the whole thing. They all had to do with South America. The first article was "Trail and Jungle in Ecuador," by H. E. Anthony, and I opened the magazine, almost sneezing as dust and mildew emerged. The pages were thick and, I could tell, had once been shiny. After decades in Professor Mannering's classroom, though, they were matted from touch.

"Peoples," Professor Mannering said from the front of the room. "This morning we will be working in pairs and reading about Amazonian cultures in periodicals of various ages, from very old to present-day. Each offers a different perspective, which is precisely what we will be discussing. Please dig in with your desk partner and take notes for said discussion."

Clutching his coffee mug in his bony fingers, he moved around the room, presumably to make certain we were reading the right stuff.

A naked-chested Shuar warrior stared out from the pages of

the *National Geographic*, his expression haughty and distant. In his hands he held a muzzle-loading gun. A caption under the photo said *He may have paid a human head for his weapon*, but the paragraph under *that* was much more informative, explaining that the musket was cheaply made, but the Shuar never tired of handling guns, for they symbolized wealth. The Shuar man in the photo wore bangs across his forehead, and his hair was tied just below his ears with pieces of something that looked like bone, or maybe antler.

"You'd think a headhunting warrior would be a little buffer than that, you know?" Marina asked.

"Totally," I agreed, forcing myself to stare hard at the magazine.

"You can relax a little," she said. "He's not here yet." She turned the page, and we started to read. The article was fascinating and full of details—everything from language to religious practices to hunting techniques to shrinking heads. But you could tell that it had been written a long time ago, because the writing was kind of stiff and, well, moldy.

Marina turned to a full-page photo of shrunken heads. 'Ewwwww!" she whispered. "Gross."

I leaned in and looked at the photo of three shrunken heads "hanging" from ropes. The hair on all three heads was crazy long, the bangs coming down to the chins because the heads were no longer full-size.

"Look at that gorgeous hair," Marina said reverently. "Even hanging off creepy shriveled heads, it reeks of Latino bombshell."

She was right, but I wasn't looking at the hair. I was looking at the heads, at the faces with their protruding lips, ornately tied with light-colored string that was left to hang, in some cases, even longer than the hair. According to the caption, the heads belonged to the American Museum of Natural History.

I glanced up to see Professor Mannering standing over us, his eyes focused on the picture of the three heads. He reached out as if he were going to snatch the magazine away, then changed his mind and pulled his hand back.

Marina leaned in to study the photo. "That is some serious awesome nasty creepiness," she declared.

Professor Mannering turned away abruptly. "Finish up, peoples," he announced. "We want plenty of time for discussion."

Just then, Penn walked in, and I caught his eye without meaning to. He looked dazed, as though he'd just woken up, which made me flare with anger. Did he even know what had happened? What was happen*ing*?

"Don't look at him," Marina whispered, closing the magazine. "Or better yet, pretend he's naked."

I turned to her.

"Oh shit, sorry," she corrected herself. "Bad idea."

Terrible idea, I thought.

Marina's dark eyes were full of embarrassment. "Oooh, I know," she said. "Pretend he's a shrunken head."

Ha! That was much better. "Exactly," I agreed. "With his eyes and lips sewn tightly shut for all eternity."

CHAPTER 30

♥

Dean Austin and his golden retriever, McNulty, who spent a fair amount of the ride with his head between the two front seats, panting and drooling on his master's ample shoulder, dropped me off at the hospital curb. "Do you want me to come in with you?" the dean asked as he slid the gearshift into park, seemingly oblivious to the giant wet spot on his chambray button-down.

I regarded the Eden General sign and tried to ignore the roiling pit of uneasiness in my stomach. "No, thanks, I got it."

He handed me an old-fashioned business card with an embossed Brookwood logo, just like the one on the acceptance letter I'd received eight months before. "It has my cell number," he explained. "Call me when you're ready to be picked up."

For a moment, I considered telling him I was ready right now, to peel the station wagon out of there. Then I considered telling him not to bother coming back at all—I'd just go back to Minnesota with Annette. Since neither was an option, I nodded and got out of the car.

Eden General looked like every other hospital I'd seen. Industrial. Ugly. Huge sign directing people to the emergency room. Ugh, the emergency room. That was where the ambulance had taken Annette.

Well, at least the driver was sober, I thought as the memory of a previous ER visit surfaced—one with a drunken Shannon at the wheel.

———————————————

It was just over a year ago. Shannon had been hosting a dinner party; Annette and I were her kitchen minions. Everything had gone perfectly until Annette slipped on the wet floor and dropped an armful of dessert plates, smashing them to bits and twisting her ankle, badly.

"How can a person be so clumsy?" Shannon hissed over her shoulder, blearily eyeing the two of us in the backseat. She slammed her foot on the accelerator and took a drag from her cigarette, the ash lengthening dangerously. As the car sped down the highway, I squeezed Annette's hand, silently assuring both of us that it would be all right.

"I tripped," Annette said quietly. Her face was streaked with tears.

"On what?" Shannon said derisively. "Your stupidity?"

"It was an accident," I said. I just wanted her to be quiet and drive, but she was on a rampage. Her dinner party had been interrupted, and she'd had a slew of gin and tonics. Never a good combination.

"It's always an accident!" She hit the gas pedal again, roaring past a pickup and veering back into the right lane, cutting him off. The pickup driver slammed on his horn and Annette clutched my arm as if her life depended on it. Shannon's behavior had been getting more volatile, especially since she'd lost her job at the insurance agency. Her drunken outbursts were more frequent and intense than ever.

Shannon took the turn into the hospital parking lot way too fast, throwing Annette and me against the inside of the car door. Annette yelped in pain as the station wagon careened up to the emergency entrance and screeched to a halt. I could practically feel Annette's frantic heartbeat through her hand as I tried to steady my own breath. We'd made it; we were safe.

The hospital's automatic doors opened wide, beckoning me inside. Pushing aside the memory, I walked to the information desk. "I'm here to visit Annette Anderson," I told the woman behind it. Her pantsuit was bright teal and she was clearly not happy about her job coming between her and the latest issue of *People*, but her expression softened when she saw my face. She quickly consulted a computer screen. "Five-oh-eight, honey. She's in the pediatric ICU. Take the elevator on your left."

"Thanks." I forced myself toward the elevators. "Floor one, elevator up," a mechanical voice said as the doors slid open. I pressed the button for the fifth floor, my gaze landing on the emergency knob as the elevator began to rise. If I had the guts to press the thing, I'd be trapped for hours, maybe days. Maybe until Annette went home with her parents. Maybe forever.

"Floor five," the voice announced. "Pediatric Intensive Care."

Maybe not.

The doors opened next to the nurses' station, which hummed with women in orthopedic clogs and cutesy patterned scrubs.

Averting my gaze, I quickly consulted an overhead sign and headed toward room 508.

"Hello?" I called, pushing open the door.

The first thing I saw was Annette's Ariel costume, crumpled on the bottom of a plastic personal belongings bag. The second thing I saw was Annette, hooked up to a bunch of machines. She had an oxygen tube up her nose and a bag of IV fluids hung over her head, dripping into her veins. Her face was a random combination of splotchy red and yellow, and her fake red hair was spread in a matted mass against the bleached white of the hospital pillow. She looked god-awful, and I couldn't believe how skinny she was. When had she lost all that weight?

The third thing I saw was Shannon. She swiveled her graying blond head like a bird of prey and looked at me with so much venom I actually felt myself shrivel. I half wanted to back out of the room, but my feet seemed to be Gorilla-Glued to the floor. "You conniving little bitch," she shrieked. "How could you do this to her?"

Oh, crap.

"Shannon," Annette's father consoled her, putting a hand on his wife's arm. "Let's not make everything worse by casting blame."

"Don't tell me how to behave, Michael Anderson." She shook him off, hard. "I gave birth to this child!" She started to sob, and I realized she wasn't sober. Annette squeezed her eyes shut and turned her head away from all three of us.

"I came as soon as I could." I stepped forward cautiously. I'd been so focused on seeing Annette, I hadn't even thought about having to deal with her parents—Shannon in particular. How did they get here so fast?

"Nobody asked you to come!"

"I did," Annette corrected in a weak, scratchy voice. Her eyes were open now, and I could see how dull they were, how empty.

"I hope you're happy that Annette almost *died*," Shannon said.

"I'm fine," Annette rasped.

That was clearly a lie, but at least she was standing up for us . . . if there'd still been an us.

"You are far from fine, young lady. They had to intubate you." Shannon's voice slithered over the word *intubate*. "You've only been breathing on your own for a few hours!" Her face crumpled, and she sobbed into her palm. No, definitely not sober.

I walked around the side of the bed and reached for Annette's hand. She grasped it weakly and looked up at me, but her eyes were so bloodshot and dazed I could barely tell what color they were, much less what was behind them. Gratitude? Regret? Love?

Love? Really? I mocked myself. *Was she feeling love for you while she was chasing after Penn? While she was kissing him? Get real, Josie.* And another voice that asked *Is that even what you want?*

"It's been a long day," Michael said. "I think a trip to the cafeteria is in order." He gently nudged his wife out of her chair. "I'm sure these two would like a little time alone."

"Time alone is what created this nightmare," Shannon snapped. "But I *could* use a cup of coffee, and you never get the order right . . ." She let her husband take her arm and lead her into the hall. "Don't get too comfortable, Josie Little," she warned over her shoulder. "We'll be back before you know it."

Still holding Annette's hand, I watched the door close behind them. When I looked down, Annette's half-vacant eyes were staring up at me and a tear was rolling down the side of her cheek into her ear. "I'm so sorry," she whispered.

"I know," I said, and then wished I hadn't. Because I *didn't* know. I didn't know at all. Was she sorry? For what, exactly? There were so many choices. *And you're not exactly free from blame, either.*

I desperately *wanted* to know, too—I wanted to know everything. But I also knew I wasn't going to. We needed hours of time, of talking, of being together to sort out what had happened to her, to me, to us. What we had was the time it took for a cup of coffee.

"They're sending me home," she said. "I've been suspended until further notice."

"Thornfeld told me."

Her eyes stared. "He did?"

I nodded. "He summoned Becca and me to his office before first period and told us what happened. I think he was looking for information."

"Did you give him any?"

Was that all she cared about? What I told the headmaster? "Should I have?"

Annette pulled her hand away, and I stared at my empty palm, startled that I didn't want to grab hold again.

"If you wanted to, yes," she whispered.

"I didn't. Besides, there wasn't really anything to tell him. I barely saw you all evening."

She swallowed painfully. "But you . . . were you outside Penn's room?"

My face flushed. So she knew after all. "I wanted to talk to him, but he was busy."

Annette's yellow-and-pink-splotched forehead filled with wavy lines, reminding me of the beach at Turtle Lake after a windy night. I could see orange hair-dye stains around her temples. "I don't know why I went to his room, I just . . ."

"It looked like you knew *exactly* why you were there . . ."

She shuddered and covered her face with her non-IV hand, and I watched her body tense. I wanted to enjoy her misery, to relish her torment. But I just felt terrible.

"Thank God you interrupted us."

Hope rose at the sound of those five words. Maybe she regretted it. Maybe she needed to make out with Penn to remember that she wanted to be with me.

"I had no idea what to do with a boy," she went on. "It was getting embarrassing."

I shot to my feet and walked to the window, which, I now saw, faced an industrial air shaft. Of course. Annette was thanking God for preserving her *reputation*. "Right. Because being discovered unconscious on a bathroom floor in a pool of vomit *isn't* embarrassing . . ."

Annette's gasp was raspy, and part of me wanted to pull the words back out of the air. Another part, though, wanted to keep hurling.

"That was really mean, Josie."

Wafts of cold air came through the window. That *was* mean. I was being mean because I wanted to punish her for hurting me. Only trying to punish her wasn't making me feel any better—it was making me feel worse.

You still love her, a voice said. I squeezed my eyes shut, wishing the ventilation system would ventilate *me*, because I suddenly felt like I was suffocating. What had Brookwood done to us, to Annette? She used to be the person I shared everything with, my best friend. I turned back to her, seeing again how thin she was, how small and frail she looked in the hospital bed. I barely recognized her. Our relationship felt small and frail now, too. But was it always? Was it once as strong as I'd believed it to be?

The door swung open and a nurse wearing ducky scrubs came in. "How are we doing in here?" she asked in a perky voice. "Have we gone pee-pee?" She lifted a plastic bag hanging on the side of the bed. I thought it was empty, but she seemed thrilled with its contents. "Good girl!" she crowed, patting Annette's arm with one hand and squeezing the bag slightly—as if it were a piece of ripe fruit—with the other. "You're up to three hundred cc's." She made a note in Annette's chart. "Keep up the good work and we'll get that catheter out before we know it."

"Thank God," Shannon said, coming through the door with a giant cup of coffee, its edge smeared with lipstick the color of Annette's hair. "There's nothing worse than peeing into a *bag*, except maybe the coffee in that cafeteria. We had to go all the way across the street to Dunkin' Donuts."

Annette gazed woodenly at her mother.

"But there was a definite upside!" Shannon wagged a paper bag in the air. "I got your favorite—Bavarian cream!"

Annette turned a shade yellower. "No junk food for our patient quite yet," the nurse said. "Her body is still recovering from the alcohol abuse."

Shannon flinched at the words *alcohol abuse* and busied herself with opening the bag. "Oh, all right," she said. "I suppose I'll just have to eat it for her."

"Or you could give it to Josie," came Annette's hoarse whisper. "It's her favorite, too."

Annette's mother pretended not to hear as she pulled a doughnut out of the bag and took a bite, squirting the vanilla cream out the holes in the sides. A giant glob splattered onto the floor, missing her shoe by inches.

I stared at the blob of creamy yellow filling, noticing that it was the same pallid yellow as Annette's eyelids. And then it was gone, smeared between the industrial tile and the sole of Shannon's shoe.

CHAPTER 31

♥

When I stepped through the hospital doors, I was startled to discover that life outside had just been going along normally the whole time I was in there, as if nothing crazy was happening. As if Annette wasn't hooked up to a bunch of machines and her pee wasn't in a bag. As if she wasn't being shipped back home.

I also realized that I'd forgotten to call Dean Austin for a ride. I pulled out his card, punched his number into my phone, and watched a woman navigate her double stroller over the curb while I waited for him to answer. He picked up on the fourth ring.

"Sam Austin."

"Hi, it's Josie. I'm ready for a ride home," I said, getting a little choked up at the sound of a friendly voice. And then, *Did I really just call Brookwood home?*

"I can leave right now," Dean Austin said. "I'll be there in half an hour."

"Perfect," I lied. Half an hour felt like way too long, but everything in Connecticut seemed at least that far away. I hung up and sat down to wait, shivering and doing my best to focus on the people coming and going at Eden General and not what had happened in that hospital room. Because something had happened, something more than what had actually transpired. And even if I wasn't ready to think about what it meant, I understood that, like so many other things, there was no escaping it.

By the time Dean Austin's blue station wagon pulled into the circle, my butt was cold and stiff from sitting on the concrete retaining wall. I slid into the front seat, completely exhausted and only just now getting that I was about to spend thirty minutes alone with the dean of students, the person in charge of student discipline. Of course, I'd spent a half hour with him on the ride *to* the hospital, but I'd been so focused on seeing Annette I hadn't registered the implication of that.

McNulty whimpered and greeted me from the backseat with a slobbery lick, and I stroked his ear while Dean Austin steered the car into traffic. From the looks of things, the drive was going to take longer than thirty minutes. We crawled along Route 122 in silence, past the commercial buildings and houses and into the country, following the line of cars as though we were in a funeral procession.

"How is she?"

I was so startled by the question, I didn't answer right away.

"Josie?"

I pressed my palms together. "I'm not sure," I said, realizing with a stab just how true my answer was. "Okay, maybe."

He flicked on his blinker and turned, passing a farm enclosed by a low rock wall. "And how are you?"

A pair of stones lay on the half-frozen ground, stones that had fallen away from the structure like fugitives. Or failures. I knew Roxanne would tell me to say that I was fine—A-OK, thanks for asking. And maybe I was. But I couldn't tell, and I didn't want to lie. I was so tired of lying. "I'm not sure," I repeated.

McNulty momentarily nuzzled my arm before getting back to his drool work on Dean Austin's shoulder. "Two honest answers," the dean murmured. I waited for him to tell me what a difficult situation this must be, or give me a lecture about the dangers of reckless behavior. But he just drove.

When we finally turned into the main circle, I involuntarily flashed back to the day Annette and I arrived. The Brookwood sign was the same. The buildings, hedges, and elm trees (with the exception of the leaf color) were the same. Everything still looked exactly like the catalog. But it all felt completely, utterly different. For one thing, there were only two of us in the car.

Dean Austin pulled into a parking space and I reached for the door handle, eager to get out, to get away. "Thanks for the ride," I told him with fake cheerfulness.

He turned to me, his eyes rueful. "You're welcome, Josie." He seemed like he might keep talking, so I quickly climbed out of my seat and closed the door between us before hurrying toward my dorm. Campus was relatively deserted, and for once I was glad that everyone spent Saturday afternoons on the athletic fields—I wouldn't have to deal with anyone.

I pushed open the door to my room and immediately saw Grandma Ruby's dress hanging on the closet door, neatly packaged in its dry cleaner's plastic. My stomach somersaulting, I shoved it into the closet without removing the plastic or checking to see if the stains had come out. When I turned around, Becca was standing in my doorway, a tiny bit breathless and wearing her cross-country uniform.

"How is she?" she asked, her turquoise eyes not quite meeting mine. "Is she okay?"

How many times would I be asked that question?

"She's recovering," I said, leaning against the closet doorframe. "It was pretty bad."

"Really?" Becca fidgeted, something I'd never seen her do. She seemed authentically distraught, which was good, because it meant she was human. And bad, because it also meant I'd have to treat her like a human, when it would have been much easier to treat her like a Soleet. "Like, how bad?"

It was just like her to want the gruesome details, as if this were fiction we were reading for Professor Drake, and not something that had happened to an actual person.

Not something that had happened to Annette.

Becca was watching me out of the corner of her eye, and I could tell she wanted me to exonerate her, to tell her that Annette wasn't her responsibility. To promise that it was fine. But it wasn't fine, and some of it *was* her responsibility. And Annette's. And Brookwood's. And mine. We all had our parts in this.

"It doesn't matter," I finally said. "She's sober and she's going home."

Becca's head shot up. "Home?"

Wait. Wasn't that public knowledge?

"Yes, with her parents. As soon as she's well enough."

That was the normal course of action, right? Annette couldn't be the first person to be suspended, or hospitalized for alcohol poisoning at Brookwood . . .

"Her parents are here?"

"Yes." It was becoming clear that Becca wasn't getting it, that she thought this was just another drunken episode. "They flew in this morning and are with her at the hospital. They had to intubate her." My voice slithered over the word *intubate* just like Shannon's had, and I felt a flash of guilt. Was I treating Becca the way Shannon treated me?

Becca's face was blank—she still wasn't comprehending.

"A breathing tube—she wasn't breathing when they found her."

Becca's face shifted into understanding and she slumped onto my desk chair. "This is bad." She looked so deflated that I found myself trying to think of something to say—something kind, or at least neutral. But she spoke first.

"What did you tell Thornfeld?" she asked, as if just remembering our meeting with him this morning.

I shoved my hands into my pockets, marveling at how quickly this girl could turn everything back to herself.

"Thornfeld?"

"What did you tell him?" she repeated, her voice rising. She sounded vulnerable now, as if I had power to wield. The realization that this was actually true dripped into me slowly, like Annette's IV fluids.

"Where did she get the bottle of Skyy, Becca? From the back of your closet?"

"Everyone drinks!" Becca shouted. "It's how we survive here." That was true, of course. Even geeks and major jocks downed shots of hard alcohol. And I knew Annette better than anyone at Brookwood—I knew she wasn't an experienced drinker, and that her mother *was*. Wasn't that a big part of why we'd come here—to get Annette away from Shannon's drinking, her abusive behavior? To keep Annette safe?

I looked away and willed myself to keep my cool, but I suddenly felt like a free diver at 150 feet—like a giant column of water was crushing down on my head. What an unbelievable mess. "I didn't tell him anything," I finally said. "I'm not a rat."

Becca exhaled through her mouth, her gratitude spreading between us. But it felt all wrong—sticky and treacherous.

Becca got to her feet. "Did Thornfeld say whether she is suspended or expelled?"

Do you actually care?

"He said she wouldn't be coming back to Brookwood when she was released from the hospital, but I'm not sure she'll come back even if it is just a suspension. Her parents are freaked, and they weren't too gung ho about her coming here in the first place. And anyway, the school might not want her. She's not a legacy, and she's on scholarship."

"They actually need the scholarship kids. They're good for PR, and—"

I wasn't sure exactly when it happened, but Becca's voice had shifted, her confident, superior cadence filling the room just in time to set the record straight, to put Annette and me in our PR, scholarship places.

I held up a hand. "You don't have to explain—I get it."

Her eyes held mine for several seconds while she fingered her pearls, considering. I reached for my own necklace, forgetting for a moment that I no longer had it. "We're going to dinner at Joe's later if you want to come."

Seriously? Other than having dinner with Penn McCarthy, that was the last thing I wanted to do. What I wanted was for her to get the hell out of my room.

"We're heading into town at seven thirty." She smiled then, the first real smile she'd directed at me in over two months.

I reeled. Had she accepted me now because she'd screwed up so badly with Annette? Did she think we were friends? Or was I some sympathy case? I curled my fingers into fists, amazed at her audacity, her confidence, her Soleetness.

"I'll see you later," she chirped.

Or not, I thought. But I said nothing as I forced my hands open and watched her disappear out the door.

CHAPTER 32

♥

Professor Drake had asked us to start our first novel, *The Heart Is a Lonely Hunter*, over the weekend, but I just couldn't bring myself to do any schoolwork. I couldn't even bring myself to get out of bed.

"You can't hide up there forever," Roxanne pronounced on Monday morning.

She is absolutely right, Josephine, my dead grandmother added.

"Wanna bet?" I replied—to both of them—into my pillow.

"Sure." Roxanne yanked my comforter off of me in one fell swoop, leaving me coverless and cold on the top bunk.

"Hey!" I threw out an arm and caught a corner of the duvet, but it slipped through my fingers. *Just like Annette*, I thought as I watched it fall in a heap at Roxanne's feet.

Was that what happened? I wondered as I shivered and sat up. *Did she slip through my fingers? Or did I force her away?* In the middle of my sleepless night, it had occurred to me that maybe Annette wanted to be free of me as much as she wanted to be free of her mother. I'd forced that thought out of my head the instant it surfaced, because it hurt more than anything else. "Can I have my comforter?" I asked.

Roxanne arched a dark eyebrow. "Will you get your ass out of bed?"

I lay there unmoving except for my eyes, which landed on the large paper sheets of gray, green, and blue that were waiting for the next stage in Roxanne's latest project—an installation—and then the shelf above her desk. I noticed right away that her self-portrait was gone.

"Hey, where is your painting?"

"I got tired of it. Sort of like I'm getting tired of trying to get you out of bed."

Roxanne and my grandmother aside, I knew I should get up. Get on with it. But that feeling I'd had when I came out of the hospital—that things were just going along normally even though nothing *was* the slightest bit normal—was making me want to stay in bed. Forever.

Annette and I had been two halves of a whole for almost a decade, and now she was gone.

"Hello?" Roxanne was getting impatient, her spiky hair looking extra spiky. "I'm hungry, and first period starts in twenty-eight minutes."

I groaned and threw myself back on my pillow.

"Josie," Roxanne said, my comforter a nest at her feet. "There's no question that this completely sucks. But life doesn't have a pause button, and right now you've got to get your butt out of bed and some food in your stomach. The administration is on high behavioral alert for all of us, and especially you. The last thing you need is to start skipping class."

Annette smiled at me from the photo of our ninth-grade school carnival. She was everywhere . . . and nowhere. Except for the sex on her terms, which I cherished and despised, things wouldn't be that logistically different without her here. And yet every fiber of me knew that she was gone, and mourned it.

You're such an idiot, I told myself. I'd somehow stupidly believed that as long as I'd been able to see Annette, to touch her, there was still an us, that we still had a chance.

Roxanne simmered in the middle of our room. "Josie, you need to get up. Now." She was done messing around.

I sat up just as she closed in, jumping past her into the comforter-nest, which didn't provide the soft landing I'd expected. "I don't suppose I have time for a shower?" I asked, raising a hand to my filthy, frizzy mat of hair.

"No way. I'd never get you out of there." She threw a pair of corduroys and a long-sleeved shirt at me and I pulled them on while she mercilessly shoved my books into my backpack. Roxanne grabbed my elbow.

"I don't need a police escort," I joked halfheartedly.

"You might when we get to Soleet central," she said as she hefted her own bag.

Something in the tone of her voice made me consider either (1) taking a flying leap back into my bed or (2) asking for alcoholic sustenance. Since the first was clearly not going to fly with Roxanne and the second was the thing that got us into this mess, I ignored both urges and allowed myself to be led into the hall. Roxanne's grip on my arm could only be described as authoritative.

"I'm good," I said, shaking her off as we approached the stairs. "Really."

She shook her head slightly but didn't reassert her hold as we started down the stairs. "Really good," she repeated. "I like it. Keep telling yourself that."

When we got to the bottom of the stairs, my head automatically turned toward room 108. She wasn't there, of course. Wasn't anywhere I'd see her.

Roxanne took my elbow again, but gently. "We need to go."

I felt leaden as she steered me across the drive and to the dining room, where everything was basically a blur. Dean Austin spotted me from his seat at the staff table, and pushed his chair back with a heavy scrape.

"He wants to talk to you," Roxanne said as he approached. "I'll get you a plate and be right back."

I felt like a marionette without its puppeteer as the dean approached. "Good morning, Josie," he said, studying my face. I had no idea what he was searching for, so I attempted to don a bland expression.

"I thought you'd like to know that Annette is doing much better." He touched my arm. "They expect her to be released tomorrow. Her parents will be coming to campus this afternoon to pack her things."

"Her things?"

"They have decided to permanently withdraw her from Brookwood."

The news hit me like a slap even though it wasn't really a surprise, and I steadied myself on the back of a chair. Of course that was what Shannon would do—yank her out of here as quickly as possible. And, at this point, who was I to object?

"Thanks," I said, staring out one of the leaded glass windows in an effort to halt the Tilt-A-Whirl I was suddenly riding. "Thanks for letting me know."

"My door is open if you need to talk, Josie. You have my cell—call anytime."

I nodded mutely as Roxanne approached carrying a tray of food I'd never be able to eat—just the smell of the dining hall was making my stomach lurch.

"Thanks," I repeated, moving away. I numbly followed my puppeteer-roommate to our own table and sat down.

"They're pulling her out," I said as she set the tray between us. Roxanne pushed my plate toward me and held out a fork.

"Her parents are coming this afternoon to pack her things."

She nudged the plate closer. "Eat. They'll be cold in a minute."

I didn't give a crap what temperature the eggs were, but I managed to fork up a bite, chew, and swallow without gagging.

"Comfort food," Roxanne said, picking up a piece of toast and slathering it with butter.

Nothing comforting about it, I thought as I forced myself to take a second bite. There was no getting out of eating—Roxanne was on me like a hawk. I felt like a little kid with a plateful of lima beans as I choked down my breakfast.

"Good," my roommate said as I took the last bite. "Now you won't pass out from lack of calories." She pushed back her chair and got to her feet. "On to first period. Need me to get you there?"

"Do I look like I'm in preschool?"

"Only your hairdo."

My hand flew to my head—I hadn't even looked at myself in the mirror before I left our room. "Shit. Really?"

Roxanne said nothing as she carried our tray to the dish drop.

"Hey, Josie," Steve greeted from behind the counter. He stopped spraying dishes for a minute and leaned toward us. "You okay?" His voice was quiet, concerned.

I nodded while Roxanne pulled me toward the main hall by my elbow—what was it with her and elbows?

"Why did he ask me that?"

Roxanne hesitated. "Because he's a good guy, and he knows about Annette," she said. "People are worried about you, Josie."

I could feel panic starting to bubble up. "People? What people?"

"Let it go, Josie. Focus on getting through the day. That's plenty to deal with."

I could see Becca and her posse up ahead, walking so close together they looked like Siamese triplets, joined at the shoulders. I almost envied their united front.

"I'll find you before assembly," Roxanne said as we came to the junction. I was going up to English, and she was going down to French. "Now get in there."

"Right." I waited for her to leave, but she wasn't having it.

"Second door on your right," she said. "Go."

"I am in preschool," I muttered as I turned to walk up the stairs. Waving like a toddler, I ducked through the door as the bell rang, and immediately regretted my slowness. Professor Drake was already scribbling notes on the board, and the only empty seat was the one next to Penn.

I walked around the table, feeling everyone's eyes on me and keeping my own on the ground until I'd pulled out my chair. Penn's copy of *The Heart Is a Lonely Hunter* sat facedown on the table, marking his page, and a second regret bubbled to the surface of my feeble brain. I hadn't even cracked the book, which basically meant I'd have no idea what the discussion was about. Which meant I'd be sitting here completely lost for the next forty-five minutes. And if I was exceedingly lucky, nobody would find out.

"First impressions?" Professor Drake asked over his tortoise-shells, a green dry-erase marker at the ready. His polka-dot bow tie was unusually askew. "Favorite characters?"

"Mick," said Macy. "She's got spunk."

Note: Mick is female despite having an assumed male name.

"Dr. Copeland," Jake Flemming added. "For his strong ideals."

Brownnoser.

"Antonapoulos," Penn piped up, tapping his pencil on the table. "He's basically a pig, but Singer is completely devoted to him. That's an impressive accomplishment."

Pot calling the kettle.

Professor Drake's scrawl started to fill the board.

"Anyone else?"

"Singer. Everyone loves him," Becca said.

"But it's based on nothing. People pour out their souls to him, but he can't hear a single word they say," Sam said.

Professor Drake nodded. "Themes for discussion, people?"

"Loneliness."

"Miscommunication."

"Self-delusion."

Great. The book is basically about my life, I thought miserably.

"Isolation," Becca said. "Everyone talks to Singer, thinking he can understand them, but everything they say literally falls on deaf ears. It goes nowhere. The characters are like tiny islands in a giant ocean."

"But they don't feel like islands when they talk to Singer," Macy pointed out. "He connects them."

"They *think* he connects them, but that's not actually true," Becca countered. "It's all an illusion."

"It doesn't matter that it's an illusion," Penn said. "The characters all believe that he understands him—that they are simpatico. For them, the bond is real."

Truth versus belief.

Penn crossed his foot over his thigh and touched my knee, and I pulled my leg away so fast I whacked my knee against the corner of the table leg.

"Josie, do you have anything to add?" Professor Drake asked, his telepathic beam landing squarely on my head.

I looked up from the sepia-toned cover of my book, painfully aware that I should be able to come up with something clever and intelligent at the drop of a hat, even though I hadn't read the assignment.

"Maybe it doesn't matter that Singer can't hear what they tell him," I said slowly. "Maybe all anyone needs is the opportunity to say it, to feel heard. Maybe *being* heard isn't the point. People don't listen, anyway."

Becca stared at me from across the table, her perfectly arched eyebrows knitting together in a rather imperfect way. Next to me, Penn's leg jiggled under the table.

"That's ridiculous. Of course being heard is the point," Becca finally said.

A look of empathy flashed over Professor Drake's face. Then he waved his copy of *Heart* in the air. "Interesting," he said. "Anyone else have something to add?"

Penn's leg stilled and he leaned back in his chair heavily. "It's depressing as hell."

I tried to pretend he wasn't sitting next to me, ignored my urge to drag him out of the room so I could scream at him in the hall. *Because really*, I told myself, *what's the point?*

Your friendship, came the answer almost immediately. *Your friendship is the point*. And then, as the bell rang, *What friendship?* It was more confusing than trying to have a literary discussion about something you hadn't read.

I got to my feet with everyone else and shoved my book and notebook into my pack, taking my time so I was the last person to leave the room. Out in the hall, though, Roxanne was nowhere to be seen. Was I supposed to go to assembly without her? Jeez, I really was like a little kid. I waited, watching the masses of students move down the hall to the auditorium. When the throngs gave way to smaller clusters and finally individual stragglers, I knew she wasn't coming and started for the auditorium.

"Josie!" a female voice called.

I turned, ready to rebuke Roxanne like a child whose mom was late for preschool pickup. But it wasn't Roxanne who had called my name—it was Lola No.

Uff-da, I thought as she strode toward me, her wool A-line skirt falling gracefully around her knees.

"Josie, I—" She looked away for a moment, hesitating and tugging down the sleeves of her cashmere cardigan, as if reconsidering. "I just wanted to tell you that I'm sorry about Annette."

Her blue eyes were softer than I'd ever seen them—almost unrecognizable.

"Brookwood isn't the right place for everyone, and I think maybe it's good that she's going home." She paused, shifting her feet. "But I know how hard it can be to be the one left behind, to lose a girl you cherish . . ."

My mouth dropped open slowly, as it dawned on me that (1) Lola No was a lesbian and (2) she knew I was, too—had probably known since the day I arrived. Did she also know what this felt like? Probably. Maybe not all of it, but a lot. Way more than I could've imagined.

"Yeah," I said, suddenly feeling like I was going to cry. Lola No, of all the freaking people, understood. How was this even possible?

"I can see how much it hurts."

I gazed down the hall through the stone archways and bit the inside of my lip to keep my eyes from welling. "I'm afraid everyone can," I admitted.

"That's not the worst thing, Josie—even if it feels like it is."

I turned back to her, to her unexpected kindness. Her face was a mixture of empathy and encouragement. "It will get better," she said.

I wasn't the slightest bit sure about that, but like I said, Lola No understood a lot more than I could have imagined. "Thank you."

She reached out and touched my arm just as Roxanne's head appeared, coming up the side stairs. "Any time."

"Oh good, you're still here," Roxanne said, shooting me a "what's this about?" look.

Lola No cleared her throat, her authoritarian air returning in an instant. "I suggest you hurry inside and take your seats, ladies," she said. "Assembly has already started."

CHAPTER 33

♥

Finally, classes were over for the day. I'd survived and could retreat to my room and avoid the world—even Roxanne, who was assigned to weekly cleanup in the art studio—until dinner, three whole hours. I was pondering my brief conversation with Lola No, as well as everything I thought I knew about her, but obviously didn't, as I skirted a red sedan parked in front of my dorm. Yanking open the door, I walked head down and fast to the stairs. Too fast, apparently, because I ran right into Shannon rolling one of Annette's massive suitcases to the door.

"Oh," I said, coming up short and feeling like an imbecile. I was so close to her I could see the broken capillaries on her nose. "Excuse me."

Shannon raised her head, a polite response on the tip of her tongue. But when she saw that it was me, her expression shifted into one of revulsion, and she stepped back as if I had some nasty, contagious disease. "There could never be an excuse for you," she spat.

I recoiled as if she had actually struck me. I was accustomed to Shannon's venom, but it was usually aimed at Annette, or occasionally the both of us. Facing her now, by myself, I felt the astounding power of her hatred.

She had always hated me, I suddenly realized, hated me with every bone in her lanky body, and had been waiting all along for something terrible to happen so that she could blame it—no, blame everything—on me.

Annette's dad came out of Annette's room with her backpack and another suitcase, and the moment I saw him, it occurred to me that it wasn't his support that had gotten Annette off the Brookwood waiting list and on the plane—it was Shannon's plan to prove once and for all that I was the one Annette needed to get away from. Could she be that calculating? Yes, absolutely. I thought Annette and I were escaping her, but in the end, they were both going to escape me. I gulped. Her plan had worked perfectly.

Annette's dad put a hand on his wife's shoulder. "Shannon," he said, "it doesn't matter. We need to focus on Annette now."

Shannon shook him off with a fierceness I rarely saw. "Don't start with me," she hissed. "I've been telling you this for years. Years! But did you listen? Did *anybody* listen? Can anybody even *hear* me?" She was shouting now, and the few students who were in the dorm dashed quickly past, heading into their rooms, so they could listen behind their doors, no doubt. "And now . . ." Her face crumpled in on itself and she started to sob. "Now she's . . . she's . . ."

In need of some serious help, I thought sadly while Michael grabbed his wife by the shoulders, half holding her up.

"Can I help you get her things to the car?"

"No!" Shannon wailed. "I don't want you to touch anything of hers." She hiccupped, dropping the suitcase handle.

Michael let go of one of her shoulders and took the handle. His expression was a collage of emotion: sadness, embarrassment, pity, and, way back behind his eyes, regret. "We just need to get to the car." His shoulders sagged. "We need to get back to the hospital."

I wanted to help them, to take Shannon by the arm and lead her out to the vehicle (How could I not have known that the red sedan was theirs—hadn't Dean Austin told me just a few hours ago that they were coming this afternoon?) that was parked in front of the dorm. But I knew she wouldn't let me touch her, and I didn't want to make things worse for Annette. So I nodded ever so slightly and stepped around both of them, pausing at the foot of the stairs to listen for the sound of the car motor and waiting until it was just a whisper on the air. Feeling like barely a whisper myself, I started the climb to the third floor, looking forward to lying on the top bunk and doing nothing for as long as possible.

The phone was ringing when I pushed through the door. "Hello?" I said, picking it up without thinking.

"Josie, is that you?" said my mom's worried voice. "Thank goodness." *Oh crap, I forgot to call*, I thought. And then a second, terrifying thought seeped into my gray matter: *She knows about Annette.*

"Yeah, hi, Mom, it's me."

"Josie, are you all right?" I didn't even know how to begin to answer that, so I didn't try. I let her keep talking instead.

"Because you didn't call," she said. "We waited all weekend and you didn't call. I've been trying your cell all day."

"You have? Oh. I'm not allowed to have it outside my room." I checked my screen—eight calls from HOME. I set my backpack on the floor and prayed she didn't know what had happened. "Sorry, Mom. It's just been really crazy here with Halloween and everything."

"Right, Halloween," she echoed tiredly. "I barely got Toby's astronaut costume done, and they came home with an entire pillowcase full of candy. Your little brothers have been having a fun-size fest for three days running."

"I believe it," I said, exhaling my relief. She didn't know.

"They're like a pair of sugar maniacs."

I pictured my brothers littering their bedroom floor with candy wrappers as they devoured their haul. I'd always loved that my parents let us pig out on Halloween candy until it was gone. "No one piece a day for the Littles," my dad would say, helping himself and laughing. "If you're gonna gorge, gorge big!"

My mouth watered, and I reached for my own, nearly depleted Halloween stash. All that was left were a couple of Three Musketeers and a Laffy Taffy. I ripped open a Three Musketeers and bit into it, my saliva mixing with the nougat, providing necessary sustenance. I was going to tell my mom the truth.

"Mom?" I said, hesitating. "Actually, I have some stuff to tell you."

Silence. Did she suspect anything?

"Mom?"

"Yes, I'm here. I was just sitting down."

Is that good or bad? I wondered feebly. I didn't know where or how to begin, so I just started talking. "It's Annette," I said. "She's on her way home with her parents."

"What? Oh my God. Why?"

I forced myself to keep going. "She got into some trouble with drinking. A lot of trouble, actually. She ended up in the hospital."

My mother's inhale sucked the air out of the phone line, and I could picture her anguished face with regrettable precision. I felt my eyes well up. "I wasn't with her when it happened—things haven't been so great between us." My voice wavered. Nougat drool dripped from the corner of my mouth, and I wiped it with the back of my hand. "I didn't know she was in trouble."

"Oh, Josie."

"But I should have helped her—I should have—" I shuddered.

"Try to breathe," my mom said. She waited for me to catch my breath, and then asked, "What happened to you two?"

So many things, I thought, closing my eyes. *So many, many things.* "Everything just sort of fell apart, I guess. It's really different here." I leaned my back against the wall and opened my eyes to Turtle Lake, which looked completely different from this angle. "Shannon thinks the whole thing is my fault."

"Shannon should take a good look in the mirror," my mom murmured, and then, "What do you think?"

"I don't know. It's all so complicated."

"Life usually is." My mom was silent for several seconds. "Are you okay?" she finally asked. "Do you want to come home, too?"

Yes! I screamed in my head. I wanted so badly to bolt—to go back to Virginia Falls, sleep in my own bed, harass my brothers up close. To go back to my Minnesota life. But deep inside I knew that was impossible—that the life I so desperately wanted to go back to was no longer there. "I'm not sure my coming home would help," I said as my chest folded in on itself.

"Oh, Josie." The sadness in her voice was palpable, and I rubbed my temples, fighting back tears. "I'm proud of you. You're hurting, but you're sticking it out, and that takes something."

I threw the Three Musketeers wrapper in the trash. "Insanity?"

My mom half chuckled. "No, guts."

"Right. Guts," I replied, "Toby's favorite." I tried to smile, but it was useless. I was too busy feeling totally, completely, utterly wrung out.

"I'll call you tomorrow," my mom said.

"Yeah, okay."

"You're a brave girl, Josie Little."

Brave, or stupid? I wondered as Roxanne pushed open the door, her arms full of pieces of painted paper of varying sizes. She stepped into the middle of the room and laid them gently on the floor.

"We're hanging the subway," she told me the second I hung up. The new cutout pieces were familiar blues and greens and grays, and I noticed for the first time that the giant pieces were no longer stacked against the walls.

"The what?"

"The subway, also known as my new project à la Monsieur Matisse."

"What happened to cleanup duty in the art room?"

"Lucky for me it wasn't dirty."

"Yeah, lucky." I watched her start to arrange and rearrange the larger pieces with dismay. I was exhausted and just wanted to lie there doing nothing, but there'd be no getting out of helping her. It was the right thing to do.

Roxanne stepped back to survey her work, then pushed the desk chairs next to each other, making a sort of bench. "Is this about the *Swimming Pool*?" I asked.

"If you mean the one you ditched me for on the other side of campus, no. If you mean the brilliant art installation created by Henri when he couldn't get to one himself, yes."

Roxanne was *Swimming Pool* crazy. Her mom used to work at the Museum of Modern Art in New York, and when Roxanne was little, she spent many an afternoon sitting on the floor of the "pool," looking up at the swimmers and divers and sea creatures floating above her on the walls.

"I knew back then that I'd have to create a cutout installation someday—my own swimming pool."

"I thought this was a subway station," I said snarkily.

She gave me a withering look and patted the seat of one of the chairs. "You're up here." She opened a jar of brass thumbtacks and handed it to me. "You're the hanger, like one of Matisse's assistants. Luckily, these old buildings still have the wood moldings. We can stick as many thumbtacks in them as we want!"

"Do you have intense love for subway stations, too?" I asked as I stepped reluctantly onto the bench.

"I like underground stuff," she said. "Which is why it's such a crime that *you're* the one tunneling all over campus."

"Not anymore I'm not," I said.

"Good. It's safer up here."

"Are you sure about that?" I asked darkly.

"A little higher on the right," Roxanne said. "Yes, I'm sure. Lots of sketchy stuff has happened down there, especially in those rooms where the seniors used to party. A little lower."

I lowered the green cutout. "Rooms?"

"Well, really just one—some kind of crumbling subbasement room under the old inn. I think it was called the jungle. My brother told me about it."

I stared at her. "The jungle?"

"Move those two a little closer together. Yes, but keep in mind that August is a pathological liar. The Ivy League fits him perfectly—he can twist his way into anything." She backed up to survey our work, until she was almost through the door. We had about a quarter of the pieces up.

"I think we have to get dressed for Vespers," I said. My arms ached from holding them above my head, but I paid no attention.

All I could think about was the possibility of an underground jungle.

CHAPTER 34

♥

I stepped through the basement door, pulling it closed behind me with one hand and taking my flashlight out of my pocket with the other. The stale, dry heat of the steam tunnels enveloped me and I stood there for several moments, breathing it in. It felt good to be back.

I hadn't thought about the tunnels in over a week. But the minute the word *jungle* came out of Roxanne's mouth, my brain started firing like crazy and I knew it wouldn't stop until I tried to find it, to see if it was real.

I checked my watch. 11:17. The guards would be on full duty in less than an hour, but getting around a few guys in uniform seemed way easier than getting around Roxanne, or having to be back by lights. I tapped the small compartment of my backpack to make sure my water bottle and the extra batteries were still there, and pulled a thick piece of chalk out of a side pocket. My online research revealed that the old inn had stood on the far side of campus on the edge of the main circle, but not much else. My plan was to try and retrace the path I'd taken with the boys the first night I'd come into the tunnels and see if I could access anything on the other side.

I cast my beam on the floor and followed the tunnel as it eased downward while pipes clanked and hissed, working harder now that the weather was colder. I turned left and descended the short ladder.

The familiar trickles of sweat were just starting to move down my back when I reached the first junction. I drew an X on the right-hand side of the passageway I was leaving and another on the left of the one I was entering, but I was starting to feel like a fool—how could I find my way to a place I'd never been, that might not even exist? I'd be lucky not to get lost.

I moved slowly down the passageway, looking for the turn that led to the entrance the boys and I had come through my first time down here. And then I was there. I shined my light to the left and saw the back of the metal door we'd come through together. To the spot where Penn had whirled me around and kissed me, and then told me how he'd fallen for me.

Just seeing the entrance made me feel lonely, and suddenly exhausted. *Turn around, you fool*, I told myself. But something else urged me onward, a force I couldn't see or hear. *Maybe it's my ancestors*, I thought as I followed the narrowing passage straight ahead. My light covered the width of the tunnel, and soon I was going down again. I passed a small passageway on the right and stepped onto a metal grate, ignoring the rank odor that wafted up from below. Up ahead was a series of bigger cross pipes, some so low to the ground I had to shove my backpack ahead of me and then shimmy under them.

The other side yielded a locked door—a total dead end without Sam and his lock-picking tools. At this rate I would never find the jungle.

I retraced my steps, my backpack removal, and my shimmy,

and shined my flashlight down the passageway I'd seen, and dismissed, on the left. It was narrow and would soon require stooping. But if I didn't want to head back to my dorm, it was the only way to go.

I followed the tunnel, bending forward and noticing that the walls here were crumbling brick and mortar instead of concrete—this section of tunnel was definitely older than the other parts I'd been in. After about twenty yards, the passage opened up to a kind of industrial dump site—piles of old rolls of insulation, broken pipes, and pieces of lumber were scattered everywhere, and at the far end the pile was so big I couldn't see beyond it.

Well, that's a deterrent, I thought. But I was determined not to be deterred. Heart pounding, I half dug, half picked my way through. By the time I got to the other side, I had sweat beading on my forehead and I could feel every speck of dirt and grime on my body. Unzipping my backpack, I pulled out my water bottle. The water was lukewarm but tasted delicious.

This is insane, I thought, eyeing the pile of debris I'd just made my way through. But up ahead, I saw some sort of hole in the ground, and I moved toward it, my water bottle still in my hand.

The hole was one end of a giant vertical pipe with a rusty ladder bolted to the side. It was just long enough to make it hard to see what was at the bottom, other than some sort of floor.

Well, at least you're not descending into a bottomless pit, I thought as I returned the water bottle to my book bag. I shoved my flashlight into the waist of my jeans, put my foot on the top rung of the ladder, and started down.

The ladder was longer than I expected, the corroded metal cooler. The rusty brown of the pipe wall shifted ominously in my wobbly flashlight beam.

Just before my foot hit the floor I heard a shuffle, and froze. Someone else was down here. I pulled my foot back up and climbed a few rungs, my heart hammering in my chest. Footsteps. Definitely footsteps. I swallowed, my mouth dry, and pulled myself closer to the ladder. A moment later I heard something close and latch. Then silence.

Get out of here! I told myself. My knuckles ached from holding the ladder so tightly, but I was frozen. Finally, after several long minutes of quiet, I lowered myself back down until my foot hit a solid surface. I held my breath and turned, shining my light around, as my jaw dropped open.

The room was small. Barely a room, really, though it did have four walls. The floor was cobblestone, but covered with decades of dust, decades of sitting idle. In the corner was a cot with a moldy mattress and an army-green blanket full of holes. It looked as though some rodents had unstuffed it and made a nest. An old writing desk with a broken leg tilted onto a chair.

At the far end was a tiny door with no handle. Closed and locked from the other side. Had someone just gone through there?

Maybe it was a rat, I thought. I tried to believe it.

The dingy walls were covered with some kind of striping. I squinted, stepping closer, and realized that they weren't stripes at all—they were vines that someone had painted. Thick, stringy vines, faded and barely visible through the dust.

The jungle. I was in the jungle. I held my breath and shined my light around, over the walls and the floor and the furniture. The head had to be here!

I shined the light over everything again, and again, s-l-o-w-l-y.

There was a drawer in the desk, I suddenly noticed. Blood rushing in my ears, I walked over and opened it. It was empty. I poked at the disemboweled mattress with my foot, then with my hand, trying not to think about what could be in there. I didn't feel anything unusual. I realized with a sinking feeling that if the mattress had been destroyed by rodents, the head could have been, too. Rat teeth could chew through just about anything.

I shuddered. What was I doing?

I didn't have an answer to that question, but I knew what I *wanted* to be doing—getting out of there. I was officially creeped out. With one final look around, I put my foot on the ladder. When I got to the top of the pipe, I noticed immediately that the air was warmer than it had been before. Much warmer. I looked at the pile of rubble with a sense of dread, then squeezed through the path I'd made on the way in. I was moving a two-by-four that had fallen aside when I thought I heard something behind me.

Turning, I shined my flashlight over the top of the pipe and down the dark corridor. Was something there?

Sweat dripped into my eyes—it was really getting hot in here. I dropped the two-by-four and wiped my face with my sleeve, but my eyes stung. I kicked aside some bricks and a wad of insulation, making my way past the pile of junk. It was getting hard to breathe.

Just keep moving, I told myself, picking up the pace. I was almost to the junction when I stumbled, knocking into a pipe. I heard a hissing sound, and the tunnel got *really* hot. I started to panic. A pipe was leaking in here, and by the time I got to the hatch to my dorm it could . . .

Kaboom! The whole tunnel shook, forcing me against the wall.

Shit. I had to get out of there, fast. Blindly rushing forward, I turned left into the main passageway and ran until I got to the corridor I'd first come through with Penn and the guys. I could see the faint outline of the door up ahead and rushed toward it.

Please don't be locked, please don't be locked, I prayed. Taking the last few steps, I braced myself for impact and hurled myself against the metal door as hard as I could.

CHAPTER 35

♥

Ooof! I landed hard on the concrete floor of the basement, my shoulder taking the brunt of the fall. I rolled off of it as quickly as I could, ignoring the searing pain, as the metal door slammed closed behind me. Fire alarms were blaring, and I could smell smoke. I got to my feet and ran toward my dorm, not even checking to see if anyone else was around.

By the time I made it back to my room, fire alarms *and* sirens were blaring. Roxanne was in bed, her back to me, looking out the window. She heard the door and rolled over.

"Holy shit, Josie," she said, her dark eyes widening. "I thought you were up there." She pointed to the top bunk, then threw back her covers and came over to investigate. "What happened to you . . . and your hair?"

My hair? I lifted my fingers, immediately finding a scorched curl, and felt my eyes start to well. Not because my hair was trashed, but because it was all too much. Penn. Annette. And now the steam tunnel. I wasn't even sure what had happened in there, but everything I touched seemed to explode.

Without saying anything, Roxanne pulled me into a hug. My legs wobbled as I sobbed into her shoulder, smearing tunnel dirt and snot all over her tee. I wanted to stay there, because for the first time in days I felt comforted. And also because Roxanne was literally holding me up. But after a minute she pushed me away slightly, studying me, her face all business.

"We've got to get you into the shower. You need a serious cleanup, and a trim. Some of those curls are material evidence . . . of something." Her dark eyes bored into mine and I dropped my gaze.

My hand reached up for a second time to touch my singed ringlets, and I turned to the mirror over Roxanne's dresser. The ends of my hair were clearly burned. I looked like hell, half-digested and regurgitated. "Fuck."

"No time for fucking," Roxanne said as she pulled a pair of scissors out of a desk drawer. "We've got a situation to take care of." I stood there numbly as reality continued to sink in. I'd just caused some sort of explosion in the steam tunnels. By accident, but still.

"Get that look off your face," Roxanne told me. "I've wielded hair-cutting scissors before." I didn't bother explaining that my expression was actually in response to the last few hours and let her steer me into the bathroom. Planting me firmly in front of the mirror, she began to trim. Carefully at first, lifting curls and investigating for damage before snipping, and then with more boldness.

The tip of Roxanne's tongue protruded from the corner of her mouth in concentration. I was glad she was paying attention, but wondered if she knew what she was in for with my locks. Then I wondered if it mattered. Given what had just happened, who cared about hair?

"This one's a disaster, but if I chop the whole thing off, I'll have a mess . . ." She trailed off and raised the blades. I closed my eyes and tried to breathe. My hair was evidence. It was charred, just like the tunnel and who knew what else. Maybe I should have blown myself up while I was at it.

I was starting to lose it. And the longer Roxanne took with my hair, the more freaked out I got. I had to let it out.

"I found the jungle," I blurted.

Roxanne stopped cutting. "You found *the jungle*?" she echoed.

I nodded.

"It's real?"

More nodding.

"Holy shit." She sat down on the edge of the tub. "Holy Brookwood shit, August wasn't bullshitting. The jungle actually exists."

Did it *still* exist? I bit my lip. Everything was so confusing down there—I had no real idea where the explosion was. "Well, it used to."

Roxanne's mouth dropped open as she realized what I was saying. "You blew it up?"

My bottom lip started to wobble. "I . . . I don't know. Maybe. I was on my way out when I tripped. Something started to hiss, and then . . ." My eyes were welling.

"That sounds scary as hell," she said. "Who was with you?"

"Nobody."

"You were tunneling by yourself?" She met my eyes in the mirror.

"Yes."

She closed the blades around the end of a curl with a slow metal scrape.

"I was looking for the shrunken head."

She shot me an incredulous look but didn't say anything.

"It makes a lot of sense, actually," I rushed to explain. I needed Roxanne to understand. "Sometimes Shuar warriors were forced to abandon their heads while they were still sacred in order to avoid having to sell them to colonialists."

"What do you mean, still sacred?"

"A tsantsa holds the spirit of the slain enemy for a year, or whenever the third ceremony takes place. After that it's just a trinket."

"Really?"

"Uh-huh."

Roxanne surveyed my head. "So?"

"So what?"

"So did you find the head?"

"Oh. No. It wasn't there."

Roxanne's eyebrows clashed in the middle of her forehead and she went back to trimming, her disappointment obvious. "Bummer." She fluffed a little, peering at each curl, her tongue clamped tightly between her teeth.

"Okay, I think I got all the serious scorch. I don't want to cut so much it's obvious, you know?" Our eyes met in the mirror. "Hey, are you okay?" Her voice was quiet.

I managed an exhausted shrug. "Probably not."

Her eyes softened, and for a second she looked like she felt sorry for me. But a moment later her face shifted again. She'd thought of something. "Did anybody see you?"

I shook my head. "I don't think so."

"Well, that's good." She scooped up the hair off the floor and dropped it into the toilet. "You need to shower, but be quick—we don't want the water running for long." She pushed the lever and I watched my charred ringlets swirl their way into the sewage system, half wishing I was next. "Not that the circus out there isn't going to distract the whole goddamned campus," she added, peering out the window.

She turned on the faucet and I pulled off my filthy clothes. I didn't usually get completely naked in front of my roommate, but she didn't seem to care any more than I did. She just scooped up my clothes and took a whiff. "Stinky, but remarkably unscathed. I'll shove them into the bottom of your laundry bag, but you should wash them ASAP."

She saw me standing there naked and frowned. "Hello? Earth to Josie. Get in the shower!"

I nodded, shivering, and lifted a foot over the edge of the tub. The warm water felt good, and the shower curtain blocked out the flashing lights—for the moment I was in my own little world. I got my hair wet, running my fingers through it as best I could before lathering it up. Then I went for some serious conditioner. I was rinsing when the hot water started to wane.

"The fire is out," Roxanne reported as the water turned unquestionably icy. She'd been in and out of the bathroom several times. "Thornfeld is out there, with Blackburn and Lola No." Her hand appeared behind the curtain and turned off the water. My conditioner wasn't totally rinsed, but that was probably a good thing—I'd need all the moisturizing and taming I could get. My towel appeared on my side of the curtain, held aloft by Roxanne's arm. I took it and dried off before slipping into my pajamas.

Roxanne took a whiff of me as she scrutinized the floor. "Not too bad," she said. "I only get a faint burn smell." She used a wad of damp toilet paper to gather up the stray hairs she'd missed earlier, then poured a glass of water and handed me half a blue pill. "You need to sleep."

I nodded and swallowed, feeling yet again like a foolish child who required looking after. Which I basically was, and had been for weeks. "Thank you, Roxanne," I said, meaning it. "You've really saved my ass."

Roxanne arched a dark eyebrow. "It's not saved yet," she intoned. "But we're giving it our best shot."

CHAPTER 36

♥

"Josie, hurry up!" Roxanne said. "Thornfeld called an emergency assembly during first period. He's going to lecture us about the tunnels."

I stood up and flushed. I hadn't forgotten about the explosion, obviously, but hearing Roxanne say it out loud made me want to flush myself down the toilet all over again. Since I knew I wouldn't fit, I cracked the bathroom door.

"Glad to see you're still conscious in there."

"I'd rather be unconscious," I said, shivering. Thanks to the explosion, there was no heat or hot water in our dorm . . . and possibly the whole school. "Maybe I should follow Annette's lead." Oh God, that was terrible.

"That's *just* what we need," Roxanne said, shoving her books into her bag. "Another hospitalization." She grabbed one of her extra messenger bags—the only one without paint all over it—and started loading my books into the main compartment. "Your backpack got pretty trashed, so I put it in a plastic bag in the back of the closet. We'll have to get you a new one, but you can use this for now. Just try to keep it organized, will you? Your old pack was a disaster even before it got fried. Oh, and I'm giving you some mechanical pencils."

"I despise mechanical pencils," I replied, snatching the bag and slinging it over my shoulder. "Should we discuss the state of your dresser?"

"My dresser has nothing to do with art, schoolwork, or grades," Roxanne retorted. "Besides, everyone needs a messy place. It's practically a proven fact."

"My entire life is a freaking messy place."

"Not your *entire* life," Roxanne insisted, "just most of it." She paraded me back into the bathroom and parked me in front of the mirror. I eyed my reflection and gulped. My hair was a *very* messy place.

"No panicking," she said, turning on the water and sticking my head under the icy stream. She toweled it, then squeezed a giant glob of gel into her hand and guided me to the toilet for a seat.

"Good luck," I said grimly as her goopy hands came at me.

"Not luck, skill." Her face was a mask of concentration, and the tip of her tongue was back in action. "And knowing when is enough." She finger combed, gelled, and scrunched all at the same time. Then she pulled out an elastic headband and slipped it on. "Take a look."

I did, and gasped. My hair looked good—really good. "How did you do that?"

Roxanne shrugged. "I've done some hair. Now let's get out of here—assembly starts in six minutes."

I silently thanked her for her omission of the word *emergency* and followed her down the hall. She moved so fast my heart was on overdrive before we even got to the pond.

"Can we slow down a little?"

Roxanne turned, incredulity all over her face. "You want to be late?"

I don't want to go, I thought, saying nothing. Her question was clearly rhetorical.

The mood in the auditorium was somber and electric at once, and I was surprised by how quiet it was, given the number of people present. I tried to relax, to breathe, but my palms were so sweaty someone could have wrung them out. Our cross-campus dash hadn't allowed time for instructions on how to get through this little event, but I knew enough to keep my head down—but not too far down—and act precisely the opposite of how I was feeling.

Thornfeld, Lola No, and Dean Austin, among others, were in an administrative huddle onstage. Lola No kept checking her watch and turning to see how many students had arrived, even though nearly everyone was already there. Finally, Thornfeld approached the lectern. "Please take your seats," he said into the microphone. His voice sounded a lot like how I felt—fried.

The few stragglers settled into the velvet rows while Thornfeld waited patiently. He looked smaller than usual behind the lectern, as if he'd shrunk a size or two.

"As I'm sure many of you know, there is no heat or hot water on campus," he said. "There was an explosion in one of the underground utility tunnels last night." He spoke slowly and clearly, like a politician making an important speech. "Damage was sustained in the eastern section of the main building. While we are thankful that no one was hurt, we must consider the possibility that an unauthorized person may have been in the tunnels. This is, as you all know, strictly forbidden." He shifted slightly, gazing out at us over the top of his glasses.

"The trustees are not going to like this," Oscar said under his breath.

"Brookwood's backbone is its Honor Code. At the beginning of each year, every one of us pledges to act with integrity, honesty, and respect. And yet it is quite clear that not everyone here is being honorable." He lowered his eyes, waiting. When he raised his head again, I swear he was looking right at me. "Anyone who knows anything is expected to come forward."

I inched downward a tiny bit, certain that I still smelled like smoke and subterranean whatever, that I may as well have had a sign that said, "It was me! I caused an explosion in the tunnels!"

Lola No leaned toward Dean Austin, whispering into his ear, and I held my breath.

"The east wing of the main building is off-limits to *everyone* until facilities and the fire department can make sure that the heating and electrical systems are functional and officials can complete a thorough investigation," the headmaster said.

My eyes found Annette's empty seat three rows up, wondering if she was already in Virginia Falls and whether I should call my mom and tell her I'd changed my mind—I wanted to come home, immediately.

CHAPTER 37

♥

Despite Roxanne's assurances that I was in fact present, I don't remember going to English or algebra after assembly. My body traveled to the humanities wing and then the science building, but it was as though I'd been anesthetized, as if I weren't actually there. And then, out of the blue, I found myself in anthropology class, sitting next to Marina.

"Can you believe it?" she asked. "I heard that there was damage all the way under the T."

"No," I replied honestly. "I can't believe it."

I watched Professor Mannering shuffle into the classroom, looking utterly unlike himself. He wore a faded blue T-shirt that my mother would have long ago relegated to the rag drawer, and his pants were wrinkled and saggy—he'd forgotten his belt. And he wasn't even *wearing* his glasses.

"Today you are going to write a personal in-class essay," he said bleakly. He walked to the whiteboard and wrote *When is what you believe more important than what is true?*

I stared at the question while blank sheets of 8-1/2 x 11 paper were passed around. When the paper was sitting in front of me, I stared some more. I wrote down my name and the question itself.

I wrote *the truth*, then erased it.

I wrote *what I believe*, then erased that.

When the bell rang, I had written each of those things a half dozen times, and had a hole in my paper. Nothing other than my name, the date, and the question remained. And I knew it wasn't because of the mechanical pencil.

"That was weird," Marina said as I shouldered the bag Roxanne had lent me.

"Yeah," I agreed as we headed to the dining hall. Roxanne was waiting, and she nodded at Marina, as if she'd arranged my drop-off. Which she probably had.

"I'm not hungry," I told her as she handed me a plate in the servery. It wasn't even her lunch period—she was supposed to be in art.

"Not the point, but you know that already. I'm heading to the salad bar. Don't come to our table until your plate is full of food."

I stood in the middle of the servery wondering what to put on my plate, what I could possibly force myself to eat.

"Everything all right?"

I turned and saw Steve, who was standing at his usual lunch-time post—the grill.

"Who can tell?"

He regarded me from behind the counter. "Well, I've got some really good stuff today. Can I interest you in grilled mahi with fresh mango salsa? Or maybe the pesto chicken?"

I swallowed.

"You don't look so good, Josie."

I don't feel so good.

He set the serving spatula down and fished around in his apron pocket. "I've got something for you. At least, I think it's for you." He held out a tiny manila envelope. "I found it in the haunted house when we were cleaning up."

"The haunted house?"

"My grandmother's house," he explained. "We haunt the first two floors every October."

"Dracula . . ." I said, realizing Steve had been the ticket taker.

He nodded sheepishly. "It's a dopey costume, but my grandmother loves it, and she lets us do the house, so . . ."

I tipped the envelope and a dirty gold chain and cracked pendant slid into my hand. I gasped. My opal necklace.

"I think someone stepped on it," Steve said apologetically. "But I thought you might be able to have it repaired."

I stared at the broken chain, at the jagged crack that ran across a corner of the iridescent stone, feeling tears gather in the corners of my eyes. I was standing in the Brookwood servery, holding my last piece of Annette. "How did you know it was mine?" I managed to get out.

"The opal is my grandmother's birthstone, and I've always liked it. I noticed your necklace the first night at dinner."

I closed my palm around the mangled piece of jewelry, swallowed, and slid it back into the envelope. "Thank you," I rasped. "It means a lot to me."

"I thought it might," he murmured, and then, in his regular voice, "Can I put something on that plate of yours?"

Roxanne appeared at my side, carrying a tray with a giant salad on it. "She'll take a piece of pesto chicken."

I was pretty sure I was the barfy green color of the pesto, but didn't object as Steve gave me a healthy serving.

"Thanks." She stopped for two glasses of water and led me to a table in the corner, where I choked down yet another meal and tried to ignore the gossip that surrounded me. Which was pointless, of course. It wasn't every day—or decade—that someone blew up part of the school. The whole community was abuzz.

After lunch, Roxanne looked me square in the face and told me she was going to go check it out. My stomach dropped.

"I just want to see the crime scene while there's police action."

"Are you crazy?"

She shrugged and got to her feet. "Maybe. Do you want to come or not?"

I knew I was going before I had a chance to exhale. "Yeah."

We dropped our lunch dishes and headed into the bleak November air to gape at the blackened trees and scorched grass. At the charred vines covering the side of the main building. A manhole cover had blown open from pressure inside the tunnels, ripping a hole in the ground, and yellow CAUTION tape cordoned off the entire area.

It looked the precise opposite of the pictures in the catalog.

Roxanne and I were standing together, our breath spilling visibly into the cold, when Becca approached. Spotting me, she reached out and grabbed my wrist, yanking me toward her. Her turquoise eyes were wide-open, exhilarated. "Talk about a boon," she said breathlessly. "Nothing like an explosion to take the pressure off. We can both heave a big fat sigh of relief."

"Relief?"

"That the administration has a real disaster to deal with," she explained. "Our potential mix-up with Annette is a tiny infraction compared to this. It'll be as if Annette never binged and got shipped out of here. Like it never happened."

Could she hear herself?

I had grown accustomed to Becca's self-absorption, but still found myself speechless. Shipped out of here, like a lifeless commodity. Like a pallet of tomato paste, or toilet paper.

And yet as I looked over her shoulder at the black earth and withered vines and scorched bricks, I felt it. I tried to pretend I didn't, because it was so awful. But I felt it—a tiny sliver of relief.

And then I remembered that I was pretty sure I'd actually *caused* the disaster everyone was staring at, and the relief was gone, replaced by self-loathing. Nausea crawled up my throat and I raised the back of my forearm to my mouth, swallowing hard.

Nobody knows, I told myself. *Nobody besides Roxanne has any idea you were even in there.* And if there was one person I could trust at Brookwood, it was my roommate. I turned to look for her, realizing only then that she was gone. I couldn't even be surprised—escaping Becca was one of her many talents.

Becca sidled away as easily as she'd yanked me toward her, and I stood in the cold with the taste of rancid chicken and pesto in my mouth, gaping like everyone else, trying to *be* like everyone else. Or at least anyone but myself. And then Penn was standing next to me, sharing my line of sight across the pond. He studied the scene with an expression I couldn't read. Bewilderment, maybe, and something else. He didn't say anything, just stood there, holding himself slightly away from me with a stiffness I didn't recognize. A stiffness that didn't suit him, didn't suit us.

There is no us, I snapped at myself.

"This is intense," Penn said abruptly. He wasn't looking at me, exactly, but was definitely invading my peripheral—I could see that curl that half covered his left eye. I had the feeling he wasn't talking about the blackened building or the gaping hole in the ground, either. Or at least not *only* those things.

And then he *was* looking at me. At my forehead, just above my right eye. He cocked his head, squinting, and I subconsciously touched the spot he was focused on, but didn't turn to face him. What did he want from me?

"I'm sorry."

The words were spoken so quietly I wasn't even sure I'd heard him correctly. But when I saw the expression on his face, I knew he'd not only said them but meant them.

I felt a flash of empathy, followed by an internal explosion of fury. He was apologizing here, in public, among a mass of gawkers? And what was he sorry for, exactly? For kissing me? For fooling around with Annette?

Everyone kept telling me they were sorry, as if being sorry was all it took. Were those two little words supposed to make it all okay? Because they didn't. It wasn't. Not even close.

I could feel my face heating up despite the cold. "Save it," I said, my voice cracking. Becca and her posse of Soleets were distracted, but not so far away that they were truly out of earshot. "Because I'm not." I met his gaze. I must have been shooting daggers, because he stepped back, a little off-balance. I hoped he'd slip on a patch of ice but he caught himself, straightening, his face full of anguish. "Not even a little," I added venomously.

I pushed past him and strode across the thin layer of snow to my dorm, the crunching under my feet matching the rhythm of my furious heart. The forty-nine steps to Cortland's third floor felt like ten.

"I expect answers from you, period," came a voice from inside my room. A man's voice—one I didn't recognize.

If I'd had a coherent thought, I might have waited quietly in the hall, listening. Getting a gauge. But my brain was obviously on a misfiring bender, because I pushed open the door instead.

A man I had never seen before was standing in the middle of our room with his back to me. He faced Roxanne, whom I couldn't see but assumed was sitting on the bed. Tall and slender, the man had a full head of dark hair that was graying at the temples. He turned abruptly, his dark eyes sharp and angry. I watched his expression morph systematically into one of cordiality.

"You must be Josie," he said with a tight smile. "Roxanne has told me much about you." I couldn't help noticing his tie, a band of dark red with miniature wolverines printed across it. A Brookwood tie.

Behind him, Roxanne looked decidedly distraught. I'd never really seen her flustered or stressed, I suddenly realized, even here in this crazy school, even with everything I'd thrown at her. Until that moment, I'd believed her to be unflappable.

"Hector Wylde, president of the Brookwood Board of Trustees." He held out his hand, which I stared at blankly for a moment before realizing that I was supposed to shake it. His fingers were cold and to call his grip firm would have been an understatement.

"Nice to meet you." The words *president* and *board of trustees* hung in the air like a cloud of gnats, thick and buzzing and nasty. I wondered precisely how and why my roommate—the one person I thought I could trust at Brookwood—had neglected to mention that her father was in charge of the people in charge around here. That he lorded over the administration. That he was the very embodiment of a Soleet. Roxanne's dark eyes met mine squarely, but looked undeniably guilty.

"I'm clearly interrupting something," I said. "I can come back."

Hector Wylde, president of the board of trustees, shook his head. "No, no, we've finished our business for now, and I have a meeting with the headmaster." He checked his gold watch and turned his presidential eyes to Roxanne. "I'll expect to hear from you," he told her. "Soon."

He smiled his tight smile as he brushed past me toward the door. "Nice to meet you, Josie," he said over his retreating shoulder.

The door closed behind him with a decisive click and we were alone with the cloud of gnats, which had invaded my head and were buzzing maniacally. "President of the board of trustees?" I said. "Are you freaking kidding me?"

Roxanne closed her eyes.

"Roxanne?"

She opened them. "I'm sorry."

"Oh my fucking God!" I shouted. "If anyone else says that to me, I'm going to scream. Annette is sorry. Becca's sorry. Penn is sorry. You're sorry. Even the damned dean is sorry. And guess what? That whole pile of sorrys doesn't change a thing. Penn still fooled around with my alcoholic mess of an ex-girlfriend whom, God help me, I think I still love. I still caused an explosion in the steam tunnels. And the one person I thought I could trust in this crazy petri dish of a school lied to me, on day one and every day after, about who she is."

"I didn't lie."

"You sure didn't tell me the truth."

"I said Brookwood was crawling with Soleets. It is. I said they don't give a damn about anyone else. They don't. I said I hate them. I do."

"You *are* one of them!"

"Not really."

"Not really?" My voice was almost a shriek. "Wasn't that your father who just walked out of here? The guy with the Brookwood tie and fancy gold watch? The president of the board of trustees?"

"Yes."

"And?"

"And I should have told you, Josie. I know that. But I can't change it now—I can only regret it. And it's not like we get to choose where we come from, either. We just have to deal."

That sort of stopped me, because it was true.

"And I *am* sorry. Even though it doesn't erase anything. I should have told you. I wish I had told you. But it didn't seem important at the time, and he's not me—he's my dad. We're not the same person."

Also, admittedly, true. And I couldn't ignore the fact that Roxanne had been nothing but good to me since the day I arrived. She'd given me sound advice, had saved my butt with Lola No, and had listened when I needed to talk. She'd been a friend.

"What did your dad mean when he said he expects answers?" I asked, sitting down in my desk chair.

Roxanne ran a hand over her spiky hair. "He wants to know what happened in the tunnels."

Even though I knew that—what else could it be?—I was really glad I was sitting down. "Why does he think you know?"

"He trained me to know, and to find out when I don't. But I'm not telling. I'll *enjoy* not telling. Let the board freak. Let the administration squirm. I don't give a crap."

I heard everything she said, but she seemed farther away than she actually was, and the hairs on the back of my neck were standing up.

"What if *I* give a crap?" I asked.

"Are you thinking of turning yourself in?" she asked, incredulous. "Josie, don't go there. It won't do any good."

"But I'm responsible."

"How do you even know that? The utility system has needed an upgrade for years—decades, maybe. And most of the damage isn't even close to where you were." She gazed at me steadily. "Explosions in utility tunnels happen all the time. I'd bet my life it wasn't your fault at all—you were just in the wrong place at the wrong time."

I gazed at her, unconvinced.

"Turning yourself in won't do any good, anyway."

"It might keep me from feeling guilty for the rest of my life."

"Guilty for what?"

I shrugged. At the moment, I wasn't even sure.

"Will you feel okay about being sent back to Minnesota? Because that's what would happen. They'd kick you out, and everything else would be exactly the same."

"What everything else?"

"The mess that is Brookwood Academy," she replied.

I waited.

"You know what I'm talking about, Josie. The board wanting perfection, the ridiculous competition, students drinking and doing drugs—" She paused for a minute, and then, "Some not knowing when to say when." Her eyes softened and I felt mine start to well.

Roxanne got to her feet and gave me a hug. "This is bigger than you, Josie. It's a tangled web of Soleetism. Let them drown in their own doctrine—they deserve it."

I sniffled. "You are seriously harsh."

Roxanne stepped back. "Maybe. But I also know what I'm talking about. I live this insanity."

"What are you going to do about your dad?"

She waved a dismissive hand. "He's been threatening me since I was three. He'll be furious, but he'll get over it." She gazed out the window. "I've been disappointing him for years."

I tried to imagine what it would be like to have a dad like Hector Wylde. To have expectations placed on your shoulders the minute you were born. To come from privilege but reject it. What was it Penn had said that night in his room? That we spent most of our time trying to meet impossible expectations. That basically, no matter how hard we tried, we were never going to pull it off.

I suddenly felt very lucky to be a regular girl from a regular family. Or at least what I thought was regular. Nobody was putting pressure on me to perform, to excel, to be at the top. I was just . . . me.

Which, at the moment, was plenty.

CHAPTER 38

♥

"I think we should go back." Roxanne's voice drifted up from the bottom bunk, jarring me from restless doze to fully awake.

"Back where?" I asked, rolling over.

"To the jungle."

Was she crazy? "There was an explosion down there, remember?"

"Lightning never strikes twice," she reasoned.

"I'm pretty sure that's a myth," I said. "Besides, people have been combing the place for days."

"We've got to make sure the head isn't there."

"I told you, I looked. It wasn't there. And I repeat: People have been combing the place for days."

"Didn't you say you got creeped out pretty fast, and left?" She was like a dog with a bone.

"Maybe," I admitted. "But since when are *you* looking?"

"Since I found out what you've been up to. Since I found out that my sleazeball brother was telling the truth. Since I heard that a shrunken head might have been abandoned in the jungle. Since I—"

"I got it." I peered at the ceiling, almost able to see Turtle Lake above my head.

Roxanne rolled out of bed and stood up, her head next to my

pillow. "Look, the hot water is back on and they aren't working in the tunnels anymore, which means the coast is clear down there. It's . . . safe. Plus, we barely even have to go *into* the tunnels. We can approach it from the other side of the building."

"And how do you propose we get to this other side?" I asked.

"Um, walk over there in the dark?" Roxanne didn't miss a beat. "People roam around here all the time at night," she said. "Just because you've been exploring the tunnels doesn't mean you have a monopoly on after-dark escapades."

Well, that was certainly a good point. One I could even verify with the pool party.

The image of Annette on the diving board flooded my brain, and I squeezed my eyes and pictured shrunken heads to force it away. I had to admit, part of me wanted to go back, to look again. To see what had happened down there. "Have you ever been in the tunnels?"

"No."

It seemed totally ironic that the well-seasoned, knew-everything-about-Brookwood Roxanne had never been in the steam tunnels.

"They're hot, filthy, and dangerous." I considered telling her about the dead rat I'd encountered, then thought better of it.

"No, really? There's no red carpet in there?" She started rummaging around in a dresser drawer. "Good thing I've got a lotta black," she quipped. "Definitely the color for jumping out of dormitory windows."

"This is madness," I muttered.

"I can steal your covers if that'll help." Her voice was light with excitement.

I climbed down and pulled on a pair of dark jeans before packing the essentials in my backpack. Flashlights. Chalk. Water. Batteries.

Roxanne was giddy as we crept down the Cortland stairs, walking so close she bumped into me more than once. When we got to the first floor, I stepped to the side.

"You're the chief window jumper," I said. "You lead."

She moved silently to the end of the hall and into an alcove with a window. Opening it, she pushed herself up onto her arms and swung a leg over the sill. She lowered herself until I could just see her face. Then she let go and jumped.

"Ooof," she said, landing with a leafy rustle.

I stuck my head out the window. Roxanne was standing between the dorm and a boxwood hedge. "Here goes," I muttered, following suit. Forty seconds later, I landed with the same "ooof" and rustle. But we were out.

I'd never been outside on campus after lights, and it was exhilarating in a totally different way from the tunnels. Instead of feeling hot and sweaty, goose bumps rose on my arms and legs, and I felt decidedly free.

Roxanne stepped out from behind the bush and looked around. "It's clear," she said, waving me forward. We crossed the circle drive and snuck behind another row of hedges, our backs to the building.

"I grilled my brother," she said. "There's a grate in the ground next to the parking lot—we can get in through there."

"It's not bolted?"

"Not anymore!" she singsonged in a whisper.

I stared at her back. "Roxanne!"

"What?" she replied innocently. "We may as well put those art room tools to good use!"

I grimaced, thinking that maybe Penn had chosen the wrong girl to join his all-male posse. "And just when did you do all this recon?"

"After assembly. It wasn't even that hard, actually. I had good cover, thanks to the meticulously pruned shrubbery."

She rounded the corner of the building and we moved along the far side in the shadows, then made a dash for said shrubbery. When we got to the grate, she grabbed ahold and wriggled it free, then set it to the side. "Voilà!"

I considered the hot, filthy tunnels I'd had to navigate and the pile of rubble I'd had to dig through underground. This seemed impossibly easy by comparison. "Do we even know where this passageway goes?"

"We have a vague idea," Roxanne said, grinning in the moonlight.

"Great," I groused, climbing into the opening and down the ladder. Roxanne followed and pulled the grate back into place.

We climbed down about eight rungs, then stooped low in the passageway, which got taller as the floor sloped down. I shined my light farther down the tunnel, imagining what was over our heads.

"Hot," Roxanne said.

I felt a little ill remembering how hot it had been the night of the explosion, and wondered if I had, in fact, gone completely insane. "This is actually tepid by tunnel standards."

Roxanne let the beam of her light move slowly over the tunnel walls and floor, over the brick and mortar and the hissing pipes. "It is super creepy in here. I can't believe you did this alone."

I can't believe I am doing it again. Was I brave, or stupid? The jury was obviously still out.

The tunnel grew narrower just before we came to a very short ladder. I climbed down and flashed my light over a small pile of construction debris that looked familiar. Bricks, old lumber, insulation . . .

"This is the kind of stuff I saw last night, just before I found—"

"What is *that?*" Roxanne shined her light on a crumbling section of wall. Hanging limply from an old nail was a wooden sign with an arrow. THE JUNGLE.

It was clear that the wire had rusted through and the sign had fallen—it pointed to the ground. I shined my light beyond the sign and saw it—the top of the pipe that led down to the jungle, and beyond that, the pile of rubble I'd come through the first time.

"Holy crap," I said. "It's right there."

"Right where?" Roxanne asked.

"That hole," I replied.

"That's the jungle?"

"Uh-uh. The jungle is underneath it."

"In the depths," she murmured.

We picked our way past the rubble, and I swung my leg onto the first rung. "Here goes," I said, and started down. Roxanne followed, nearly stepping on my hands. A moment later, we were both standing in the jungle.

"Welcome, ladies," a raspy voice called through the darkness. I jumped, then whirled, shining my flashlight toward the cot.

"Holy shit," Roxanne murmured.

Holy shit was right. Professor Mannering was lying on the cot. (Gross!) He sat up gingerly, swinging a leg to the floor. "Welcome to the jungle."

I stood there, flabbergasted. What was my seventy-five-year-old anthropology professor doing in the depths of the steam tunnels?

"What are you doing here?" Roxanne blurted.

"I could ask you ladies the same question," he replied as he turned on a lantern and set it on the desk. "But in fact I am quite sure we are here for the same reason. Or at least, similar ones. Indeed, I suspect that our dual arrivals at this particular location on the Brookwood campus are interconnected." I heard him sigh and then pull something out of a small satchel, setting it on the desk with a muffled, glassy clunk.

I shined my flashlight on the item, which was wrapped in burlap and gathered at one end. A piece of cotton string dangled from the top—part of the coarse cloth had slipped out of the knot, exposing a section of glass underneath. I blinked and stepped closer, trying to focus. Was that a nostril?

"What is that?" Roxanne asked, shining her light toward the desk.

Professor Mannering's thin fingers reached out and tugged on the edge of the burlap, and the glass container slipped out, rolling sideways. He stopped it with his other hand and righted it.

"That, I'm afraid, is a shrunken head."

CHAPTER 39

♥

"You had the head?" I blurted before I could stop myself. I could hear the accusation in my voice, and felt ashamed of it.

Professor Mannering pushed the jar toward me. "Yes," he said. "Yes, I did."

I looked at him, then the head, then back at him. I was too shocked to speak.

"And for a long time. Too long, in fact. But I told him I would retrieve it, that I would keep it safe." His voice faltered. "And given what happened after that, it seemed the least I could do."

"Told who?" Roxanne wanted to know.

"Edward Hunter, of course." He nudged the jar toward me again. "Go ahead. Take a closer look."

I picked up the jar and turned it slowly in my hand while Roxanne shined her light on it for added illumination, as if it were on exhibition at a museum. About the size of an orange, the face was a wrinkled, dark, leathery blue-brown and had tufts of long, very dark hair sprouting from its crown. The nose, lips, and eyes were sewn shut and tied with coarse cotton string that was repeatedly and ornately knotted. It was hideous and beautiful all at once.

"Freaky," Roxanne said.

I turned the jar upside down. Written on the bottom, in faded black ink, were the words *Shuar Tsantsa, September 14, 1942.*

"It's quite something, isn't it?" Professor Mannering said.

I felt the weight of the head in the small jar, which was growing warm from the heat of my hand. Part of me wanted to put it down, but another part refused. "Why did he give it to you?"

Professor Mannering shook his head. "He didn't, exactly. He told me where he had hidden it. Edward was one of my very first students, and certainly my first star student. He had a brilliant mind, and I admired him. I suppose I was even in awe of him . . ." His voice trailed off. "I was young myself—just a boy, really. More like my students than the rest of the faculty."

The oversize lips pressed against the inside of the jar, kissing my palm. I set the jar down with a shudder.

"I so wanted the boys to like me," Professor Mannering went on. "And I didn't know where the line between student and teacher was supposed to be. By the time I realized that some of my students were determined to have their own hallucinogenic parties, how they wanted to use Edward's scientific talents for their own purposes, well . . . I was too late." His words lingered in the air, and neither of us said anything for a long time. When I looked back at Professor Mannering, he had tears in his eyes.

"If I'd been wiser, I might have been able to intervene, to . . ." His voice wavered. ". . . save him."

I reached out and put my hand over his. "It was a long time ago," I said.

He nodded, then shook his head. "Indeed. But I only remember that when I am in front of a mirror and see an old man looking back at me. If not for that, it would seem like yesterday."

"Why didn't you tell anyone you had it?" I asked quietly.

Professor Mannering balked. "What good would that have done?" he asked. "Edward had already died. His grandfather had already died. And he and his father, Edward Hunter II, never got along. He actually told me he came to Brookwood to *escape* his father."

"I think a lot of us want to escape our fathers," Roxanne said resignedly. This shook me a little, as it was also true about Penn. *And if you added mothers, Annette,* I thought with a pang.

Professor Mannering picked up the head and returned it to the burlap sack. "I came here a few nights ago to leave this here, quite certain that you would soon find it, Josephine. But someone interrupted me, so I had to depart the moment I arrived."

"That was me," I said.

"Ah, you were ahead of my projected schedule. Not surprising, really. At any rate, I returned as soon as the tunnels were safe again. Or at least relatively safe." He paused to look me square in the face. "I assure you that I understand the allure of these tunnels. But the truth is that no one is safe down here."

I nodded.

He held the burlap sack out to me. "I want you to take it."

"What? No, I—"

"I want you to take it and decide where it should be. Except for the other night, I haven't been down here since Edward died, and I won't ever return. It is time for me to leave this place, to let go of Edward and his head, and of Brookwood." He smiled ruefully. "I am ready to go," he added, "now that I know the head is in safe hands."

I felt a wave of panic. "What makes you think my hands are safe?"

"That is hard to explain. Perhaps because you were the first student in half a century to find your way here," he said. "And by yourself, the first time," he added with a nod toward Roxanne. "That takes a great deal of courage. But it is also because in spite of your wordless essay, I can see that you are not letting Brookwood change who you are, or what you believe. Which, given what was at stake and the truth that had to be faced, takes even *more* courage." He coughed lightly. "I suppose, then, that it is the combination of factors, as so many things are."

The burlap sack was still dangling in the air, held by string and Professor Mannering's fingers. I put my hand underneath and he let go, dropping it into my open palm. He reached out with both hands and closed my fingers around it.

"Congratulations, Josie Little," Professor Mannering said. "You are now in possession of Edward Hunter's Shuar shrunken head."

CHAPTER 40

♥

"What the heck am I going to do with it?" I asked Roxanne the next morning. I was sitting on her bed, holding the shrunken head. Since taking possession the night before, I'd barely put the thing down, or stopped talking.

Roxanne leaned toward the bathroom mirror and swiped her lashes with navy blue mascara. "Give it to the administration?"

"Why would I do that?"

She shrugged. "Because they'd love to have it," she mused. "They could put it on display in the main hall with a sign under it proclaiming that it only cost them one student."

I burst out laughing. "You are positively evil."

"Maybe." Satisfied with her lashes, she pulled back from the mirror and turned in my direction. "But here's the thing. Brookwood hasn't exactly been on the best of terms with the Hunters since their legacy genius son died on campus. Giving back the head might change that."

"Really?"

"Totally possible. It's been half a century since Hunt died, and time heals. I'd be willing to bet that the Hunters want to be reunited with Brookwood as much as Brookwood wants to be reunited with them."

This made total sense to me in a twisted way. All I had to do was hand the head over to the Brookwood administration.

Problem was, I didn't want to. It seemed too easy. If it were the right thing to do, wouldn't Professor Mannering have done it years ago?

I looked at the face in the jar—eyes and lips tied shut, as if it were in pain, as if it had a secret it was afraid to let out. I thought of Edward Hunter—bullied and manipulated. I wondered how, exactly, he died in the tunnels. Why he and his father didn't get along. Edward Hunter II was an old man now. Was he full of regret?

I pictured Annette in that hospital bed, on her way home with her abusive mother. The mother we'd tried to escape. I'd thought that by bringing Annette here, by getting her away from Shannon, I'd be keeping her safe, setting her free. But now it seemed that maybe Annette was too broken inside to know how to be safe or free. She had wounds that were invisible—even to me.

Maybe the same was true of Edward Hunter.

I felt the warm glass against my fingertips. Poor Edward Hunter. Poor Annette.

"Are you all right?" Roxanne asked.

Annette is still alive, I reminded myself.

"Unclear," I said, gazing at the long dark hair pooled in the bottom of the jar. It was so shiny, like black corn silk.

Professor Mannering hadn't saved Edward Hunter, and I hadn't saved Annette. *Was it possible for one person to save another?* I thought. Maybe, but only if that person *wanted* to be saved.

Did Annette want to be saved? I inhaled sharply as the question formed in my head, because I was utterly unable to answer it. And, I realized, it wasn't my job to know. It wasn't my problem to solve. It was Annette's.

"This doesn't belong to me or Brookwood," I suddenly said.

Roxanne was at her desk now, loading up her book bag.

"Do you think I could send it to the Hunters myself?"

Roxanne tapped her finger on her chin. "That's a little risky," she said. "We'd have to figure out where to send it, and pray it arrives safely. And it probably wouldn't help the school very much." She turned to me, a mischievous smile spreading across her face. "Which is precisely why I like it."

CHAPTER 41

♥

"Hey," I said as he approached.

"Hey," Penn said, his gait halting and awkward as he ambled up to me. He almost looked like someone else, even in his blue blazer and button-down, his red striped tie flapping a little in the cold. Vespers was starting any minute, but I'd asked him to meet me by the baseball field.

He drew close and stopped, waiting.

I'd had a hundred things to say to him, but now that he was standing in front of me, the words were suddenly stuck inside. I looked up at the curl hanging over his eye, and it was as if he'd just walked into my room, carrying my suitcases. As if I'd just arrived.

"Josie?" he said.

"Yeah, I'm in here somewhere," I replied. "I just can't figure out what to say to you."

He half smiled. "Well, I know what to say to you," he replied. "Josie, I'm sorry. Sorry for being a jerk. Sorry for kissing you. Sorry for fooling around with Annette."

Ouch. Did he have to bring that up? The words *You're an asshole* took shape in my head, but I didn't say them aloud.

"We'd both been drinking, and she, well, she made the first move."

My gaze moved past his shoulder to the blackened hole in the ground.

"That's no excuse . . . I shouldn't have . . . I should have just said no."

"Yeah, you should have," I agreed. "But you didn't." Part of me wanted to punch him, to tell him he was a total jerk. Did he think he could get off this easy? But another part of me knew he wasn't getting off easy, that nobody who paid attention did. And if there was one thing I knew about Penn McCarthy, it was that he paid attention.

Still, it would have been ridiculously easy to blame him for everything. To pretend that Annette had been mine until the night she ended up in his room. Except that wasn't the truth—it was merely something I wanted to believe.

"There's something you should know," Penn said. "Something she said when we were together."

I winced a little when he said that last word.

"It was that she didn't want to be such a follower. That she wanted to be herself. But then she said she didn't know who she was anymore."

I closed my eyes and tried not to make that my fault.

"She said she wanted to be authentic, like you."

My eyes shot open. "I'm not so authentic."

"Also . . . we didn't have sex. I couldn't." He looked away. "She's not you."

He did not just say that.

I glanced up at him, at his eyes, which were full of hurt. "It wasn't bullshit, Josie," he said quietly. "I totally, completely fell for you. Like it or not, you *are* authentic. Pretty much the most authentic person I know."

And there it was again. It wasn't bullshit. He saw me, and wanted me anyway. Maybe even loved me a little. I momentarily wished I wanted him back.

"A girl who authentically likes girls."

"Well aware of that fact," he said.

"I know how it feels to want something that's impossible," I offered. "I know how much it sucks."

Penn ran a hand through his curls. "It sucks all right," he agreed, his eyes clouding as he added, "but not as badly as Annette's situation. She is a major mess."

A slow, sickening feeling spread through me like water seeping into a moldy sponge. He was absolutely right—she was. And no matter what I'd told myself or had wanted to believe, the truth was that there was very little I could do to fix it.

I inhaled raggedly, trying to get the air in. When it came out again, it was a sob. Penn reached out and touched my arm, but didn't try to talk me out of it. There was no *I'm sorry*, no *It's not your fault*, no *It will be okay*. He was just there with me, propping me up with his proximity, while I gave in to my anguish. And somewhere in the midst of my tears and Penn's quiet presence, I realized that, in spite of everything—or maybe because of everything—Penn was a friend. A real friend, and one I wanted to keep.

Finally, I wiped my eyes on my sleeve, pulling myself back together. "Ugh," I said. "It's too much."

Penn held out a rumpled tissue. "Way too much."

I took the tissue and blew my nose, feeling like I'd just been through the spin cycle, but also a little bit better. "I have something to show you." I unzipped the small bag I was carrying, took out the burlap-covered jar, and unwrapped it. Cradling it in both hands, I held it out to Penn.

"Holy shit," he breathed. "Is that the head?"

"That's the head."

"You're carrying it around campus?"

I chuckled. "It's an old trick Roxanne taught me—sometimes you can get away with things that aren't expected."

He took the jar gently, turning it. "So it *is* real." He studied the leathered skin, the sealed eyes and lips, the still-shiny dark hair. "This is definitely the creepiest and coolest thing I've ever seen." He flipped it over and read the bottom. "Where did you find it?"

"I didn't, exactly. It sort of found me."

"Really . . ." I could hear the question in his voice, the disbelief.

Just tell him. "Professor Mannering had it."

"Mannering?"

"Yup."

"You're shitting me."

"Nope."

"How'd he get it?"

"Edward Hunter gave it to him, essentially. He's had it for fifty years."

"How did . . . oh my God." He did a quick calculation of

years and slapped his forehead. "How did I not realize that Mannering and Edward Hunter were here at the same time?"

I shrugged. "It was Mannering's first year here."

"Yeah, but I should *totally* have known that." He held the jar up to the dim light one last time before wrapping it in the burlap and handing it back. "Edward Hunter III was my grandfather's best friend."

"What?" The words circled in my brain, mixing with my own questions, and then, an odd sense of relief for the science geek who died too young. *Hunt had a best friend*, I thought. *A real one.*

"Do you have the address for Edward Hunter II?" I said.

"Sure," Penn confirmed. "Our families have been friends for generations. Grandfather wasn't here when Hunter died, though. He went to Sutton."

"The rival school?"

"My maternal grandfather," he said, half rolling his eyes. "The Watsons are a Sutton family."

I shook my head. "I don't think I will ever understand this stuff."

"That might make two of us," Penn agreed.

I remembered the little rhino—Sutton's mascot—sitting on the shelf above Penn's desk, how Penn had declared that it wouldn't go into a trophy case. It could only be his grandfather's. "Is that why you were looking for the head? For your grandfather?"

"Yes, and the Hunters." His eyes traveled the wall of the damaged building. "And also because, I don't know, I guess I wanted something more out of being at Brookwood—something more than a diploma and admission to the right college."

I felt the corners of my mouth rise. "You just might be authentic yourself, Penn McCarthy."

"You think?"

"Absolutely." I tucked the shrunken head into my bag and smiled up at him. We were ready to go to Vespers.

CHAPTER 42

♥

"Annette?" I said, unable to believe she'd answered the phone. I'd called a dozen times, hanging up every time Shannon's voice had come at me, like a razor blade, over the telephone line.

"Josie, hi. Yes, it's me. Have you been calling? Someone keeps calling and hanging up. Shannon says it's you, trying to get to me."

I gazed out the window at the pond while melancholy dripped into me. Because it was me calling, but not to get to her. Just the opposite. "Yes, it was me." I hesitated, not quite sure what to say. After so many failed attempts, I really hadn't expected to reach her. "I needed to talk to you."

"Oh, Josie, I'm so glad you called. I was afraid you wouldn't."

A string of silence stretched between us.

"I'm sorry," I blurted, my heart heavy with knowing that saying those two words wouldn't fix everything. Or anything, for that matter. But the truth was, I *was* sorry, for a lot of things.

"I miss you," she said.

Had she heard me? I wondered as I waited for my heart to pound, my breath to catch—for Annette's missing me to move into my body and make it react. Or for a sarcastic comment to come flying out of my mouth. Neither happened.

"Are you all right?"

A slow exhale made its way across the phone line. "I don't know," Annette said, her voice cracking. "I can't believe I'm back in Virgina Falls, in this house, with my mom . . ." She shuddered, and I knew in unfortunate detail how her green eyes had just turned a shade closer to gray, how her bottom lip curved as it wobbled and she started to cry.

Say something! a voice in my head said. *Make it better!* But another voice reminded me that it wasn't my job to make it better anymore, that really, it never was. Annette was caught in her own web, and I couldn't get her out. She'd have to untangle herself.

So I didn't say anything. I just waited quietly on the line, letting her cry. "Oh God," she finally said, her voice a squeaky mess. "Can you believe how stupid I am?"

"You're not stupid—you just have some stuff to figure out." It was so strange. I'd felt terribly confused over the past couple of months but was really just finding my way. It was Annette who was getting lost.

"I don't know how everything got so messed up."

I wasn't entirely sure myself. Was it me? Brookwood? Her mother? Herself? *It's all of it,* I thought. *It's all of it, and a zillion other things. It's life.*

Annette sniffled. "Do you think I should try to come back?"

I didn't. Not because I didn't want her to—I actually wasn't sure whether I did or didn't—but because I thought maybe Lola No was right. Brookwood didn't seem like a good place for Annette to be. "I don't think you should decide now. I think you should focus on taking care of yourself. You and your dad have to figure out what to do about your mom. You can't let her keep hurting you, Annette."

"I know," she said. "My aunt Sarah is coming to live with us for a while." I could hear the hope in her voice. "But, Josie?"

"Yeah?"

"I think we died."

I felt a giant wave of loss wash over me and into me, settling in my bones. I hadn't put what had happened to us into those exact words but knew it was true as soon as I heard them. Whatever Annette and I had been, we weren't anymore.

"Do you think I'm going to be okay?" she asked, her voice wavering.

I rolled away from the window, willing myself to tell the truth. "I can't answer that," I said. "But I know I believe in you."

CHAPTER 43

♥

Mr. Edward Hunter II
942 Fifth Avenue, PH2
New York, NY 10075

November 9, 2015

Dear Mr. Hunter,

I believe the enclosed item belongs to you. It was
found in an underground room at Brookwood Academy. I
realize this will not bring back your son, but I hope it will
bring you some peace nonetheless. It certainly is a remarkable object.

With Best Wishes,
Anonymous

I set the head in a box that Roxanne had absconded with from the
mail center, cradling it in several layers of crumpled newspaper.

"It's weird," I said, "but I'm going to miss my little head."

"Be glad it's *not* a Little head," Roxanne said with a tiny shudder. "That would be a bit gruesome."

I laughed and silently said good-bye to the leathered face and tied features before closing the box flaps and taping it securely. Carefully copying the address Penn had gotten for me, in indistinguishable block letters, I addressed the mailing label and stuck it on, using Penn's home address as the return and covering it with a piece of packing tape, just to be safe.

"Are you sure we shouldn't go with FedEx?" I asked for the tenth time.

"Uh-huh. We're going old-school, just like the recipient. My mom's gallery sends original USPS registered insured all the time—reliable but not showy."

I nodded and picked up the box, noting that it was light for its size. "Ready?"

Roxanne slipped her feet into her ancient boots and we headed out the door to the post office in town—the school mail center was closed on Saturdays, and was risky, despite the theory that you could get away with a lot of things right under the administration's nose. The explosion in the steam tunnel had been declared a random accident and the activity at the east end of the main building had mellowed considerably; there were only a few gawkers and the crime scene was devoid of firefighters. Students had recently finished classes and were heading up to the fields for Saturday afternoon games. Brookwood life was moving forward, recapturing its rhythm. I had no idea what was going to happen once the package under my arm reached its destination, but I was okay with that. I'd cross that bridge when I came to it.

As we passed the pond and the science building, Professor

Mannering's essay question popped into my head—the one I still owed him about truth versus belief. There were so many things I'd believed to be true when I arrived at Brookwood. That it was my job to get Annette away from her mother. That at Brookwood, Annette and I would thrive. That our relationship was strong and beautiful. And authentic.

The truth, I'd come to realize, was made up of other things—things I'd learned and experienced, and things that shaped my new life here. It was never my job to save Annette from her mother, or from the world, or from herself. That was up to her, and I could only offer help, and only then if she wanted it.

We didn't thrive here. Or at least we didn't thrive here as a couple. I wasn't even sure we'd ever been a couple at Brookwood—even behind closed doors. I think we were two people simultaneously hanging on, but trying to break free in our own ways.

Was our relationship strong and beautiful? Parts of it, yes. But on the whole, not so much.

I was still sorting out how I would put these mental ramblings into words, and then down on paper. The thing was, I was still letting go of old beliefs and getting used to the truth. It felt a little bumpy, and yet kind of okay.

"Will you come to the studio with me when we get back?" Roxanne asked. "I want you to help me paint new paper for my next project. It's going to be all green."

I stopped in my tracks. "Let me guess."

"Yup," she said. "A jungle." She sighed. "It's too bad I can't install it *in* the jungle."

I thumped the box under my arm lightly. "And too bad we're not keeping this thing," I said. "We could use it as decoration. Hang it right from the center of the room."

She grimaced. "Grisly."

"And yet, weirdly appropriate."

She nodded. "After we paint, I was thinking we should go up to the fields and watch the soccer game." She pulled her coat collar up around her neck. "Just to check it out."

My head swiveled toward her. "Did something happen with Hank?"

The corners of Roxanne's lips rose in a tiny smile, but she shook her head. "Let's just say that being near him no longer makes me want to punch him in the stomach."

"Well, that's a start," I agreed with a laugh. And, I realized, I had similar feelings about Penn. I was still upset with him but could already feel my anger starting to lift. I didn't have to carry all that mad around—I could choose to let it go. And though Annette had ripped out half my heart and taken it back to Virginia Falls, it was clear that I was going to survive, that I was choosing to stay at Brookwood and move forward right along with everyone else. Not because I was trapped in the petri dish, but because I had decided that right here was where I wanted to be . . . even, unbelievably, without Annette.

ACKNOWLEDGMENTS

This book was several years in the making, and very definitely wouldn't exist without:

Judy Blundell, who told me to write a book,

David Levithan, who told me I should definitely write *this* book,

Anica Rissi, who told me she *knew* I could write this book,

Sarah Stephens, who propped me up when I was sure I *couldn't* write this book,

and Hilary Zaid, who gave me a place at her table and proved an invaluable sounding board while writing, and rewriting, much of this book.

I am indebted to countless people who make my life rich and whole. I'd like to thank Josh Adams for saying yes, and for believing in my work, as well as the lovely Lisa Sandell, who understood what I was trying to say, sometimes before I did. My poker playing posse for their plentiful food, drink, humor, and patience. Steve Schieffelin, both a remarkable teacher and a wise soul who provided insight into many things boarding school, literature, and life. Olivia Prud'homme—I would not have survived boarding school without you. Richard Bassett, who always knew which questions to ask and when to laugh heartily—you are no longer here but your spirit and your voice are as strong as ever. To my mother, Elisabeth Mason, for allowing her children to be their true selves, my siblings Christopher, Elisabeth, Mary, Robert, and especially Emily, who consistently tells me she loves me . . . even when I am being difficult. And finally, my husband Brian Vaughan and my crazy and wonderful children Nora, Elliot, and Oliver, who put up with having a writer for a wife and mother, make my heart swell and break as only a human heart can, and tether me to the world. Thank you, thank you, thank you.

ABOUT THE AUTHOR

Jane B. Mason lives in Oakland, California, where she spends her time adjusting to her teenage children, open water swimming, and writing. Her most recent titles, written with Sarah Hines Stephens, include A Dog and His Girl Mysteries and the Candy Apple titles *The Sister Switch* and *Snowfall Surprise*. *Without Annette* is Jane's YA debut.